Whatever Happened to Mary Janeway?

A Home Child Story

Mary Pettit

DUNDURN
TORONTO

Editor: Jane Gibson
Copy Editor: Jennifer McKnight
Design: Jennifer Scott
Printer: Webcom

Library and Archives Canada Cataloguing in Publication

Pettit, Mary, 1948-
Whatever happened to Mary Janeway? : a home child story / Mary Pettit.

Issued also in electronic format.
ISBN 978-1-4597-0171-7

I. Title.

PS8581.E8554W43 2012   C813'.6   C2012-900074-4

1 2 3 4 5   16 15 14 13 12

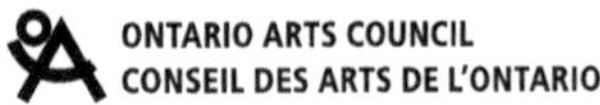

We acknowledge the support of the **Canada Council for the Arts** and the **Ontario Arts Council** for our publishing program. We also acknowledge the financial support of the **Government of Canada** through the **Canada Book Fund** and **Livres Canada Books**, and the **Government of Ontario** through the **Ontario Book Publishing Tax Credit** and the **Ontario Media Development Corporation**.

Care has been taken to trace the ownership of copyright material used in this book. The author and the publisher welcome any information enabling them to rectify any references or credits in subsequent editions.

J. Kirk Howard, President

Printed and bound in Canada.
www.dundurn.com

Dundurn
3 Church Street, Suite 500
Toronto, Ontario, Canada
M5E 1M2

Gazelle Book Services Limited
White Cross Mills
High Town, Lancaster, England
LA1 4XS

Dundurn
2250 Military Road
Tonawanda, NY
U.S.A. 14150

For Paul, who patiently waits for me in the wings

Table of Contents

Acknowledgements		11
Background on Mary Janeway		15
From *Mary Janeway: The Legacy of a Home Child*		17
Prologue		19
One	London	23
Two	Summer in Goderich	29
Three	Back in London	37
Four	Mrs. B. Gets Sick	46
Five	Woodstock	51
Six	Hamilton	65
Seven	The Lunch Pail Town	77
Eight	Queen Victoria's Birthday	84
Nine	The Church Family	91
Ten	Infantile Paralysis	99
Eleven	Unexpected Visitors	104
Twelve	Life Goes On	117
Thirteen	A Dream Comes True	125
Fourteen	Hamilton: A City of Firsts	131
Fifteen	Missing Person	137

Sixteen	Centennial Celebrations	145
Seventeen	A Wedding and a War	151
Eighteen	A Bitter Cold Winter	164
Nineteen	Armistice	171
Twenty	The Roaring Twenties	176
Twenty-One	Mr. Jacques's Funeral	181
Twenty-Two	A Child Is Born, a Child Is Lost	190
Twenty-Three	Picking up the Pieces	196
Twenty-Four	A Knock on the Door	205
Twenty-Five	Kingston Penitentiary	209
Twenty-Six	Ottawa Street	214
Twenty-Seven	Stony Mountain	219
Twenty-Eight	Freedom at Last	224
Twenty-Nine	The Great Crash	230
Thirty	The Turning Point	237
Thirty-One	A Family at Last	244
Thirty-Two	A Milestone	259
Thirty-Three	The Final Chapter	266
Epilogue		271
Notes		272
Bibliography		281
About the Author		285

"Change, which was to become the great characteristic of the new century, began its acceleration in those early years. When the first decade dawned, kitchen and parlours were still lit mainly by candles and coal-oil lamps. Out west, families still crouched in huts of sod or poplar. The baroque, cast-iron stoves, constantly a-bubble with soups and porridges, were fired by wood. Save in the larger cities the roads were rutted nightmares. It was still the age of the livery stable, blacksmith shop and hitching post. Men shaved their beards with straight razors and women's skirts, plumped out with petticoats, trailed in the mud, dust and slime of the streets. Prices were low enough by today's standards: you could buy a turkey dinner for twenty cents and a muslin nightie for nineteen; you could rent a furnished room by the day for half a dollar."[1]

— PIERRE BERTON, *Remember Yesterday*
A Century of Photographs

"Words which could be used so prodigally in conversation had now to be weighed and measured and set down in a more orderly fashion. Words on paper suddenly assumed a permanence hitherto denied them."[2]

— RICHARD B. WRIGHT, *The Age of Longing*

Acknowledgements

Many people have contributed to the telling of Mary Janeway's story. I am grateful for their contributions and ongoing support.

To the Janeway family: Emma Janeway's daughter, Lois Lamble, and grandchildren, Wayne Lamble and Gail (Lamble) Horner; Emma's sons and daughters-in-law Bob and Merle Touchings and Walter and Arlene Touchings for their enthusiasm to share their family history; Gail (Lamble) Horner, for welcoming me into her home in Edmonton and her willingness to lend me family photographs so carefully preserved; Caroline Janeway's granddaughter, Rowena Lunn, for lending me Mary Janeway's wedding portrait.

To the Jacques family: Joseph Jacques, for being my friend and remembering Mary at his grandfather's funeral when he was ten; Donna Skillings, granddaughter of Daniel Jacques Jr., for saving Annie's letter written in 1907; Barbara Luft and Bill Zinkan, Annie Jacques's grandchildren, who helped fill in the blanks on the Jacques family tree.

To Ivan Black, for walking me through an "ice man's delivery day" in Hamilton.

To the staff at Hamilton Public Library: Stella Clark, retired librarian assistant, for advising me on grammatical correctness and helping me in my search for "old stuff" in Canadian history books; Laura Lamb, Leslie

Powers, and Mariann Horvath, Local History & Archives, for finding answers to my never-ending questions.

To Anne Gow, Ivey Family London Room, London Public Library, for providing archival images of the London streets in 1900.

To Susan Ramsay, curator of Battlefield House Museum, Stoney Creek, for contributing to descriptions of clothing worn in the early 1900s.

To the late Dr. Ruth Shykoff (Dr. Sky), polio survivor, who readily shared her polio stories of the 1920s based on her medical practice and personal experience.

To Allan Easson, retired production manager for the former Vernon Directories Limited Publishers, for providing information about the Hamilton City Directory.

To Theresa Westfall, deputy warden at Warkworth, who searched her computer database of registered convicts at the Kingston Penitentiary in 1925.

To Dave St. Onge, curator of Correctional Services of Canada Museum for providing insight into "life behind bars" at the K.P. and making available "The Convict Register and Description Book" — Kingston Penitentiary.

To Doreen Thomas, chief, Administrative Services Stony Mountain Institution, Winnipeg, Manitoba, for enlightening me about prison life in 1926.

To Kathleen Latulippe, volunteer for the British Family History Society of Ottawa, for researching the Janeway family tree.

To Ron and Diane Lindsay, now of Ingersoll, for sharing the heritage of their hometown Woodstock and providing a roof over my head when I visited.

To Catherine Steel, my dear friend, who pretended that she wasn't when she critiqued my first draft.

To Dundurn: Barry Penhale, my publisher emeritus, who never lost faith in me and believed in the importance of telling the rest of Mary's story; to Jane Gibson, my editor, who never tired of asking me when, where, and why; to Jennifer McKnight, my copy editor, who worked very hard to make sure all was intact.

Acknowledgements

To my family: Catharine Dochstader, my sister, for remembering some of our childhood memories that I'd forgotten; Steve Silva, my son-in-law, for his willingness and ability to scan all the illustrations; Paul Pettit, my husband, for patiently listening to me think out loud and responding to my constantly asking for his opinion.

And to Mary Janeway, who came to Hamilton as a young bride and never left.

Background on Mary Janeway

Since the publication of *Mary Janeway: The Legacy of a Home Child* I have continued to research the Janeway family. Much to my delight, I located some of Mary's relatives in Alberta. Her sister Emma Janeway's children, Gordon Touchings (deceased), Lois Lamble (deceased), Robert "Bob" Touchings in Edmonton, and Walter Touchings in Westlock; Emma's grandchildren, Wayne Lamble in Edmonton and Gail Horner now in Lethbridge, Alberta; and her sister Caroline "Carrie" Janeway's granddaughter, Rowena Lunn, now living in Kelowna, British Columbia.

I also learned that Mary Janeway's parents, William and Martha, along with their children Caroline, John, William, and Mary, relocated from Scotland to London, England, before Mary's younger sister Emma was born in Lambeth, England, in 1888. Two years later, their mother Martha died in childbirth and her sisters came and took the newborn back to Glasgow, leaving William in London to raise Caroline, John, William, Mary, and Emma.

Eleven-year old Carrie was "ready to be trained for service" and helped raise two-year-old Emma. John, age ten, was sent to an orphanage, then ran off to Vancouver, British Columbia, to work in the coal mines. William, age eight, and Mary, age six, were sent to an orphanage in Liverpool, and then to Canada as home children, and were placed on farms in rural Ontario. Their father passed away in 1902. Carrie worked as a nanny to pay for Emma's keep in an orphanage in London, married Frank Lunn, the gardener at a well-to-do home in London where she worked as a maid, and had two sons, Francis "Frank" and Harvey, while living in London.

Carrie, along with her family, and Emma were the last Janeway children to immigrate to Canada. Prior to leaving Britain in 1908, Carrie traced Mary and Will through the Red Cross and found them to be living in Ontario.

In this sequel to *Mary Janeway: The Legacy of a Home Child*, which traces Mary's life up to age sixteen, the Janeway family, the Church family, the witnesses at the weddings, the woman who helped raise Mary's son, the Jacques family, and the Hewson family are real people. The rest are fictional characters, threads of the author's imagination interwoven to create a backdrop to the story in an attempt to tell and understand Mary's life. The places, cities, town, streets, and identified buildings are real. Mary lived her adult years in Hamilton, fondly referred to as the Electric City, the Lunch Pail Town, and the Steel City.

From *Mary Janeway: The Legacy of a Home Child*

July 25, 1900

Mary headed for the station with the same determination that had helped her get this far. She never looked back. When she arrived at the wicket, she found she had enough money, the money Will had given her, to go as far as London. And that is how she decided her destination. The station master could not help wondering where the little curly-haired young woman with the straw hat and tiny red suitcase was really heading as he helped her board the train.

With the exception of one elderly man and a couple, there was no one else aboard. Mary chose a window seat and felt wistful but not sad as the train pulled out. She watched the fields roll by and allowed herself to be gently lulled by the slow lateral motion of the train rolling down the tracks.

After about thirty minutes the train stopped at Beachville to pick up some passengers and mail. A young girl in her mid-twenties boarded the train and stopped beside Mary's seat. Mary panicked briefly. Was this someone from Innerkip who recognized her?

"Do you mind if I sit with you?" she asked.

"No, I don't mind," Mary replied.

"I've a long trip ahead and I hate travelling alone," the girl admitted, smiling as she sat down, removing her large brimmed hat and setting a train case in the aisle beside her. Mary guessed that the girl was around Annie's age but nothing like Annie. This young woman was friendly.

"Where are you going?" Mary asked with curiosity.

"I go as far as London, then I catch another train to Montreal," the girl explained, still a bit out of breath from hurrying. "I'm to meet my cousin Elizabeth there. She's coming to live with us," she said excitedly. "What about you?"

"I'm going to London," Mary answered truthfully. "My sister Caroline just had a baby and she needs me," she said without hesitation. She turned and looked out the window.

And I will be free, she thought.

Cornfields, pastures, rivers, and trees flashed past, but all Mary could see was her own reflection in the glass.

Prologue

> "Most home girls had had at least four years' introduction to Canadian domestic routine by the time they had completed their indentures. Most were weary of other people's babies and other people's housework. They did not go to the city in order to exchange the informality of the farm household for the strict hierarchy of service in a large city establishment or the aprons of the country kitchen for the starched uniforms of the city parlour. They wanted their own room, their own wage and their own choice of what to do on Saturday night."[1]

July 1900

The train ride from Innerkip to London was peaceful in many ways, but also frightening. Mary stared out the train window. A casual observer might have thought that the young girl was taking in the pretty countryside, rolling hills, winding riverbeds full to the brim with creek water from too many rainfalls, and the densely wooded foliage that separated cultivated fields ripening for harvest. Mary may have been looking out at her surroundings, but her mind was elsewhere.

Running away was the culmination of eight long years of loneliness and desperation. No matter how she had dealt with each uncomfortable situation inflicted on her while living on the farm, her thoughts invariably came back to the same fundamental question: "Should I stay or leave?" Today was the first day she would no longer ask herself that question. That was behind her now — forever. She couldn't help but reflect on the events that had unfolded in her short life to bring her to this place in time.

Born in Rutherglen, Scotland, on August 2, 1884, Mary, at the age of five, and her older brother Will had been sent to an orphanage in Liverpool, England. Two-and-a-half years later, she and her brother were put on a ship bound for Canada. They docked in the Montreal harbour, where an agency inspector named Mr. Murray took her, along with a handful of other girls approximately the same age, to a "Distributing Home" in Stratford, Ontario — a temporary shelter until suitable placements could be made.

While awaiting her fate, Mary observed the visitors who arrived to scrutinize the girls in the hope of finding a suitable domestic servant to take home with them. Mostly rural folks in need of help on their farms, some left with a child, some left empty-handed, but most had opinions about home children. It was difficult to forget the comments she overheard while dusting the hall banister.

> Everybody knows those Home Kids have nits.
> Most of the waifs and strays shipped over by those British do-gooders are subnormal at best.
> They're subnormal. That eye colour tells its own tale.
> Nathan's father says the Home Children are all tainted from birth. If they had a Home Boy, he'd sleep in the back shed. Otherwise, he might burn the house down in the night.[2]

Mary knew they were not necessarily talking about her, but the words were still hurtful. Sometimes she'd study her face in the mirror and begin to wonder if they were right. Were home children subnormal? She'd check her hair for nits and look at her eye colour with skepticism. Despite the overheard comments, she hoped that someone would come soon and want a little girl to be part of their family.

Less than two months after her arrival in Stratford, the Jacques family contacted the home and indicated the "need for a girl." Mr. Jacques picked her up in his horse and buggy one sunny afternoon in June 1892 and headed for Innerkip, a small town nearby. Annie, the eldest and only girl in the Jacques family, had three brothers: Thomas, Chris, and the youngest, Daniel, named after his father. Mary had lived on their farm as a domestic servant for eight years, until today when she finally decided she'd had enough.

As the train rolled along with a steady, predictable *clickity-clack*, she began to relax. She thought about her family, those she'd left behind in England, and her brother, whom she'd been separated from after arriving in Canada. Her roots had been in an emotional tangle from the time that she was a young child. She often wondered if it was a coincidence that she'd ended up in Innerkip, named after a river flowing through Renfrewshire, Scotland, near her birthplace. Was her Scottish heritage watching over her like a guardian angel?

After leaving Scotland, her family had gone to London — London, England. And now she was leaving Innerkip, the place she'd called home for half her life, and was heading for another London — London, Ontario.

Mary desperately wanted her freedom and independence, yet having her own room and earning a wage seemed so unattainable to the young girl just a week shy of sixteen. She had $3.61 and a small red valise with a broken strap containing all her worldly possessions, including her Bible, a gift from Reverend Ward, the rector at St. Paul's in Innerkip. He was a very special man, since he'd found her brother Will and made it possible for them to spend a whole day together when she was ten.

She got into the habit of tucking a memento or scrap of paper that was significant in the pages of her Bible. It was where she'd hidden the small white envelope that Will had given her. She would never forget walking home from school that afternoon in late fall, when he'd appeared out of nowhere on the dusty county road with a small horse-drawn wagon.

> *He lowered his voice as though someone might be listening. "I have a plan. As soon as I get settled, I'll come back for you. And we'll find John, we will." He added, "I promise. In the meantime I want you to take this," he said and handed her a small white envelope.*
>
> *"What's this, Will?" she asked.*
>
> *"It's money, not a lot.... it's part of what I earned at the Lounsburys. I want you to keep it, Mary. If for some reason you can't wait for me to come and get you, you'll need some money. Hide it in a safe place and don't tell anyone!"*[3]

ONE
London

> "Work for domestics in private homes was pure drudgery: long hours, lack of social freedom and privacy, and negligible pay."[1]

1900

The gentle swaying of the train and the sound of the metal wheels clicking on the tracks reminded Mary that she was heading to London. She'd never been there before and had nowhere to live once she arrived. When the train pulled into the CPR station on Richmond Street, she was tired and apprehensive, but determined.

Having located a *London Free Press* discarded on one of the benches in the station, Mary quickly scanned the "Female Help Wanted" section. She had no clerical experience and while she was able to cook, no hotel would hire her because she only knew how to make apple butter and Johnnycake. A live-in domestic position was the only choice, especially since it was considered unacceptable for a young, single woman to live alone.

Several ads looked promising. One was for a kitchen girl, $14 per month, and a general servant willing to go to Goderich for August.

Ivey Family London Room, London Public Library, London, Ontario.

In the 1890s, Richmond Street is a muddy streetscape spanning several blocks. Pedestrians are boarding the streetcar and a team of horses are waiting patiently on a side street. Note the horse trough in the right foreground.

Another was for a dining-room girl that paid $12 per month, and the third was also looking for a general servant to go to Goderich. Mary had no idea where that was but would go anywhere if it meant she'd have a job.

It made sense to answer the ad at 501½ Richmond first since she was already on that street. Mary was the most hopeful about this one since two positions were available, but she wondered why a house would have half a number. Shortly it became clear. Two buildings were crammed in the space that should have been for one. She walked up to the narrow, tall brown frame house, third one from the corner. The sign out front read "Fancy Goods, McEwen's Intelligence Office."

Mary knocked on the door timidly. No one answered so she knocked harder. A smallish woman wearing a crisp white uniform appeared. "Can I help you?" she asked kindly.

"I'm here for a job," Mary replied, waving the folded newspaper.

"Oh, you must be asking about the summer home. Can you come back tomorrow morning after ten o'clock? Mrs. McEwen should be home by then."

"Does that mean the positions aren't filled yet?" Mary asked, hopefully.

"I really don't know. I have my hands full looking after things right here."

"I'll be back tomorrow ma'am. Thanks just the same." The lady nodded and closed the door. Mary wasn't discouraged — one of the positions might still be vacant. Her preference was the kitchen girl since the other one was only for a month and probably paid less.

She headed down Dundas Street, walked five blocks, and found 406 Burwell. Taking a big breath before lifting the knocker, she lightly tapped the bright blue door three times. Nothing happened so she did it again with a little more enthusiasm, looking around for signs that someone might be there. Her eyes darted from window to window as she wondered if this place might become her new home. Finally, someone peeked through the front curtains and a moment later a rather stout woman in a plain dress came to the door.

She was told that Mrs. J. Smith McDougall had filled the position two days earlier. "The ad went in the paper a week ago. You might have stood a chance if you'd not been so tardy," she said as she closed the door, leaving Mary standing on the front stoop. She thought the woman had been unnecessarily rude and also thought it might have been a mistake to work for someone who had two names.

"Smith McDougall," she said under her breath, "probably means she's rich."

Mary was too tired and hungry to tackle the last ad, so decided to wait until morning to try her luck again before returning to 501½ Richmond. She stopped at a bakery, bought a cheese bun, and sat on a bench to eat it while she looked at the paper again. Where could she stay for the night? The European Hotel on Dundas Street had special rates for weekly boarders, but when she found it, it looked too fancy and she didn't even bother walking up the steps. She headed down Clarence Street. Ladysmith Hotel had a nice ring to it and Mary hoped that it would be more suitable. She ended up staying two nights, but Charles

Stevens, the proprietor, felt sorry for the young girl and only charged her for one.

Mary was up bright and early the next morning, her first full day in London. It was a beautiful city but so much bigger than she had ever imagined. She'd never seen so many churches and banks. She walked past the post office, police station, and courthouse, overwhelmed with the hustle and bustle of the crowds and rather intimidated having come from such a small place as Innerkip. She wasn't sure whether city life was going to suit her, but one thing was for certain, she wasn't going back to the farm.

She walked eleven blocks before she found St. James Street but within a few minutes was climbing the stairs to #346. Mary felt less optimistic. This ad was only for one position, a good general servant to go to Goderich for the summer. A man answered the door. At first he seemed confused. "You'd have to speak to my wife. She's the one who hires the domestics. Step inside and I'll get her," he said.

A well-dressed woman in her late forties appeared. "Are you here to apply for the position?" she asked, as if there might be some other reasons why she'd be there.

"Yes ma'am. Has it been filled?"

"Not yet. I never hurry when I hire new girls. It's far too important. Do you have references?"

Mary's eyes fell. "No ma'am, I don't but I …" Mary was at a loss for words. She tried to collect her thoughts. "I have a lot of experience cooking, cleaning, and sewing. I know how to make apple butter too." As soon as she said that, she felt foolish. Being able to make apple butter was not going to secure a job.

"Without references I can't possibly consider you. That would be a risk I'm not willing to take," she said decisively and ushered her out.

Mary wandered around for a while and waited until exactly ten before returning to Richmond Street. The smallish woman who'd spoken to her yesterday remembered Mary and invited her into the front room. Mrs. Ellen McEwen appeared and introduced herself. She was tall woman with a tidy bun of chestnut-brown hair and she wore beautiful jewellery.

"I've hired a kitchen girl but still need a general servant. You do realize that it's just for August," she paused. Mary nodded. "It pays $9 and you'd have to travel to Goderich, our summer home on Lake Huron. It's a long trip, about sixty miles by train, but the scenery is splendid." She stopped to take a breath. "You'd have half a day off in the month and Sunday, the Lord's day. Everyone should rest that day including the servants."

"It sounds perfect," Mary replied hoping to hide the desperation in her voice.

"Can you leave the day after tomorrow?"

"I can go sooner if you like," Mary answered. She didn't want to stay in the hotel any longer than necessary.

"If you can leave on Friday, so much the better. And your name is?" she paused.

"Mary … Mary Janeway, ma'am."

"Very well then Mary. The job is yours. Be here by eight o'clock in the morning. I'll already be gone but Elsa can go over a few things with you."

Mary was thrilled. As of tomorrow she had a job and a roof over her head. She strolled down the street, went into a grocery store to buy an orange, then back to the bakery for another pastry. She even bought some licorice to celebrate her good fortune and her birthday that was right around the corner.

The next morning at five to eight, Mary knocked confidently on Mrs. McEwen's door. The same lady that she'd already met twice gave her a second-class train ticket to Goderich and directions to the Grand Trunk Railway station. The lady, whom Mary assumed was Elsa, chattered away as if she had all the time in the world. "Since you're new in town, you probably don't know that we've got two train stations. Would you believe that we live exactly half way between them? It's very convenient if I do say so myself. Now, let me see, where was I?"

With that she walked out on the front stoop and pointed to the right. "Just stay on Richmond and walk a fair piece until you come to York. You can't miss it, the station's right there as big as life, across the street from The Grigg House Hotel. There's no danger of you getting on the wrong train, since there's only one line into Goderich. I suspect that will change.

Ivey Family London Room, London Public Library, London, Ontario.

A group of people are standing on the platform at the Grand Trunk Railway Depot. The inscription erroneously gives the location as Richmond Street, but it was situated on the south side of York Street between Richmond and Clarence Streets.

I'll bet it won't be long before the CPR goes into Goderich too." Mary wasn't the least bit interested in how many trains went into Goderich since one was all she needed.

"If you get lost just ask anyone directions to the Grand Trunk. You'll find folks around here pretty friendly." She explained all this without seeming to ever stop for a breath of air.

Mary nodded, never indicating that she'd already familiarized herself with the main streets. She felt that it was wise not to share all her business or appear too knowledgeable. The woman went on to explain that it was about a three-hour trip and someone would be there to greet her. Mary was growing accustomed to taking the train. This trip wouldn't seem nearly as intimidating as the last one.

TWO

Summer in Goderich

> "'Goderich, the prettiest town in Canada,' its city fathers apparently taking as true, a compliment paid by visiting royalty in the 19th century."[1]

August 1900

Mary looked out the train window with anticipation. The town of Goderich was perched on a bluff looking west over Lake Huron, not unlike a robin's nest high up in a tree branch close to water. She could see some houses, big beautiful houses, and suspected that she'd be living in one of them.

She was met by Emil, the young boy the McEwen's had hired to run errands. It was a short buggy ride to the lakefront cottage on Essex Street. A peaked, cedar-shingle roof extending over the main veranda and the bevel-edged, wooden horizontal exterior siding added to its character. Mary thought it was pretty enough to be in a magazine. She was introduced to Sadie, the kitchen girl, and given a cot in the servant's quarters. There were a few awkward moments at first so she busied herself unpacking what little she owned. Sadie showed her a cupboard designated for the "general servant."

She was given her instructions on Saturday morning. Mary followed closely at Mrs. McEwen's heels as she walked down the hallway, pointing out the small bedrooms. "The first thing you'll do every morning is empty the chamber pots." She couldn't help but cringe. She was then shown the proper way to make beds and told to change the sheets every Monday. "I'd like the bedrooms swept every other day, the others can be done the day in between." Mary quickly realized she'd be sweeping six days a week.

"Yes, ma'am."

"If you have any questions ask Sadie. She did your job last year. For now, let's concentrate on the washing since that's your main job and it will probably take the best part of your day. Follow me."

Mary walked silently behind her. The woman's long grey cotton skirt made a swishing noise as it moved from side to side, brushing the walls as she headed into the kitchen. Sadie looked up and smiled, then continued rolling pastry on the dough board for a raspberry braid she was preparing for lunch. The kitchen was full of good smells that brought back a wave of memories for Mary, memories that weren't all that pleasant.

"Fill the copper boiler with well water every night and put it on the stove. That way it's ready for morning when you light the fire and bring it up to boil. Put the clothes in while it's heating and grate some Sunlight soap. It's over here." She held up a small cornflower-blue granite bowl with a stub of a soap bar in it. "I never have the girls use anything but Sunlight, it's guaranteed to be a good cleaner." Mary watched in silence, her eyes occasionally glancing over at Sadie.

"Once the water is good and hot, you must podge it. You do know what that is, don't you?" Mary shook her head. Mrs. McEwen reached over and picked up what looked to be an upside-down funnel with holes in it and pushed it up and down in the pot. "This is a podger and what it does is cycle and circulate the water through the clothes.[2] Be careful not to touch the water, you might get burned." Mary looked down at the scar on her right arm.

It had been a cold winter's night that December, just a few days after the Christmas concert. The wind howled like wild dogs and the drafts through the clapboards made the house cold, damp, and uncomfortable. More heat was needed.

"Where's that girl? Get some wood in the stove," Mrs. Jacques demanded from across the room. Mary never answered. She was sitting on her milk stool by the end of the stove with her head down. "What are you doing there, Girl?" Mrs. Jacques continued to prod. The oldest boy, Thomas, gave her a kick, which toppled her off the stool causing her right arm to fall against the hot stove. At first no one realized that Mary had fainted. With sudden realization, young Daniel screamed for help as he pulled her inert body away.

"Thomas, run and get the cream quickly," Mrs. Jacques ordered as she wheeled across the room toward Mary. All Mary could remember when she came to was lying on the floor and Annie putting cream on her right arm, which had blistered from the extreme heat. It was the only time she thought Mrs. Jacques looked frightened. She was a great believer in herbal remedies like poultices, tonics, and hop tea, but even she began to panic when she saw the extent of the burn on Mary's arm. "Put lots of cream on her, Annie. We don't want her scarred."[3]

Mary covered the scar with her other hand. "Then you put them through this wringer," Mrs. McEwen said, pointing to an antiquated hand wringer that was screwed to a nearby table top, with a laundry tub full of water sitting on the floor underneath it. "One rinse isn't near enough, so you should podge the soap out of them again or put them through two rinses. Any questions so far, Mary?"

Mary was surprised that she called her by name. "No ma'am, I think I understand."

"Good, let's move on then. After the rinses, put them in one of these wicker baskets and hang them outside. Always start with bed sheets since they take the longest to dry, even on a sunny day."

Mary had hoped her job would be more than sweeping, washing, and making beds, but she soon realized there was a distinct pecking order among servants. Just before Mrs. McEwen left the kitchen, she handed Mary a blue-and-white stripe dress and cotton pinafore.

Sadie could tell that the "new" girl was overwhelmed and felt sorry for her. She got a little closer and whispered, "I was scared too when I first started. Maybe you can have my job next summer. I've already given my notice 'cause I'm leaving at the end of the month." She paused and grinned, "I'm getting married this fall. Working in here isn't so bad and the pay is better." She smiled and went back to her pastry board. Mary didn't need to be reminded that her job was paying $5 less.

The next day, the Sabbath, meant little or no work was permitted. Mrs. McEwen told the girls that they were welcome to go to church provided they sat at the back. Sadie had already offered to take her into town to show her around and Mary thought it sounded like a lot more fun than listening to a minister's sermon.

"Let's go into town first and save the best for last," Sadie said, tossing her apron over the back of a chair. She couldn't wait to get out of the kitchen.

"What's the best?" asked Mary.

"You'll see," she grinned and grabbed her by the arm. The two girls headed in the direction of Goderich's famous octagon-in-the-square known as the Court House Square, which was actually round. A rumour had spread that the town had accidentally been given the plans for the city of Guelph — an interesting theory but not true.[4]

They walked through the park, past the post office, a green grocer advertising a dozen apples or oranges for fifteen cents, and a second-hand shop, all with "closed" signs in their windows. At the west end of the square, Mary saw an impressive sign on top of a building that read "G.N. Davis." He was a dealer in hardware, stoves, tinware, and general house-furnishing goods and his store was referred to as the Stove Depot. As they continued round the square, she could see several hotels, livery stables, and carriage shops in the distance.

"You'll notice that none of the stores have verandas," said Sadie, as though she were an official tour guide. Mary shrugged. Sadie continued,

"Some folk say a store collapsed after a heavy snowfall a few years ago so other shopkeepers were afraid and tore them down.

"We could go that way," Sadie pointed in a northerly direction, "if you're interested in seeing the jail." Mary shook her head. "It's a strange-looking building. It gives me the creeps to think that bad people live so close by. They've had two hangings there," she whispered. Mary looked skeptical. "Don't tell me you've never heard of the Black Donnellys?"

"No, who are they?"

Sadie headed for a bench under a large tree in the park, sat down, and patted the seat beside her. "An Irish family by the name of Donnelly lived not too far from here. They had seven boys and one girl named Jenny. They were very bad, all of them," she paused, "except for the girl. James, the father, killed a man and the local authorities posted a $400 reward for anyone who would bring him to the Goderich jail. They never got him but he turned himself in. He was very mean and so was his wife Johannah. Everybody was afraid of them."

"What happened?"

"He ended up going to prison in Kingston and when he got out, he came back. Eventually the local people ganged up and hunted down the family. The men that killed the Donnellys were all Irish, all Catholics, just like the Donnellys, and were some of their closest neighbours. It was called the Donnelly massacre and they all got killed except three brothers who didn't live in town," Sadie said dramatically.

"Do you think anyone has ever escaped?" Mary asked, showing more interest in the jail than the Donnelly family.

"I think they've tried but no one's ever done it. The walls are huge. I heard that they're something like two or three feet thick." Sadie chattered away. "I wonder what the food would be like, probably not great but at least it'd be free." She laughed at her own joke and jumped up. "Come on, Mary, we've got a lot more to see."

"Do they have a library here?"

"Yeah, it's the next block over on Lighthouse Street, but it wouldn't be open today."

"Do you ever go there?"

"No," Sadie hesitated, "I don't like to read." Mary sensed she was uncomfortable and wondered if Sadie knew how to read. Not everyone had the opportunity to go to school, and nothing more was said.

"Come over here," she said impatiently, grabbing Mary's arm. "Have a look in the window." The girls moved closer to the glass, cupping their faces with their hands to block the sun. "Hannah's Bakery is the best! Now you won't get the full effect today, so you'll have to use your imagination. But honestly, you have to walk past on a workday. I swear you can smell the hot-cross buns a block away. They're six cents apiece and worth every penny." Mary was starting to feel hungry, which reminded her that it had been a while since they'd eaten.

They continued on and came to a place where there were no homes, just a little hill that led to the beach below. Sadie ran down with Mary close at her heels, and to her delight there was the lake — Lake Huron. Other than when she crossed the ocean to come to Canada, the closest she'd ever been to water was the Thames River and the quiet little pond beside the gristmill when she lived in Innerkip.

"I told you I saved the best for last," Sadie explained, breathless. They walked along the town beaches watching picnickers and Sunday strollers enjoy the warm mid-afternoon sun. Sadie ran to the water's edge, plunked herself in the sand, and took off her shoes. Mary followed close behind like a duckling with its mother. Both began to wade in the cool water. It felt so good.

Mary knew she'd be happy in Goderich, if for no other reason than being so close to the water. She picked up some shiny beach glass and a few interesting stones, weathered smooth from time, and pocketed them. They'd end up in her faded red tea caddy, the one she'd found in the hayloft while living on the farm, along with her other treasures.

They went as far as the lighthouse and Sadie pointed out the bluffs high above them. "You wouldn't believe the view from there. And if you're lucky you might see a steamer squeeze through the breakwater into the harbour. They come in quite often." It was getting late so she suggested they head "home." Mary hadn't really thought of Goderich as home and was a bit anxious about tomorrow morning, her first day on the job.

Her day began at seven, making beds and emptying the chamber pots. Mary was no stranger to this chore; she'd done it for the past eight years. As far as she was concerned, it was the worst job. Sadie had shown her the privy, tucked behind a large oak tree in the back corner of the yard. She also had explained that the servants were accustomed to going down to the lake to bathe. Mary was familiar with privies but washing in the lake was new to her and seemed strange at first.

Cleaning and laundry took the whole day and Mary was exhausted when she went to bed that night. Her muscles ached but it was a good tired. After a couple of days, she got into a routine and was able to get her work done a little sooner. At first Mary had been afraid that if she finished too quickly, another chore would be waiting for her. But Mrs. McEwen assured her that if her tasks were properly done, she was free for the rest of the day. That alone was her incentive to work hard.

She celebrated her sixteenth birthday, if you could call it a celebration in a house full of strangers. She'd been there exactly one week. Mary finished her chores early, which meant she had time to walk into town. Her licorice was long gone so she treated herself to one of her favourite candies, a pound of buttercups, which cost ten cents and a package of spearmint gum. She never chewed more than half a piece at a time to make it last longer.

She walked down the escarpment and along the beach, reflecting on past birthdays. This was one of the better ones. Mary was determined to make the best of her situation. The people were kind enough and her surroundings were beautiful. The outdoor work of hanging up the clothes proved to be the best part of her job so she always took her time. She was happier than she'd ever been in the past eight years.

Sadie was a friendly girl and Mary was glad they'd met. She thought she seemed young to be getting married, but perhaps was a bit envious as well. She looked wistfully across the lake and wondered if there was a fellow out there somewhere for her. She hoped so. She closed her eyes, turning her face in the direction of the warm gentle August breeze, and wiped a strand of hair out of her eyes. She thought a great deal about her future. It made it easier to bury the past. She hadn't given up hope that someday, somehow she'd meet her brothers and sisters again.

Since Sunday was a day of rest, all kinds of preparation had to be done the day before. It meant having to do two days' work in one. But it was Mary's favourite day of the week — a break in her routine that gave her a chance to walk along the beach with Sadie. Newspapers and magazines were put away, and people were encouraged to read only "Sunday" things, things that had to do with a person's Christian faith. Mary could never figure out why God would object to anyone reading a good book or writing a letter to a friend.

On her half day off that she had earned after working for two weeks, she went into town to browse in the second-hand store and buy a milk-chocolate nut roll. Then she headed to the beach to walk barefoot in the sand. She watched a family of five having a picnic under the shade of a tree, a dog chasing a stick, and a young couple strolling hand-in-hand down the shoreline toward the piers. Mary was amazed at how quickly she had adapted to her new place. It felt as if she'd been there longer than a few weeks.

Sadly, at the end of August she had to say goodbye to Sadie and the little town of Goderich. Mrs. McEwen offered Mary a temporary job in her London home because her dining room girl had come down with a fever. From the train window she watched the harbour, the tall wooden grain elevators, the piers, breakwaters, and break wall grow smaller and smaller. Mary knew she would miss this picturesque little town and more than likely would never return.

THREE

Back in London

"In the first decade of the twentieth century, men made up almost 90% of the labour force, and in the good years there was no scarcity of jobs."[1]

September 1900

Mary was back in London just in time to observe the Labour Day celebrations. It rained in the morning but by noon the skies cleared and the sun came out. The rain had affected the number of spectators along the parade route, which went from Market Square downtown to Queen's Park. But at Queen's Park, the crowd was estimated to be about three thousand. Mary was content to catch a glimpse of the parade, as she'd only seen one before when she was living on the farm in Innerkip.

Mary learned more about Mrs. McEwen after she moved back to the city. She had a fancy goods shop and her husband was a private investigator, hence the sign on the front lawn. It was no secret that a well-to-do auntie had left them her summer home in Goderich.

The job, however, only lasted two months until the girl she'd been replacing was well enough to return. She found another general servant position and spent her days cleaning and doing laundry for a family of seven. It was similar to her job in Goderich, but without Sadie's company and the advantage of a beach and beautiful lake.

Mary celebrated Christmas alone in her room above the kitchen. She strung popcorn and cranberries and draped it across the top of her window. Red tissue paper over the lamp and a small green candle in a jelly jar she'd picked up at the market gave her tiny room a festive look in spite of the absence of a tree and gifts. She felt fortunate in many ways. She had a job, a little money, and a roof over her head, but, more importantly, she had her independence.

January was a chilly month and everyone worked hard at keeping warm. She remembered the day that she'd stopped at the busy newsstand on the corner of Dundas and Richmond for a package of gum. People were mulling around, talking about the headlines in the *London Free Press.* Queen Victoria was dying. Mary remembered singing "God Save the Queen" at the orphanage and had been taught to show respect for Her Majesty, the lady whose portrait hung on the wall in the dining room. She didn't know how to react to the latest news but sensed a general sadness in the air.

> As evening shadowed London on January 22, 1901, a tired old lady slipped out of the world. Victoria, Queen of England, had ruled one-quarter of the earth, one in every five persons on the planet. One could travel around the globe secure in British law and custom, the nearest thing to a world government that man had ever known. Values were stable, business expansive, and progress was more of the new gospel. Victoria had always tried to keep things as they were. But now Victoria was gone, and with her an age.[2]

The Queen's passing made the headlines of newspapers and magazines across the country and was the topic of conversation on every street corner. Journalists penned their thoughts and tried to do justice to the passing of a Royal figure, a Queen who had meant so much to Britain as well as other countries in the Empire. It wouldn't be until four years later that Mary thought about Queen Victoria again. At that time her late Royal Majesty took on a more personal meaning.

Mary flitted from job to job like a bee searching for nectar. When things became intolerable in one situation, she had no choice but to look for another position. It was Mary's lucky day when she saw Mrs. Balfour's ad in the paper: "WANTED — AT ONCE, A GOOD GENERAL servant; in exchange for 3 meals a day, own room, $9 a month. Apply 440 Maple Street."

She arrived at the woman's doorstep, having walked fifteen blocks. Mary was down to her last fifty cents. Her present job was babysitting two-year old Henry, "Henry the handful." Although he was a little monster, that wasn't the reason she wanted to leave. Henry's mom, a waitress who worked evenings, was often unable to pay Mary.

"I'm a little short tonight. I'll pay you the day after tomorrow. You know I'm good for it and Henry loves you so." Mary had stayed longer than she should have, for the little boy's sake.

Mrs. Jenny Balfour, a short, round, plumpish lady with beautiful white hair, wiped her hands on her faded blue gingham apron and answered the gentle knock. Mary quickly inquired if the position was still open.

"Oh, I assumed someone more … mature would answer my ad," she said.

"I'm almost seventeen and I've worked as a domestic since I was eight," Mary replied. The woman ushered her into her quaint but cluttered front room. After brief introductions, she was invited to stay for morning tea. Mrs. Balfour said very little about the job and seemed more interested in chatting about her personal philosophy on life.

A small black cat appeared in the doorway. Mary's heart skipped a beat remembering Mustard, the yellow barn cat she'd befriended on the farm. The cat meandered into the room ignoring both of them, climbed up on the windowsill, and fell asleep in the sun.

"What's his name?" Mary asked.

"It's Barney, but he went without one for quite a while. I found him curled up on my doorstep one cold, snowy morning last December. Felt kinda sorry for the little fella, just skin and bone. I gave him a saucer of buttermilk; he curled up by the warm stove and pretty much decided to stay. Everybody called him something different. He got Blacky, Midnight, and Patch for the white spot on his paw, which made sense, but none of them suited him. He was quiet and didn't bother much with people, probably been a stray too long."

"So how'd you end up with Barney?"

"I'm coming around to where I want to be," she said, letting out a big sigh. "About the same time he arrived, I had a boarder by the name of Barney Huntley … the old codger. He wasn't the friendliest sort, kept to himself, real quiet, but paid his rent on time. I asked him one day if he had any kin and he shook his head. So I said, 'how would you like a cat named after you?' It was one of the few times I'd ever seen him smile." Mary remained silent, knowing there was more to the story.

"Poor man had a heart condition and a few months later he died, in that room right above your head," she said, pointing upward with her index finger. Mary looked up and silently prayed that that room wasn't going to be hers. "That's how Barney got his name."

"I had a cat once, his name was Mustard. It was a long time ago."

"You said you'd worked as a domestic for a number of years."

"Almost ten," she said, realizing she was exaggerating slightly. "I cleaned, dusted, prepared meals, helped at sewing bees, and even baked bread and canned preserves," she replied with confidence.

"I'm curious as to why would you'd have done all those things at such an early age."

Mary was cautious about sharing her past and paused momentarily. "My parents passed away and I was left to fend for myself," she said, having no intention of telling her that she'd been sent to an orphanage and become a home child. "I went to school and I can read," she paused, realizing that that probably wouldn't help secure the job, "and I'm a good worker," she added. Mary thought Mrs. Balfour looked a little too old to have children at home but asked anyway.

"I have a son and a daughter." She picked up a small pewter frame housing an old black and white photo of a young couple holding hands. She wiped the dust off with a corner of her apron and handed it to her. "My daughter Martha and her husband Malcolm live in Toronto. It's too far for many visits but my son-in-law is in the coal business and had to go where there's work. No children unfortunately, which means no grandchildren for me," she said sadly putting it back on the bookshelf.

"And your son?"

She shook her head and looked out the window. "He died three years ago, three years next month, down at the docks in Hamilton Harbour. Thomas was a chainman in the foundry. They said it was a freak accident with the electric brake on an overhead crane. Lost my husband too, a long time ago. Life hasn't always been kind, but I've learned to put my faith in the Almighty."

She took a breath and continued, "That's when I started to take in boarders. Thomas used to help out but he didn't have a lot to spare. I've always done the cleaning myself but my arthritis has been acting up lately. Never had help before, kind of hate to admit I need it. Martha wants me to come and live with them. I'm putting it off as long as I can manage," she smiled. "Would you like to see your room?"

"I'd like that, ma'am," she replied and they headed upstairs, thankfully walking past the room that had been occupied by Barney Huntley. Mary's room was small but not tiny, tastefully decorated in pale lilac with soft white muslin tieback curtains framing a tall, narrow window. She wondered if it had been Martha's but didn't dare ask, for fear that it would lead to another long-winded story.

Mary settled into her new home quickly. Whenever things were going well, she thought about her family. Her sisters were back in England, John had gone out west, and the last time she'd seen Will was the summer she turned eleven.

"Are we almost there?" she asked, looking up at her travelling companion with her soft blue eyes. The Reverend hoped and prayed that Will was Mary's brother.

Upon their arrival shortly after ten in the morning, Will was called in from the barn. He was visibly shocked to discover his sister standing in front of him.

"Mary, is that really you?" he asked. His face went pale as he dropped his cap and ran to hug her tightly.

Reverend Ward slipped out the kitchen door with a nod of his head and mouthed the words, "I'll be back later." The Lounsburys suggested that Will show his sister around so they headed for the barn. Once outside, Will wrapped his strong arms around Mary and clung to her.

For a minute neither Mary nor Will spoke. "Mary, I can't believe it's really you. Is this a dream? Let me look at you," Will exclaimed, releasing his hold. He grabbed both of Mary's hands and took one step backward as if to soak up every detail and put to memory what he saw. Mary was so overwhelmed, she never said a word. She couldn't take her eyes off her brother.[3]

Ivey Family London Room, London Public Library, London, Ontario.

On November 26, 1895, a large, three-storey red-brick library building was opened at Queen's Avenue and Wellington. Note a raised, moulded cement sign above the double-arched entrance saying Public Library and the small balcony above the entrance.

Mary desperately wanted to find Will. It took a great deal of courage to go to the public library and ask for help. The sign perched on top of the desk said "Robert J. Blackwell, Librarian," but a woman was standing behind the counter. Miss Rothsay, one of many assistants, was a stern little lady with short reddish-brown hair. Once you were inside "her" library, no talking was allowed — just a whisper. Miss Rothsay told her that the government had sealed the records of Canada's home children and "she best forget about it." Mary thought it was more likely that she couldn't be bothered to accommodate a young girl's request for information.

Since she was there, she decided it would be a good opportunity to borrow a book. The public didn't have free access to the shelves prior to 1908, which meant the staff had to retrieve the books and a certain amount of interaction was necessary. Mary was intimidated by Miss Rothsay but refused to give up her favourite pastime because of a grumpy old librarian assistant.

Sometimes on her way home she'd stop to pick up a little penny candy. She couldn't wait to lose herself in a good book while enjoying some red licorice or a few black balls. She could never completely finish one without taking it out of her mouth periodically to check the colour, and she was convinced it was a life-long habit.

It was surprisingly quiet at 440 Maple Street considering there were six boarders living in close quarters. This was probably due to the fact that Mrs. B., a nickname that Mary came up with, insisted on clean, respectable, non-smoking adults without pets even though she had Barney. Mary got used to people coming and going but was careful not to grow too attached to anyone, since the length of a boarder's stay was never certain.

Some were easier to get along with than others. Miss Freeman, a spinster schoolteacher, had this annoying habit of correcting everyone's grammar. Mary waited for the day that she'd make an error herself, but it never happened. When the woman was agitated, which was a great deal of the time, she'd take one of the small tortoise-shell combs from her cropped-off, tinted red hair, which she wore straight back, and scrape her scalp vigorously. As strange a habit as this was, it seemed to calm her down.

Mary preferred Mrs. Polanski, a very sweet lady who sat in the front room and would knit for hours. She always seemed so happy and content. Harvey Langdon, who everyone nicknamed Handy Harvey, thought he was both a comedian and a repairman. All his jokes began with "Did you hear about the guy who …" and even if you nodded, he'd still tell you. When Harvey fixed one thing for Mrs. B., two more were broken. Strangely enough, she never got upset with him.

Mrs. B. was a kind, caring woman with a unique sense of humour. When someone came down with a winter cold, she'd say, "If you ignore it, it would last two weeks and if you pamper it, it would last a fortnight."[4] She had home remedies for everything from colds, catarrh, ague, ear, and toothaches, and swore by her little "cure it all" book if barley water or consommé soup didn't solve the problem. Here is some of the advice that she followed:

- To ease the pain of a toothache, clamp your teeth on a clove.
- If you had an earache, drop warm oil called electric oil in the offending ear or hold a small bag of salt, which had been heated, against the ear.
- To induce a good night's sleep, warm milk with a teaspoon of honey was the answer.
- A croupy cough called for a teaspoon of sugar with turpentine dripped on the sugar.
- For a bad cough, eucalyptus on the sugar was the treatment as well as the inevitable mustard plaster.[5]

Mary would have to be quite ill before subjecting herself to a mustard plaster. She remembered Mrs. Chesney preparing "a plaster" for her son Jimmy who had galloping consumption. She made a paste of mustard, flour, and lukewarm water, spread it on a piece of flannelette from an old sheet, and covered it with a layer of butter muslin. It had only been on his chest ten minutes when his skin started to blister. She seemed pleased with the results, quickly removed it, and put Vaseline on the blisters. The anguish on Jimmy's face told a different story.

Pamphlets full of medical advice based on good intentions found themselves in people's homes. Word of mouth was powerful advertising. It wasn't uncommon for people to see their neighbour's names in a hand-delivered pamphlet endorsing something to promote healthy living. That's how Mrs. B. heard about these hard black blocks called Spanish Cream for dry mouth and a hacking cough. She'd hammer them into small pieces and was convinced the pungent little nuggets had a medicinal quality when placed under the tongue. Mary was suspicious that they were nothing more than licorice.

Mrs. B. purchased liniments from the Raleigh or Watkins man at the door but refused to buy cough medicines since honey and lemon juice were just as effective and far cheaper. She also used a product derived from the deadly nightshade family called "belladonna." She'd put a drop in each eye if she was tired and believed that it helped her to see better. In reality, all it did was dilate her pupils.

She often shared her opinions with Mary while they prepared supper. "I think people expect Dr. Phillips to make house calls when it isn't necessary. If he charged more than fifty cents, they'd think twice about it. He's too nice for his own good. I've heard that he's made house calls to people who couldn't pay and he's still their doctor. That isn't right." Mary knew from living on the farm that many times rural folk couldn't pay the doctor. "I remember when one of our neighbours on the farm couldn't pay Dr. Chesney for delivering their baby ... the fifth one! They gave him chickens instead. I often wondered how they decided that little Elijah was worth three chickens," she said and then continued peeling potatoes.

"At least *your* neighbours gave him something," Mrs. B. replied. "Mary, are you feeling all right? You look peaked."

"I'm okay, just a bit of a sore throat."

"I want you to forget about the rest of your chores today."

"But I haven't dusted or swept the front room."

"A little dust or dirt won't hurt anyone. Why a man on a galloping horse would never see it and a blind man would be glad to." Mrs. B. insisted that she go to bed right after supper with a wet handkerchief wrapped around her neck, covered with a thick wool sock. Mary was surprised how much better she felt the next morning.

FOUR

Mrs. B. Gets Sick

"By the turn of the century electricity was becoming a normal part of city life."[1]

1903

Living at #440 wasn't always easy. Although Mrs. B. was fussy about whom she "took in," a certain amount of tension was expected among boarders in a rooming house. When things got harried, Mary would go to her room and curl up on her bed with a book. Thanks to the electric light bulb, she could read well into the night with far more safety than candlelight.

She decided that living in the city had its advantages, like being close to the library, having mail delivery, and a newspaper left at your door six days a week. Even though she didn't get any letters and it was usually yesterday's news by the time she got the paper, it was still better than being on the farm. She could always find a magazine lying around with glossy advertisements of the latest gadgets and beauty creams.

Mary also enjoyed trade cards, the hand-delivered colourful cards that expounded on the wonders of a product. She was intrigued by the things that someone would dream up to sell and the promises made on the little cards dropped at Mrs. B.'s door. By today's standards a great number of these trade cards would be considered in poor taste. Black people were often pictured in a derogatory way and even something as innocent as "Daisy Rubbers," footwear for the rainy season in 1902, would have a different connotation by the twenty-first century.

By far the most exciting invention was the horseless carriage. Mrs. B. got talking to Mary about the "motor vehicle craze" one Sunday afternoon. "I can tell you that the first man in Canada to buy one lived in Hamilton. I can't recall his name but I remember one paper said it cost him a thousand dollars and another one claimed it was sixteen hundred. Either way that was a lot of money five years ago." Mrs. B. was referring to John Moodie, the Hamiltonian who bought the first four-wheeled gasoline-propelled motor vehicle to be owned and operated in this country. The little one-cylinder Winton was manufactured in Cleveland and could do twenty-five miles an hour.

Hamilton Public Library, Local History and Archives.

Moodie's Winton was one of only twenty-one hand-crafted vehicles produced by Winton Motor Carriage Company Cleveland in 1898, their first year of production.

"Have you ever been in one, Mrs. B?"

"A motor vehicle?" she asked. Mary nodded. "No, I don't know anyone that well-to-do, and besides, I wouldn't trust it anyway."

"I would," Mary replied, sipping her tea. "It looks like fun."

Mrs. B. smiled. She enjoyed Mary's company and wished she could have paid her more. She encouraged her to look for a part-time job. Mary found one minding the Parson girls around the corner on Kent Street while their mother taught singing lessons in the local church basement three evenings a week. She'd heard that Mrs. Parson told the children to "practice 'till you're blue in the face and blood spurts out of your nose," and was glad she wasn't one of her students. She enjoyed Jessie, the six-year old, but two-year old Larissa was another story. Once in a while their dad would come home from work early and he'd let the girls do whatever they wanted.

"Where are my little angels?" he'd ask, and they'd immediately pop out of bed.

"Mrs. Parson wanted them in bed at seven, sir."

"Mrs. Parson isn't here. Girls, wouldn't you like to stay up and keep your dad company?" Naturally they'd squeal with delight.

"Can we have a treat, Papa?" Larissa would croon in her father's ear. He always complied, knowing full well that his wife was strict with candy and never allowed it before bed.

Mary preferred babysitting when he wasn't around but knew better than to complain. Jobs were difficult to find and it meant an extra twenty-five cents a week. Time passed quickly and she was content for almost two years when her life took a sudden turn.

She was walking home from babysitting one night in late November, enjoying the Christmas lights folks had wrapped around their verandas. As she approached Mrs. B.'s house, she knew that something was wrong. Instead of just the single porch light and soft glow from a hurricane lamp in the front room, there were lights on everywhere. A pale, agitated Mrs. Wyse greeted her at the door.

"I have bad news Mary. Mrs. Balfour was taken to the hospital a little while ago. She took a spell."

"What do you mean a spell?"

"We don't know yet, dear," she said, gently putting her arm around her. Mary felt numb inside but managed to save her tears until she got to her room. For most of her eighteen years she'd remained aloof from others but she'd grown to care deeply for the lady she called Mrs. B.

Mrs. B. stayed in the hospital two and a half weeks. Mary, with the help of Mrs. Wyse, ran the boarding house, making sure the rents were collected on time. The doctor said that she'd had a stroke but was lucky it hadn't been too serious. Before she was discharged, Dr. Phillips came to see her.

"Let this be a warning sign to slow down, Jenny, and let others do the work."

"Should I be selling my house and moving in with my daughter?" she asked.

"I think it's time." Mrs. B. had placed Dr. Phillips on a pedestal four years ago when he'd been there for her after she lost her son. She wouldn't think of questioning his advice nor would she let anyone else. She spoke to Mary the day before her house went on the market.

"Let's have some tea," she said, having waited until everyone else had left the kitchen. Mrs. B. poured her famous blackcurrant tea from the dainty pink rosebud teapot and handed Mary her cup. "This isn't easy for me but I have to face facts. Dr. Phillips wants me to move in with Martha. He thinks it's time I slowed down."

Mary tried to steady her hand as she set her teacup on the table. She vaguely remembered a similar situation when her father had told her that he couldn't cope after their mother had died and some of them were being sent to an orphanage. Mary had only been five at the time but it had been a traumatic experience that she'd never forget. Mrs. B.'s words reminded her that she was being abandoned all over again.

"I've given a lot of thought to you," Mrs. B. said quietly. "After all, you're the reason I was able to stay here as long as I have. An old friend of mine, Lottie McKinnell, who lives in Woodstock, came to visit me in the hospital. She told me that a friend of a friend is looking for kitchen help. I thought of you right away. It would mean moving to Woodstock, but I've heard it's a nice town. Sleep on it a night or two, dear. In any case, it'll take me a while to sell my house."

Mrs. B. asked a fair price and #440 was sold within a few weeks, which meant that Mary had to find a new place to live after Christmas. She had no choice but to accept the position that Mrs. B.'s friend had offered her.

"You'll do fine. You're a bright girl and I know they'll like you."

"It's not the job I'm worried about; it's missing you, Mrs. B." Mary replied.

"I feel the same way, but I'm an old woman now and need to be taken care of," she handed her a paper. "Here's my daughter's address in Toronto. You can always come to visit me."

"I'd like that very much," Mary said, pocketing the slip of paper. They both knew it would never happen, but somehow it made saying goodbye a little easier. Gradually the boarders moved out. Mary kept hoping that something would make Mrs. B. change her mind, but it was not to be.

She packed her things and left early Thursday morning, the last day of December. As she headed down the street in the direction of the GTR station, she turned back to wave to Mrs. B. But this time she wasn't standing on the front porch or looking out the window. She was already gone and Mary knew there was absolutely no reason for her to stay.

FIVE
Woodstock

> "Van Ave., as it is now commonly called, has always been considered as 'the Avenue' and to live on the Avenue was the final step up the social ladder of the elite of Woodstock at the turn of the century. A glance down the list of residents turns up a fair collection of doctors, lawyers, merchants, gentlemen and town and county officials. The owners of these homes engaged many servants including gardeners, parlour maids and kitchen help. Yes, it was something to live on the Avenue."[1]

January 1904

Mary walked down Vansittart Avenue with an address carefully handwritten on Mrs. B.'s fine Wedgwood Blue stationery. She felt certain that the people living on this beautiful tree-lined street were very, very rich. She did stay with the Thompsons two months, then took a job as a parlour maid down the street, and by early May was ready to move on again. After finding it so hard to say goodbye to Mrs. B., Mary vowed she wouldn't get that attached to people.

Her next job was as a nanny for the Heppletons for $10.50 a month plus room and board. Mr. Heppleton was a well-respected jeweller on Dundas Street. In Mary's free time, which didn't usually amount to much, she loved to leaf through Mrs. Heppleton's Eaton's catalogue. "Widely circulated across the country, the Eaton's catalogue was referred to as 'the wishing book' by struggling families. You could have your goods delivered quite cheaply by freight to your nearest railroad station, or sent by mail at a cost of sixteen cents per pound. Five cents extra guaranteed safe delivery."[2]

Mary tried to imagine herself in an Irish linen skirt worth $1.75 or a printed duck shirtwaist suit. Shirtwaists (blouses today) were one of the first widely sold affordable ready-made items ranging in price from 65¢ to $2.25. The lined cashmere waist, available in ten colours, was the most expensive, and garments costing a $1.50 or less only came in black. "I hate black," she said under her breath, flipping the catalogue shut.

A walk to the park over on Light Street would help her forget about the beautiful clothes that she couldn't afford. Victoria Park was a whole city-block square with big trees around the perimeter, a large cannon at one end, a few benches, and a lot of green grass. It wasn't a particularly pretty park but it was a quiet place where she could go to read and no one could find her to do another chore.

One of the first things Mary did when she arrived in Woodstock was to find the local library. She was given directions to the corner of Perry and Dundas. When she saw no evidence of a library, she asked an elderly lady, who pointed above a drugstore. "There it is, up there, dear. I heard it was temporary but who knows for sure," she said as she trundled off in the opposite direction. Mary spotted the door sandwiched between two storefronts and climbed the narrow staircase to find a small room with stacks of books piled everywhere. She didn't care what it looked like, as long as she could borrow the books. To the left of the doorway was a tidy little desk with a sign on it that said *Miss M. I. Robb, Librarian.* Mary wondered if the librarian's first name was the same as hers, but had no intention of asking.

After she had read the "Library Borrowing Policy" on the wall, Mary was issued a library card. She signed two books out, the limit for a first-time borrower. As Miss Robb stamped the due date on the back of each one, it reminded Mary of the time she'd gone with Mr. Jacques to pick up their mail at the rural post office. Every article of mail had to be stamped with the day's date and either AM or PM. She'd been fascinated watching the postmaster insert a rubber pad beneath each envelope before striking it with his cancellation hammer, creating the muted thumping sound so characteristic of the post office. Mary, only eleven at the time, thought that that job would be fun.

"Your card, Miss," a voice said, "be sure you don't lose it." There was no chance that would happen for fear there might be a replacement fee.

Whenever Mary was downtown she got into the habit of going to the Market Square, a few blocks past the old post office, behind the town hall. She loved to wander under the low-lying roof and wide canopies so typical of a farmer's market and watch people barter. Woodstock had thirty-three butchers, seven on Dundas Street and twenty-six right in the daily market. When her boots needed repair, she headed to the cobbler's on the corner of Dundas and Wilson, two stores past the tinsmith and

The Woodstock Post Office (city hall today) with its exterior stone carving, decorative gable trim, and a bold corner tower with four clocks was an impressive sight in 1901.

The Pettit Collection.

The town hall (museum today) was built on Finkle Street in 1853 with unique semi-circular windows and a domed cupola.

The Pettit Collection.

The market (a restaurant/theatre today) had a low roof and wide canopies, typically built for an outdoor marketplace in that era.

right beside a confectioner's. It was a bit of a walk, but his prices were the best. If she had a little money left over, she'd cross the street to Hall's Bakery for a raisin cinnamon bun or a gooey butter tart.

On one of Mary's outings to the park she met Ethel Kipp, who was a few years older than herself. Ethel, daughter of Orvie L. Kipp of Kipp & Schultz Butchers on Dundas Street, had a part-time job in a ladies dress shop. The two young women became good friends, and on her day off she'd meet Ethel and they'd sit in the park and chat or go window-shopping along Dundas. Sometimes Ethel would treat her to a cone or a pastry, but Mary was careful not to take advantage of her friend's generosity too often.

Ethel knew everyone in town and would point out important people, like John White, the town's mayor; the newly appointed postmaster, Henry J. Finkle; and Sid Coppins, owner of the local plumbing shop. "Mr. Coppins must be a very rich man. He owns an automobile," Ethel said. Little did she know that not only did Mr. Coppins own one of the first motor cars in town but that he would own them for almost sixty consecutive years.

Later that day Mary overheard Mrs. Heppleton talking about the new hand-pumped vacuum cleaner in the window at the King Co. down on Peel Street. "According to George King, not only will it do the job far better, he'll stand behind his invention."

"Why would you need one, when we've got a girl to do the cleaning?" asked her husband.

Mary was annoyed at his remark, but at the same time curious to see this newfangled invention that would make her job easier. She invited Ethel to go along, hoping that they'd be brave enough to go inside the shop. The girls pressed their noses against the store window to get a better look.

"I wonder how it works," Mary said.

"Why don't we just go in and ask?"

"They'll never believe we can afford to buy one."

"Why?"

"Because we look poor," Mary replied sadly, and started to walk away. Her friend followed closely at her heels.

"Well, it's just a dumb old vacuum cleaner, who wants one anyway?"

"I do," she replied stubbornly, "someday when I have my own place."

Ethel shrugged her shoulders. "Let's get a grape soda, my treat," and she ran ahead of her down the street towards the ice-cream parlour. While they sat at the counter sipping their sodas, Ethel suggested going to the dance hall in the Market Square on Friday night. Mary was shy and reluctant to go but finally agreed to meet Ethel in the park.

She pinned her hair up and wore her newest dress, a blue percale shirtwaist that cost eighty-five cents. Mary had never been to a dance and felt awkward until she noticed a man standing over in the corner looking at her. She hadn't been there fifteen minutes when she met her future husband, Jim Church. Mary fell in love with his dark, mysterious, grey eyes and slight hint of aloofness, and started going to the dances with Ethel every Friday night knowing Jim would be there.

"He isn't like anyone I've ever known," she said to Ethel. "He's had lots of different jobs and his stories are interesting."

"What sort of stories?"

"He saved a man's life once by breaking up a fight and he's seen waves on Lake Erie as tall as the Bank of Hamilton Building. Have you ever been to Hamilton?"

"No, the farthest I've been is Stratford," she replied wistfully. Mary had been there too but never said a thing. "Anyone can make up stories. How do you know they're true?" she asked suspiciously.

"I don't," Mary shrugged, "but there's something about him … something different. You act like you're my big sister."

"I am three years older. Just be careful, I don't want to see you get hurt."

Mary started seeing Jim more often. They took evening strolls along Light Street, walks in the park, or wandered down Dundas. Mary loved going downtown at night when possible, usually a couple of nights a week when Mrs. Heppleton didn't need her. People hurried down the street to the Market Square while horses, tied to steel-wrapped wooden hydro poles, waited patiently in front of the Opera House (now Capitol Theatre). The new electric streetlights cast a warm, romantic glow on the young couple walking hand in hand, occasionally stopping to glance in a shop window.

If Mary admired a pair of wool gloves or a scarf, Jim would insist on buying them. She knew that she shouldn't accept gifts, but store-bought things were so beautiful and sometimes the temptation was too great to resist. Her petal-pink cashmere scarf was one of those gifts. Each time she wore it, she remembered the night that Jim had bought it. He'd wrapped it around her neck, then turned to the salesclerk and said, "Don't bother putting it in a box, my favourite girl will wear it home."

Sometimes they sat in Harvey Pendleton's restaurant sipping cold sodas or they headed to Long & Co. for a homemade ice-cream cone. Occasionally, Jim would take her to the theatre. The shows lasted about an hour and cost five cents, the price of a cigar. On Saturday nights, weather permitting, a travelling salesman set up his stall in the northwest corner of the town hall square.

"Let's head over to the square and see if doc's out tonight," Jim would say, grabbing her hand.

> Woodstock was fortunate in having a Pitchman in permanent residence who saved many from an early grave. He was a little man with a scraggly beard and wore square lenses in his spectacles. Dr. Kinsella, better known as "doc," would stand on a soap box and expound the wonders of his products. The Doc was of Irish extraction and was possessed with a knack of delivering an endless spiel of Irish wit, while educating the crowd on the wonders of Dr. Kinsella's Elixir of Life Compound and Dr. Kinsella's Corn Cure.[3]

It didn't take long before Doc would be well into his "platform of promises" as if he was a messenger sent from God. With his hands outstretched, he claimed that his elixir of life compound, a concoction of herbs that tasted like root beer, could cure anything if taken regularly. (Doc had a ready audience until a law, passed five years later, prevented him from selling "his wares" on the street.) If the weather was bad and he didn't show up, Mary and Jim could always count on a show over at the Perry Street fire hall. The bell rang at 9:00 p.m. sharp, the horses came out of their stalls, raced around the premises, backed themselves into their places, and waited to be harnessed by the firemen who slid down the pole. Any other time the tower bell in the fire hall rang, it signified fires, curfews, or lost children.

Occasionally they went to Fairmont Park for a picnic. Mary would buy nippy old cheese, an apple, a pear, and even splurge on white-flour buns at Poole & Co., a family-run grocery store. Jim would meet her at the corner of Dundas and Vansittart, take the picnic basket from her, and they'd grab a ride on Estelle, the streetcar.

> The youth of the day considered the trip down Dundas St. hill a source of entertainment as it was always a question, "Would Estelle make the curve?" Just in case she would make the curve at Mill and Dundas some brave young buck would run up behind the car and pull the trolley off the overhead line and leave Estelle at the mercy of the foot brakes, which required sand to help stop her progress. As a result she quite frequently left the rail. There was always the problem of climbing the hill on the return trip. On different occasions passengers had been asked to disembark and walk up the hill in order for Estelle to make the grade.[4]

On their first trip out of town Jim pointed out his boarding house and the Canadian Furniture Manufacturing Company, the factory where he worked. It took up twenty-five acres along the river. After the streetcar crossed the tracks, it turned on to Park Row, heading for Ingersoll Road and finally Fairmont Park. Estelle went as far as Ingersoll, stopping en route at Beachville, but most folks got off at the park. Band concerts and weekly dances were held in the pavilion built in a grove of trees and a small theatrical stock company put on three performances a week in July and August.

The more time Mary spent with Jim, the less she saw of Ethel. One afternoon the girls decided to meet downtown for a soda. Ethel started in with her usual concerns. "What do you really know about him? Does he ever talk about his family?"

"I know his birthday is March 18th and he's twenty-one. He's from Bright, which is near Innerkip where I was sent to …" she stopped, remembering that she'd never told Ethel about being a home child and working as a servant, "where I lived as a child."

"That's it, that's all you know about him."

"He said he'd had a sister named Minnie and some cousins that live in Hamilton."

"What happened to his sister?"

"He pushed her down the well one day after they'd had a little disagreement," she said sarcastically. The look on Ethel's face made Mary feel badly. "She died from acute appendicitis last year just before Christmas. Jim had already left home and was living in a boarding house on Dundas Street. He's still there."

"You've been to his room?" she asked, in shock.

"Of course not. All I did was walk past," she replied innocently.

Ethel laughed. "So what else do you know about the man who's stolen your heart?"

Mary's face was flushed as she continued to defend Jim. "He use to work for Bain Wagon Company and now he's at the Canada Furniture Manufacturing Company over by the river."

"That's Mill Race Creek you're talking about. What's he do?"

"He's a trucker, whatever that means."

"It means he moves furniture around."

"He said it was temporary until he finds work painting," Mary let out a big sigh. She had no intention of telling her friend about his dream to have his own decorating business someday or that some of his money had been won playing cards.

"He hasn't said much about himself," Ethel persisted.

"I think he's a private person and I'm not going to pry. He doesn't ask me personal questions either."

"You mean he doesn't know that your parents died from typhoid fever," she paused. "And you and your brothers and sisters were sent to live with different relatives."

Mary shrugged. "Of course he knows. I told him what I told you." She didn't like making things up, but justified it if it meant hiding the fact that shed been a home child. What harm could come from pretending to be related to the Jacques instead of being their domestic servant? At least her last comment to Ethel was the truth. She had told Jim exactly what shed told her. "Why can't you just be happy for me?"

"I am, but I can't help but worry a little."

Mary could not remember a time when shed been happier. As May turned into June and the cherry blossom trees came out in full, she fell deeper in love. She was turning twenty that summer and was anxious to get married. Shed finally found someone who cared for her and she wasn't about to let him slip away.

One hot sultry Friday evening in early June, they rented a canoe and paddled down the Thames. Jim found an isolated cove and suggested they get out and sit on the riverbank. He took a flask of whisky out of his pocket. Mary sensed he had something on his mind.

"I've met a lot of girls but none that mean as much to me as you do," he said softly. He stroked her hair and kissed her, like hed done so many times in the past. One unruly lock of dark hair kept falling over her left eye. Her heart raced. Is this the moment that she had waited for, the moment most young girls dream about for years? Was he going to ask her to marry him?

"I love you Mary," he paused. "I want you to be mine."

"It's all I've ever wanted," she replied without hesitation. He started to unbutton her shirtwaist. "What are you doing?" She screamed and splayed her fingers across her chest.

"You said it's what you wanted."

"I didn't say that at all. I said I wanted to be yours … your wife is what I meant."

"Wife! Who said anything about getting married? I'm talking about … you know, becoming closer."

"You mean …" she stopped mid-sentence. Mary couldn't bring herself to say the words. She was shocked. Ethel had been right. She jumped up and ran to the canoe. "Take me home, I've nothing more to say to you."

Jim paddled back to the boathouse, returned the canoe, and without a word spoken they headed back into town on the streetcar. As they approached her street she said, "I never want to see you again," ran up the steps, let herself in, and slammed the door. She ended up confiding in Ethel, who was very sympathetic. Her friend honestly believed that she'd been spared inevitable heartache down the road.

Mary turned twenty finding little to celebrate. Her job would end in September since Matthew was starting school and a live-in nanny was no longer needed. She read the signs posted in shop windows looking for help but most wanted restaurant or office experience and didn't provide room and board. What a servant girl knew best was babysitting, cooking, and cleaning.

Ethel finally talked her into going back to the dance hall again. It was the last weekend of the summer and an exceptionally humid evening. She'd only been there a few minutes when she felt a hand tap her on the shoulder. Mary, taken by surprise turned quickly toward the voice. "Will you dance with me?" Jim asked with that innocent boyish grin, the one that she'd never been able to resist in the past.

She shook her head and whispered, "No, it's over. Please leave me alone."

"Just one dance for old times' sake. You won't regret it Mary." She hesitated long enough for him to continue. "One dance, that's all I'm asking."

"Then you'll go away?"

"If you still want me to, I'll go." He took her arm and they moved out on the dance floor. The musicians were playing "Love's Old Sweet Song," a well-known tune that'd been around since the year she was born. "I've missed you so much," he said softly in her ear. "I can't tell you how much. I made a mistake, a terrible mistake. I should have known you weren't that kind of girl."

The air was stifling and she felt short of breath. Voices around her, intermingled with young girls' laughter, seemed to be getting louder in order to be heard over the music. The smoke from men's cigarettes curled up toward the ceiling in spirals making Mary light-headed and confused.

"I have something to show you," he said, taking her by the hand. They left the dance hall and headed down the street to the park. It was quiet there, almost serene. It would have made the perfect photograph, a young couple sitting in the dimly lit park, framed by large stately trees moving slightly in the wind like the fringe on a winter scarf. They were oblivious to the sound of the tower bell ringing in the fire hall. Was a fire out of control, a child lost or was it just a reminder of a curfew?

For a moment Jim held her hand and then he reached into his coat pocket. "I've been carrying this around for over a month, hoping to see you." He held up a small box. "I want you to be my wife. I don't want to live without you anymore." Mary looked down at the gold ring with a modest, pear shaped bluish-violet stone. She was speechless. "If you still want me to go away, I will," he said quietly.

"I never want you to leave me … I never did." Tears ran down her face as he quietly slipped the amethyst on her shaky finger and wrapped his arms around her. Mary gave Mrs. Heppleton two weeks' notice and happily quit her job. She sent a note to her sisters in England, glad that she'd hung on to Carrie's last letter, and hoped they hadn't moved in the past four years.

Mary had dreamed about her wedding day and knew exactly what she wanted. For her "something old" she clipped her ivory-tusk comb in her hair. She chose sateen in a creamy, rich ecru fabric at John White &

The Pettit Collection.

This contemporary photo of the courthouse still boasts a massive building of sandstone with a complex roofline. The building directly behind was the county jail, which houses the Oxford County Board of Health today.

Co., and along with a picture she'd snipped out of the Eaton's catalogue, went to Elizabeth Farrington the dressmaker over on Wellington Street. She borrowed Ethel's timepiece broche and found a dainty linen hanky edged in cornflower-blue embroidery to tuck into her sleeve.

Since Jim already owned a dark suit that he'd bought a year ago for Minnie's funeral, he went to Amos Harwood, a well-known boot and shoemaker to have a genuine leather pair of boots custom made. As soon as Joseph A. Copps, the local barber, opened his shop the morning of their wedding, Jim got a haircut, a shave, and a cigar, and he was ready to get married.

Mary studied herself in the mirror. She'd been born in a leap year and hoped that getting married in one was a good omen. She brushed a lock

Courtesy of Rowena Lunn, Caroline Janeway's granddaughter.

Mary Janeway looked elegant on her wedding day in a laced-trimmed shirtwaist with pouched sleeves, boned-standing collar, and a skillfully arranged pleated skirt just clearing the floor.

of hair out of her eyes, hair that had darkened over the years. A tiny silver pair of pince-nez gave her eyes more distinction; perhaps she was realizing her own maturity. She took off her amethyst ring, believing that once a wedding band was placed on her finger, it should never be removed.

They exchanged their vows at the courthouse on Hunter Street. Mary had walked past the huge stately building many times. She'd never noticed the monkey heads hidden among the capitals of the red marble pillars at the two front entrances or stepped inside to see the ornate interior cast-iron stairways until the day she got married. And she didn't notice them that day either.

At eleven o'clock in the morning on Wednesday, October 5, 1904, with more than a hint of fall in the air, Mary Janeway became Mrs. James Church. F.W. Hollinrake officiated, Ethel was her maid-of-honour, and Harold Teetzel, one of Jim's co-workers at the Canada Furniture Manufacturing Company, was his best man. It was a civil ceremony that lasted fifteen minutes — the happiest fifteen minutes of Mary's life.

SIX

Hamilton

"In 1903 the Hamilton Automobile Club was founded, the first such club in Canada. Yet the impact of this technological revolution was slow to develop, largely because of the lack of adequate roads. Up to 1914, motor vehicles were curiosities or luxuries more than essential components of the transportation system."[1]

October 1904

Three days after they got married, the newlyweds headed for Hamilton. Jim had worked there before and was optimistic he'd find something. Mary knew very little about Hamilton except its nickname, the "lunch pail town." She soon learned how the city that she'd be calling home forever got this name.

Jim grabbed a *Hamilton Spectator*, the newspaper that everyone called the "Spec." It was a balmy 62 degrees at noon according to the thermometer outside Parke's drugstore. He looked up his cousins Walter and Arnold Church, two bachelor brothers who lived downtown, so they'd have somewhere to stay while they looked for a place to live.

Jim was anxious to try out the incline railway, a newfangled man-made contraption that scaled the side of the mountain. Two sets of tracks ran side by side up the face of the mountain and a horizontal platform was attached to each set of tracks. At one time there'd been a toll road up John Street, but later James Jolley built what came to be known as the "Jolley Cut" and donated the road to the city with the stipulation that there be no tolls. However, horses had great difficulty climbing the steep mountain and the first incline railway was built on James Street in 1892.

Mary and Jim arrived just in time to watch a platform descend and empty its cargo, at least twenty people and several bicycles. Jim knew that the James Street incline was unique because the cars were powered by steam engines instead of balancing each other by cables. Technology that used horsepower fascinated him.

"Mary, we've got to try this."

"There's a charge," she replied, squinting in the sunlight as she read the sign on the hut. "It's two cents a trip, school children a penny. Look over there," she pointed. "There's steps. We could walk up, save our money, and get some exercise."

"It's not the same, besides I've had all the exercise I need today and we still have to walk back," he thumbed in the direction they'd come.

Mary's eyes followed the incline as it slowly edged its way to the top. "It's looks so steep. How do you know it's safe?"

"You're afraid to go."

"No, I'm not. We just don't need to be spending money unnecessarily."

"Tell you what we're going to do, my pet." He took her by the hand, swinging it in time with his stride as he headed down the street. "We'll wait for my first pay," he turned back. "We'll be back, very soon."

Within a week they found a little frame bungalow on West Avenue, wedged between two larger ones. By today's standards the house lacked "curb appeal," but Mary fell in love with it. She knew how to "make do or do without." All it needed was some white lace curtains, window boxes, and a couple of red geraniums.

Shortly after moving to Hamilton, Mary ran into George and Dan Mundy, cousins of the Jacques family where she'd been a domestic servant for those eight long years. While she was most interested in hearing

The Pettit Collection.

In 1904, Mary's house at 100 West Avenue North was considered to be the east end of the city. It was a modest bungalow (aluminium-sided today) conveniently located close to the Barton streetcar line and the City Hospital.

about young Daniel since he'd been the nicest to her when she lived on the farm, she discovered that Daniel's sister Annie and her husband Elias Zinkan had moved to Drumbo, about eight miles from the Jacques homestead. While Mary was still afraid of reprisal for having run away from the farm, she was lonely and decided to write her. Annie wrote back, which told her that the past had been forgotten, and the girls began to correspond.

Jim found work at the American Can Company, close to home. He walked down Barton Street, three blocks to Emerald, and down to Shaw. When the weather was frigid, he jumped on the streetcar. Passengers were kept toasty warm by sitting close to the stove that was being stoked by the conductor.

"The pay isn't great but it'll do for now."

"I can find something too you know," Mary replied.

"No wife of mine is going out to work. That's my job!" Jim wasn't alone in his thinking. "A woman's real place, it was almost universally agreed, was 'in the home.' A working husband who permitted his wife to work was open to criticism for 'not wearing the pants in his family.'"[2]

After Jim got his first pay, Mary bought a couple of yards of white cotton voile to make curtains and some red gingham for her kitchen table. Someday she hoped to have an electric sewing machine, but her eight dollar second-hand treadle would do a nice job. And it wasn't long before the lady next door befriended her. Mrs. Tolten, a widow with time on her hands, was looking for a friend. It was nice to have someone to talk to or invite over for afternoon tea, but the elderly lady was no substitute for Ethel.

On Friday night Jim came home from work in good spirits. "Unless it's raining Sunday morning, my pet, you and I have a date," he paused, "with the incline." He got up from the table and headed to the porch to light up a Player's while Mary tidied up the kitchen.

Two days later the sun was streaming in their bedroom window. Jim woke up early, like a young child on Christmas morning. He was anxious to try out the incline. Mary, on the other hand, was dreading it. They grabbed a streetcar at the James and Gore turn-back that ran south on James Street to the base of the escarpment. Streetcars had been running on Sunday for ten years since it was no longer considered a violation of the Lord's Day Act.

"Look at that," Jim said. "It must have known we were coming." The strange metal thing was descending almost filled to capacity with passengers plus a horse and wagon loaded with produce. They stood patiently in a small queue at the foot of the mountain. Jim was impressed with how it handled such a steep grade with a heavy load, but he'd heard of people being afraid to take the incline and wasn't surprised at his wife's reluctance.

As people got off, they walked past a small hut where an attendant collected the fare. It saved having a second one at the top. Once it was empty, Jim and Mary along with about a dozen others passed by the same hut and paid their fare. Mary was thankful there were no large wagons waiting to get on the adjoining platform attached to the narrow covered passenger car. She felt that it would be less of a risk without all that additional weight.

Hamilton Public Library, Local History and Archives.

The incline railway (circa 1910) enabled Hamiltonians to travel from the city to the mountain. The incline became obsolete by 1931 largely because of the popularity of the automobile.

People filed into the enclosure but didn't bother sitting down, since the trip to the top didn't take long. Everyone around her seemed so complacent and acted as if it was no different than taking a streetcar or train. Mary started to relax as it began to climb. She saw things from a different perspective for the first time in her life. The panoramic view was breathtaking and she soon forgot about her fear.

"There's the hospital," Jim pointed straight down, "the one you thought looked so big. What'd you think now?" She smiled.

"Can you see the tall building?" he asked as Mary squinted in the sun. "The one with the clock and further down the bay?" She followed his finger. "They'll soon be ice fishing, curling, and skating on it. Ever gone skating?" She shook her head. As a child she remembered watching kids strap blades to their shoes and skate on Mr. Allenby's pond but she didn't own any.

"I can't believe how tiny everything looks, even the horses and wagons. The people look like little ants running around," she said. "What are those bare spots, there and there?"

"Those are parks, Hamilton has lots of them. There's Lansdowne Park at the bottom of Wentworth Street, Sherman's Inlet, and Huckleberry Point."

"Lots of railway tracks too."

"Yeah. The TH&B will take you as far as Toronto or Buffalo." He put his hands on her shoulders and turned her around. "And those tracks go to the beach strip. See those tracks way over there?" She nodded. "They're for the radials. They'll take you to Beamsville, Dundas, Brantford," pointing in different directions as he spoke, "and even as far as Oakville."

It only took several minutes to reach the top. They found a bench in a park-like area and sat down just long enough for Jim to have a smoke. "I feel like I'm on top of the world," Mary said, linking her arm through his.

They walked along the mountain brow, enjoying the tranquillity and beautiful wooded areas. By noon they were getting hungry. Mary regretted not bringing a picnic basket. They took one last look at the view before getting back on the incline to head down the mountain.

"I take it you changed your mind about the incline. Did you get your two cents worth?"

"And then some," she replied.

Life slipped into a quiet, comfortable routine. Mary made friends with two ladies down the street when they were out shovelling their front walk. Viola and Affie Berezowski had immigrated to Canada from Poland as youngsters with their family. They were close to each other, having lost both parents to typhoid fever a few years earlier. Affie was a seamstress and worked out of their home. Viola, who went by the name Vi, had a part-time job in the church office.

Neither had married, but Affie, who was thirty-one, had had a serious relationship with a fellow from out east. He'd come to Ontario to work on construction and install power lines for the hydro company but once the job was gone, so was he. It was obvious that she'd resigned herself to spinsterhood like her sister.

Mary soon learned that the girls were very different. Vi had a knack for "stirring the pot" and Affie was the peacemaker. Little things like hanging the clothes out or folding the laundry could turn Vi into a fit of anger but it was usually short-lived. Although only one year older, Affie seemed far more mature. Mary preferred her company but enjoyed chatting with both over a pot of tea.

Hamilton was an interesting city. The brightly painted electric streetcars with their two-man crew smartly dressed in their HSR uniforms were an impressive sight. Mary usually walked downtown and rode home with her parcels. Saving the nickel streetcar fare meant that she slowly accumulated enough to buy a pearl necklace, a pair of stockings, or a glass candy dish.

She liked shopping at the Arcade, a department store on James Street that sold groceries as well as meat in the basement. She was most familiar with the bargain basement merchandise. A uniformed, gloved operator manned the elevator and salesclerks wore black, brown, or grey since bright colours weren't considered to be proper attire. Customers wore the same basic colours, usually accompanied by hats and gloves.

Stanley Mills, another department store, was on King just east of James Street. It had lovely wide aisles and beautiful things displayed in glass showcases. One spring Mary found the prettiest straw hat there with pale pink artificial flowers on its big, floppy brim. She wore it with pride to church on Easter Sunday for many years. Young children loved this store, especially the enchanting Toyland around Christmas.

Woolworth's, four stores down from Stanley Mills, was just as popular. Seemingly, many years earlier in a Woolworth Store in Lancaster, Pennsylvania, the first purchase made had been a five-cent fire shovel, which was why the store came to be known as the "five and dime." Advertisements of the time tell of "lots of bargains and lots of products — from toilet paper to cream pies to parakeets."[3] They established fixed prices at a time when bartering was commonplace. It was one of the first stores Mary had ever been in that had their merchandise on the counters for customers to handle. Woolworth's was renowned for its great lunch counter and her favourite meal was the hot creamy chicken on a patty shell.

Mary was impressed with the number of services available to city folks. There were home deliveries for milk, bread, ice, and fish. Her milkman, Pat O'Neill, worked for the Hamilton Pure Milk Company. Since opening its plant two-and-a-half years earlier on John Street North, it had earned a good reputation for producing sterilized, pasteurized milk at a time when unsafe milk was a concern. Customers were no longer satisfied to have farmers ladle milk out of large cans into receptacles left outside their doors. The company organized its delivery routes so efficiently that they eliminated a hundred milk wagons, proving that twenty-five could deliver milk anywhere in the city early in the morning. Pat knew exactly what Mary wanted by the number of washed milk bottles she left out. If she wanted something extra like butter, cream, or ice cream, she left a note with the money in her milk box. Cottage cheese was only available on Wednesday and Saturday.

Every so often Mary would place an order with the Canada Bread Company, known for its good quality bread, oatmeal raisin cookies, butter tarts, and cinnamon squares. But most of the time she baked her own since it was cheaper.

Courtesy of Ross Hunt.

Hamiltonians enjoyed bread delivery right to their front door, just one of the many conveniences offered to folks living in the city. Aubrey Hunt is holding the first horse's bridle and Horace Hunt the third horse's bridle.

It was common for fuel companies to deliver coal in the winter and ice in the summer. Competition for ice storage was keen since it was only gathered and stored once a year. Several companies stored the "cold stuff" that became invaluable in the warmer months. Every February the farmers went out on the frozen bay to cut blocks of ice with a crosscut saw and float them up onto ramps. Sometimes a team of horses and the bobsleigh would go through the ice and the entire team would be lost. The ice blocks, about four feet long and three-to-four feet deep were taken by sleigh to one of the ice and fuel companies and stored in buildings insulated with sawdust walls. They were stacked eight rows deep with sawdust sandwiched six to eight inches thick between each layer of ice. There was enough ice harvested in four weeks to accommodate the needs of Hamiltonians for that year.

Elijah Dunbar, a friendly man with a Scottish accent, was Mary's ice and coalman. Like the milkman, he was considered family. He picked up his load from the Abso Pure Ice Company down on Bristol Street early in the morning. By the time he got there, the ice blocks had already been removed from the building, gone through the scoring machine, and were waiting on the platform. After loading his wagon, he was on his way. Elijah sold tickets, charging half a penny for a pound. Ice was sold in blocks of twenty-five, fifty, seventy-five, or one hundred pounds and delivered three times a week. Mary would place a card in her front window to indicate the size of ice block she needed. Her card was usually on the "50" side, unlike some of the rich folks in the west end who had larger iceboxes.

The neighbour kids loved to watch Elijah wield his ice pick. Sometimes he'd chip a little ice off the block and give it to them as a treat. Then he'd go on about his business, carrying the block through the back door into Mary's kitchen. Her pine icebox, fortified with a metal liner to act as an insulator, had a pan underneath to catch the water. Still, the ice would only last two days.

Mary found it much simpler to keep food cold in the wintertime in the three-sided metal box that hung outside her kitchen window. All she had to do was open the window to get the food that Mother Nature was protecting. When refrigerators became popular in the early 1930s, people gladly got rid of their iceboxes.

Hamilton had three daily newspapers, the *Spectator*, the *Times*, and the *Herald*, as well as postal delivery twice a day, six days a week. The "pillar box red" mailboxes, which some called "royal red," were a common sight on street corners. Tom Patton, Mary's talkative postman, informed her that mail had been coming to the doors of Hamiltonians since 1875.

"Where else could a man work that would give him clothing year round? I've got a serge tunic, pants, two jackets, not to mention an overcoat and raincoat," he paused, and Mary reached out to get her mail. "Three hats if you include my kepi" (military-style cap). Finally, he handed over her letter and as she turned to go back inside he added, "They even gave me a belt and a clothes brush." Tom wore his uniform with pride and Mary wasn't surprised that he shined his shoes every night. She'd never once seen his jacket unbuttoned.

At first Mary was afraid that Tom might know too much about her business from delivering the "penny postcards," those hastily written but very public notes exchanged before the telephone became popular. At one time they had "reply postcards," which meant if the postman were inclined, he'd get more than just snippets of gossip.

Mary walked to Carroll's at the corner of Emerald and Wilson to buy her groceries. She couldn't afford fresh-grass butter, but his second grade was usually three cents less than elsewhere. His prime new cheese was two-and-a-half cents cheaper a pound if she bought two pounds at a time. Greengage plums were nine cents a tin and raspberries just a penny more. His lamb chops and sausage were reasonable if they were on sale.

Mary compared the grocer's prices with those at the Hamilton Market, also called the Central Market and the Market Place. Weather permitting, she'd strike out Saturday morning, her brown leather purse looped through one arm with a carefully folded, crocheted shopping bag tucked inside. On her way she usually stopped at the butcher's on York Street for some fresh bacon or a pot roast. She bought his butter in bulk at Christmas and Easter for baking. The market was open year round and usually crowded, but that was part of its charm. She found some produce overpriced and sometimes would return home with little to show for the day but a loaf of bread and a head of lettuce.

City of Toronto Archives, Fonds 1244, Item 1032.

The Hamilton Farmer's Market, opened in 1837. By the turn of the century, the idea of an outdoor market square had earned its place in the city.

Her first stop was the baker's stall. She loved the aroma of freshly baked bread and raisin scones. There were other places in the market that didn't smell nearly as nice. Sometimes she bought a loaf of sourdough bread if they weren't already sold out. It was hard to resist the oversize chocolate chip or oatmeal raisin cookies and coconut macaroons. Occasionally, she bought one to eat right on the spot. A quart of honey cost ten cents, maple syrup, which Mary preferred, was more than double the price. She loved to dip fingers of bread or chunky slices of banana in the sweet syrup. Eggs and shelled walnuts were cheaper at the market. Mary knew her prices and wasn't about to be fooled by false advertising.

It was hard to pass the puppies and kittens without stopping to pick one up. She would have loved to take one home, but Jim didn't want a pet. Rabbits hanging from the side of the farmer's wagon reminded Mary far too much of cats. Since her only friend on the farm had been Mustard, a scruffy barnyard cat, she vowed never to eat rabbit meat. But a visit to the market wouldn't be complete without the sound of squealing hogs and squawking chickens. The poor things were crammed into small crates awaiting their fate. The chickens, usually sold in pairs, went for less if they were still alive. Buying livestock "live" never appealed to Mary. She'd seen too many animals end up in a pot on the stove for the evening meal when she'd lived on the farm. She was a city girl now and preferred to buy meat in a more civilized manner. She either bought the middle grade of beef, No. 2 carcass, a pound of veal or mutton depending on what was available.

Mary always bought apples, usually Russets or Greenings, for "eating out of the hand" but nothing compared to Spies in a fresh apple crisp or a pie. The only time she didn't buy them was when she could get Mr. Birchall's. He lived several blocks from their house and had a large apple tree. No one could beat a six-quart basket of his delicious snow apples for fifteen cents.

Parsnips and beets were nutritious, only cost ten or fifteen cents a basket, and helped to fill up a plate. She bought potatoes by the bag even though a bushel or peck was cheaper. Anything larger than a bag would have been difficult to carry home on the streetcar. Mary usually went to one particular stall for most of her produce, convinced that nothing compared to the fresh leaf lettuce in the big crates stacked on the back of the vendor's wagon. Having made her last purchase, she jumped on the streetcar, purse looped over one arm, cradling her heavy shopping bag in the other and headed down Barton Street. Mary could hardly wait to get home to make her favourite, an egg-salad sandwich on sourdough bakery bread, piled high with the freshly picked lacy-edged lettuce.

SEVEN

The Lunch Pail Town

> "Thousands of factory workers were the backbone of the city's economy. The multi-million dollar income of those who carried lunch pails was the foundation on which all other commercial endeavours in the city were built. Enterprises such as stores, banks, restaurants, theatres, car dealerships and real estate agencies could not survive without the city's labour force to support them. The lunch pail carried by many of Hamilton's steel workers was a proud symbol of the city's industrial might."[1]

November 1904

The temperature began to drop, sometimes as low as twenty-five degrees Fahrenheit at night, but the days were comfortable, often reaching forty on the thermometer. Mary thought things were going smoothly for Jim at work, but suddenly he was let go. He said that he'd had "words with the boss."

After reading the classifieds for a couple of weeks with no luck, Jim warmed up to the idea of Mary working part-time. He made it clear it would be temporary, just until they got over the "hump" and he found a decent job. With the morning paper folded under her arm, Mary answered several ads. The first one was for a general servant but turned out to be a full-time position. The next one was looking for a housekeeper four hours a day but the pay was poor, and the last one was for a housemaid. That job paid the most but Mary thought the woman would be hard to please. She went back and accepted the housekeeping position five days a week, eight until noon.

She did the cleaning, laundry, and ironing without a break and then came home to do more of the same. Mary didn't complain because she knew Jim felt badly. But she became discouraged when she'd often arrive home to find him asleep on the sofa. When he was out, she suspected he was at the racetrack. As time went on, the situation seemed to bother him less. Mary had no time for herself and hardly ever saw Affie and Vi.

The weather turned colder as winter was fast approaching. Some evenings if she wasn't too tired, Jim would suggest that they take a stroll downtown through Gore Park. A light dusting of snow had a calming effect on the hectic city as it draped itself around the trees and covered park benches. Hamilton was a pretty city at night, especially at this time of the year. Lampposts surrounded the fountain, lights from the retail stores reflected on the snowy city streets, and the tall, stately Hamilton Bank Building and Sun Building provided an impressive backdrop. The "Lunch Pail Town" was gearing up for the Christmas season.

The first week in December Mary got sick. She was rundown and hoped that it was nothing more serious than catarrh, with its weak, flu-like symptoms accompanied by extreme fatigue. After several sleepless nights, she tried the "cayenne pepper sandwich," another remedy she'd seen on the farm. She put a liberal sprinkling of the red pepper between two generously buttered crackers and ate the spicy concoction before bedtime. Other than a burning sensation in her mouth, which thankfully didn't last long, she still had trouble sleeping.

When it lingered on without showing any sign of improvement, she had to find a doctor. Mrs. Tolten recommended Dr. H.D. Storms on Bay

Street South. He examined her, did several simple tests, and quickly diagnosed that she was "with child." Mary didn't tell him that her husband was out of work and she was the breadwinner. She went home with a heavy heart, afraid that Jim would be upset. They hadn't planned to have a baby before they'd even been married a year. If the truth were known, the subject had never even been discussed.

She prepared dinner quietly so she wouldn't disturb Jim, who was resting in the living room. She waited until after supper before she told him the news.

"How can we possibly afford another mouth to feed?" he spit the words out angrily. "How did you let yourself get in such a state?"

"I didn't do this on purpose nor did I do it alone," she answered with a calm voice.

"As if we don't have enough problems," he replied. "What next?" he said and stormed out the door.

Mary cleaned up the kitchen, went to bed, and cried herself to sleep. She never knew what time Jim got home because she was past caring by midnight. She continued to go to work, waking up each day at 6:00 a.m. to face a bout of morning sickness before heading out to catch the streetcar. Jim slept through it all. She never questioned what he did while she was at work and they never discussed the baby.

In the past she'd always enjoyed the month of December. She found people on the street were friendlier and store clerks more generous. But this year was different. She was also aware that Jim had lost his sister about this time last year. Their first Christmas together wasn't as special as she'd hoped it would be.

In late January, an enumerator knocked on their door to gather information for the city directory that came out every summer. Names and street addresses were very important before the telephone became a commodity. Jim Church had his first listing in Vernon's *City of Hamilton Directory* for the year 1905. A woman's name was only listed if she was a widow.

By the third week in February, Jim's mood changed drastically. He came home one evening with a smile on his face and a bouquet of yellow roses. He didn't complain about the weather, the slippery front walk that

Mary hadn't swept, or Jake, the yappy dog who lived next door. Instead he greeted her with open arms and flowers. She hadn't seen him in good spirits from the time she'd told him about the baby.

Mary put the flowers in water and they sat down to dinner. "Why are you so happy?"

"I'm a lucky man," he replied as he scraped the last of the rice pudding out of his fruit nappy. "What would you say to going out tonight?"

"Where?" she asked cautiously.

"I'm taking you to the theatre."

"Can we afford it? The rent is due in five days."

He opened his wallet and pulled out a wad of bills. "Go and get ready, just leave the dishes and wear something nice!" he said grabbing her hands, practically lifting her out of the chair and gently turning her in the direction of the bedroom. Mary only had one thought: Jim must have won some money at the track. Life would be good as long as the money lasted. Once the cash was gone, she knew that he'd hit rock bottom and start drinking too much.

"Where did you get that money?" her voice carried from the bedroom to the front room.

"I robbed a bank, my pet ...what do you think?" he said sarcastically.

"You've been at the track, haven't you?"

"Why do you insist on spoiling everything? I have a surprise and I know it'll please you. Never mind the chatter. Get dressed before I change my mind and find another lady to take out on the town."

Mary put on her Sunday dress, a rose-coloured floral print shirtwaist. It was a fitted style and obviously a bit snug around the middle. Four months of pregnancy was becoming difficult to ignore, even though it hadn't been discussed. Jim took her to the Grand Opera House on James Street where they sat in the second row of the gallery holding hands, watching Ethel Barrymore. It was after ten o'clock by the time they got home. While Mary took her coat off, Jim went to the liquor cabinet and poured two glasses of sherry.

"Jim I can't drink. Have you forgotten?"

"You don't have to, just pretend," he said, handing her the glass and at the same time raising his own. "I have a job, which means you can quit yours," and clinked her glass. She quickly touched it to her lips and set it down, eager to hear more about his good news.

"It's in the shipping yard down at the dock. It'll be steady work, five days a week."

"How did you hear about it?"

"Through a friend who owed me a favour from a long way back. I tell you, what goes around, comes around," he said, smiling that boyish grin that had won her heart.

"Maybe I shouldn't give my notice just yet," she said cautiously. She knew how difficult it would be to get another position if for some reason his job didn't work out.

"My darling … my little wife, you have so little faith," he said, gulping down his drink. "Keep your job for now if you want but once our baby's born, I want you to stay home with *him*." He laughed at his joke but wanted her to know that he hoped it would be a boy. "I want my child to be raised proper, by his own mother, not somebody else's."

Mary couldn't have asked for sweeter words. What she heard was Jim's acceptance of the baby and his concern for its well being. She ignored the comment about wanting a son, hoping that a daughter would please him just the same.

Jim grew more attentive as the weeks went by. They had conversations well into the evening about the baby and how their lives would change. Mary's concern was that it would be healthy.

"Let's worry about important things, like who he'll look like," he'd say. Mary would laugh, her way of handling this constant reference to the baby being a "he" rather than a "she."

"What do you think about calling him James?"

"I like that but what if James turns out to be a girl?"

"Then we'll try again until we have an heir to carry on my name," Jim replied. Mary never knew if he was kidding but it didn't really matter. She believed that only God could determine what the baby would be and that was that. She was determined to raise her child, whether it was a boy or a girl, in a loving Christian family … something that she'd never had. She didn't know much about Jim's childhood since he never talked about it, but suspected that it hadn't been very good.

By early April Mary was finding it difficult to get up and go to work so she gave her notice. Along with her last pay, she was given a tiny, pale-yellow flannel nightgown for her new baby. It had little blue flowers the colour of morning glories hand embroidered around the neck. She hurried home, anxious to show Jim the gift.

"I can't see a boy wearing that."

"For heaven's sake, a baby's a baby. He or she can wear anything. The point is, they didn't have to give us anything."

"They're rich, Mary. Coming from rich people, it doesn't mean much."

"Well, it means something to me," she said, tucking the tiny nightgown in the bottom drawer of her dresser.

Two weeks later she had a surprise visit from Ethel, who was moving to the States. She brought her several receiving blankets and some cloth diapers. Ethel expressed her disappointment in not being around when the baby was born but insisted on reading Mary's tea leaves. She was absolutely convinced that the baby would be a girl.

Hamilton Public Library, Local History and Archives. Image donated by Robert Gardner per CHCH-TV, August 16, 1963.

This 1913 photo of the Hamilton Jockey Club track was an impressive site extending from Ottawa Street to Kenilworth, north of Barton. The site provided a social outing as well as an opportunity for Hamiltonians to bet on their favourite racehorse.

As time went on, it started bothering Mary that Jim met his buddies at the Royal Hotel to have a drink and play cards several nights a week. He was also going to the racetrack every Saturday. Mary had no idea that Jim had become obsessed with track betting at the age of sixteen and was a well-known regular in the crowd. Mary hoped that this would all change once the baby came.

When they first moved into their house, she'd salvaged a child's cot that the previous tenants had left behind. Besides the cot, the only other thing in the baby's room was a small vase perched on top of a wooden crate turned end to end, which she'd covered in a remnant of pale yellow cotton. Mary had picked up the multi-coloured vase made out of "end-of-day" glass at the market in a moment of weakness. It had cost eighteen cents. She knew all about that particular kind of glass. Back in Innerkip Mr. Jacques had explained that at the end of each day the glass blower threw all the remaining colours into the pot and made one last piece. It was always unique and could never be duplicated. However, at that time it was considered the "dregs," much like the last cup of coffee on the stove, slightly bitter with age. It wasn't until many years later that end-of-day glassware came to be considered a rarity and was in great demand.

The baby's due date was July 7. There was still time to sew blankets and knit bonnets, but Mary was reluctant. She'd heard that it was bad luck to make things before a baby's arrival, or as some would say before "the blessed event."

EIGHT

Queen Victoria's Birthday

"Before 1900 only unwed mothers and poor women gave birth in the hospital."[1]

May 1905

Mary decided to have her baby at home. Dr. Storms made arrangements for Hannah, a certified midwife with years of experience, to be on hand for the birth.

"What if something goes wrong at home?" Jim asked.

"I read that there is more risk of infection if you have a baby in the hospital." In fact, Mary was wrong. By the turn of the century hospital sepsis had decreased dramatically and home births were no longer safer.

She'd given a lot of thought to the pros and cons of going to the hospital. Dr. Storms told her about a new drug that was replacing ether and chloroform for women during childbirth. He reassured her that "twilight sleep" was perfectly harmless to both the mother and the child. He explained that she wouldn't be completely unconscious, merely unable to recall the pain later. His concern was that this drug wouldn't be available to her if she had the baby at home. If a doctor was called in, he couldn't give her a full anaesthetic and a certified midwife wasn't permitted by law to administer pain-killing drugs. Still, knowing all that, Mary was reluctant to go to the hospital.

Her concern was for the welfare of her unborn baby. Wasn't childbirth supposed to be a natural occurrence in a woman's life? She was hesitant to take drugs, even for pain. At times like this Mary was reminded that she had no one to turn to for advice. Her mother had been part of her life for such a short period of time. Mary had a slight headache and closed her eyes. She could hardly even remember what her mother looked like. How had she managed to give birth to five babies? Mary stopped. Her mother didn't have five; she'd had six children. It was the birth of her last baby that had changed the direction of their lives forever.

> *"Oh my God, William!" she cried. His nose was hanging broken and he was bleeding badly. Before he could explain how the colt had reared up and kicked him, his pregnant young wife, overcome with emotion, fainted on the kitchen floor.*
>
> *"Catharine!" he screamed as he bent over her. "Help me carry her to the bed," he shouted at the children. "Will, run to Packard's farm and tell Lyle to get the doctor quick. Mama needs help real bad."*
>
> *Little Mary had been watching everything. She stepped down off the stool, backed into the corner, crouched down, and buried her face in her knees. Emma began to cry.*
>
> *The next morning Papa called all the children, including Emma, to the table. He had bandages on his face. "We lost Mama in the night. The baby came sudden — far too soon for your mama. She wasn't strong enough." He paused to steady himself, and then continued reluctantly. "The doctor was too late to do anything. The baby's gonna live but it's small and sickly. He thinks it isn't quite right so they're sending it to Glasgow. Just as well I expect." He continued, but spoke quietly. "I love you all and I'll try to take care of you, what with Mama gone now."*[2]

Mary didn't remember anything about the baby except that it was a boy. She didn't even know his name. What she did remember was losing her mama because of him. As an adult, she found it difficult to explain the feelings that she harboured toward this innocent baby. Mary had been left with the memory of a terrible accident and fleeting images of her mother.

Now as a grown woman of twenty-one, she sat at the kitchen table and covered her face with her hands. She wept for her mother that she'd barely known, wept for her father who'd sent her to an orphanage, and wept for brothers and sisters she hadn't seen in years. But more than that, she had tears because she was afraid. If only she could forget that her mother had died having a baby. What if her baby came early and the same thing happened? Mary knew that childbirth involved some risk. She could die giving birth just like her mother or succumb to child-bed fever shortly after the birth. Infant mortality was high and it wasn't uncommon for children to die in infancy. She'd read that for every ten babies born, one didn't make it to their first birthday.

Mary curled up in Jim's armchair in her faded pink bathrobe and drank a cup of warm milk that settled her stomach and had a calming effect. She regained her perspective and came to the conclusion that her mother's death was purely accidental. The baby wasn't ready to be born and the trauma of her father's accident must have brought on premature labour. She reminded herself that it had happened fifteen years ago and her mother had been considerably older than her. Today's doctors and midwives were more knowledgeable.

She decided to talk to Hannah about her concerns. Mary liked the petite, soft-spoken woman who was about forty and who had already visited her a number of times. Sometimes she'd put her arm around her in a comforting motherly way and had a sense of knowing when this kind of affection was appropriate. Perhaps it was because she'd already delivered over twenty babies and had four of her own.

"Hannah, what if my baby comes early?"

"Babies know when the time is right. Remember your calendar date is only an approximate time and it can be six weeks either side of that."

"What if the pain gets really bad?"

"I'll be right there by your side and can give you a little something if it becomes necessary." Mary looked up at Hannah, swallowed, pressed her lips together, and nodded in an unconvincing manner. "What happened to all that confidence you had? Where has it gone, dear?" she asked kindly, reaching over to pat her hand.

"You're right. I need to be stronger."

Hannah squeezed Mary's hand and smiled. She finished her cup of tea and stood up to leave. She had other women to tend to and while her visits were brief, she was always willing to stay a little longer with a first-time mother. She sensed that Mary was still anxious. "Is everything all right now?" she asked.

"I think so, but I'm still a bit scared," she said quietly.

"Having a baby is the most natural thing in the world," she paused. "And so is being afraid. I'll see you next week," she said, and let herself out.

Mary was glad that City Hospital (today's General Hospital) was only ten minutes away, just in case. The four-storey red-and-white patterned brick hospital had a central tower and two detached brick wings extending southward, connecting with the main building by open corridors. It had well-lit wards, adequate ventilation, heating provided by central fireplaces, water closets similar to those in English hospitals, speaking tubes, and dumb waiters. Considered quite modern for its time, it was equal to anything of its kind in Canada.

Mary had no difficulty filling her days while she waited for her baby's arrival. Laundry took the better part of a morning. She baked bread every Wednesday and went to Carroll's a couple of times a week. She was starting to buy canned goods to eliminate some of the trips to the grocery store but was cautious. Children had been known to die from "summer complaint," food poisoning from botulism. She made sure that her house was clean and a hot meal was waiting for her tired husband at the end of the day. A visit to the market rounded out her week.

Mary and Jim were fortunate to have some of the modern day conveniences including electric lights, a water closet, and an icebox. Jim dreamed about owning an automobile and was convinced that someday cars would take over the roads and the horse and buggy would be gone forever.

> Driving was an adventure in 1905; a twenty-mile drive was a conversation piece. Outside cities the roads were improved dirt or unimproved dirt. In summer the dust was so blinding that passengers wore goggles and dusters. In spring the mud was axle-deep and some farmers made a living hauling motorists out of potholes (which the farmers themselves kept watered). On cloudy days a man drove with one eye on the ruts and the other skyward; it took fifteen minutes to get up the canvas top and the side curtains.[3]

Mary's dreams were not as grand. She looked forward to the day when she could soak in a cast-iron bathtub with claw feet instead of bathing in a tub in the kitchen. She also hoped to have a telephone, central hot-water heating, a gas range complete with a warming oven, and a washing machine that was cranked by hand. She was thankful for her treadle machine, knowing that she wouldn't be able to afford "store bought" clothing for her baby. Mary was adamant that her son or daughter would dress like other children. She knew how painful it was to look different and was relieved that her child wouldn't grow up with the stigma of being a "home child." Conversations that she'd overheard at the Strathcona Home for Girls still bothered her:

> That girl is scrawny as a picked chicken. How the doctor thinks she will be any real help with the work, I fail to see.
> What use will she have for book learning?
> I thought this Home Girl was to be a help, not just an extra mouth to feed.[4]

One evening in late May, Mary was feeling particularly tired and curled up on the sofa to leaf through a magazine while Jim read the paper. She saw an ad for the new portable vacuum cleaner.

"Take a look at this," she said turning the page around. "It's so much smaller than ours."

"Are you telling me you want a new vacuum?"

"Of course not. I'm just amazed how quickly things change. I'm happy with mine." Although her vacuum was big and cumbersome, it signified that she was a modern day housewife and sweeping was a thing of the past.

"You can thank Mr. Polanski for that. I worked so damn hard on painting his house and if he could've paid his bill, you'd never have had that vacuum. It was his idea to do a little horse-trading, not mine. I'd have much rather had the money."

"And if he didn't refurbish old things, we might have ended up with nothing," Mary added. All of a sudden, she doubled over, clutching her belly and gasped. "Jim, it's the baby! I think it's time!"

He ran to the neighbour's and made a frantic call to Hannah. She came immediately. It was obvious that Mary was in labour.

"Hannah, is everything alright?" Jim asked.

"Everything is fine. We're having a baby!" she answered with certainty, holding Mary's hand all the time that she spoke. Jim went outside and waited on the porch while Hannah did what was necessary. The time passed slowly for the young man who was about to become a father.

When Mary's contractions were about two minutes apart Hannah gave her "one teaspoon of a tincture of laudanum, an extract with opium in it, which could be administered by a certified mid-wife."[5] Almost immediately the pain backed off.

Despite her husband's wish for a boy, Mary delivered a healthy five-pound, four-ounce baby girl on Wednesday, May 24, at 6:15 a.m. Eighty-six years ago on the same day, Queen Victoria had been born. Her late Majesty had been a popular royal figure and the longest reigning Queen in English history. Mary couldn't have been happier that her daughter was sharing her birthday with the Queen, a day that had been declared a statutory holiday in Canada. For years she'd tease her little girl by telling her that the day she was born, the country was so excited they didn't print a newspaper. And every year on her birthday, there would never be a paper.

Mary felt a contentment that only a very proud first-time mother would understand. Wednesday was her lucky day. She'd been re-united with her brother, run away from the farm, and married on a Wednesday and now her daughter had chosen that day to enter the world. But she was exhausted after eleven-and-a-half hours of labour. Hannah brought her a cup of tea and a few crackers on a tray, but they went untouched. Mary's job was done and she promptly fell asleep.

"Would you like to hold your daughter, Jim?" Hannah asked.

He looked at the tiny sleeping infant in her arms. She had definitely inherited his dark hair.

"Maybe later," he replied quietly, leaving the room to go outside for a smoke.

They'd never discussed what to call the baby if it was a girl, so it wasn't until several days later that she was given a name. Their daughter was christened Gloria Victoria, named after her paternal grandmother and Queen Victoria. Although the baby's name was chosen with care, soon after her birth the little girl inherited the nickname Mona. It stayed with her for life.

And Jim soon forgot about wanting a son.

NINE

The Church Family

"In 1906, Hamilton's first major strike, and one of its most dramatic, involved the Hamilton Street Railway, when 180 employees walked out to enforce demands for an increase in pay rate, then eighteen cents an hour, and union recognition."[1]

1906

Jim managed to find a couple of painting jobs after he was laid off from the shipyard. He liked being his own boss and continued to dream about having a decorating business.

When Mona was nine months old they moved to 36 Charles Street, a two-family dwelling a couple of blocks west of James (Hamilton Place and the Art Gallery today). The rent was two dollars more but Jim insisted that "this re-location" would improve his prospects of finding customers. Both residences and businesses had made their home on Charles Street, which created an interesting but rather unusual neighbourhood.

Mary left West Avenue with reluctance, promising to keep in touch with Affie and Vi. She found another Carroll's at the corner of Hunter and Queen, within walking distance of her new home. Luckily they'd moved before the city enumerator came around, and for the first time, Jim listed himself as a painter.

Mrs. Tolten's offer to mind Mona was still good, even after they moved, but Mary rarely left her and was content to stay home to witness each little milestone in her daughter's life. She had waited in anticipation for Mona to hold her head up, had delighted in trying to interpret each of the tiny infant's facial grimaces, and had circled her calendar on the red letter day that Mona cut her first tooth. Mary couldn't have been happier and more content. Unfortunately, her husband didn't feel the same.

Jim desperately wanted to buy an automobile. His friend owned a Model T Ford and was in the habit of picking him up to go to the racetrack. He got the courage to ask Joe if he could borrow his car on Sunday afternoon. He promised to drive it with care and supply his own gasoline. Joe was hesitant until Jim slipped him a five dollar bill.

Mary was excited about the family outing. The fall had brought cooler temperatures and the leaves were just starting to turn. She may not have been so enthusiastic if she'd known what it was costing. The following weekend they set out on an adventure in the country, with little Mona dressed in her Sunday best, bundled securely in the back seat. They headed out of the city in the direction of Woodstock. With Jim having grown up there, he was familiar with the concessions and sideroads of Blandford Township. Although they didn't go as far as Innerkip, each time they approached a hill or curve in the road, Mary anticipated seeing the silhouette of a large school bell around the next bend. It was difficult to forget the six years that she'd spent at the little country school, for it represented her only formal education.

The fresh air, the Queen Anne's Lace, and other wild flowers nodding their heads in the breeze along each side of the winding county roads reminded Mary of her walk to school on the days that she'd been allowed to attend. She wondered if the schoolhouse, nestled beside a grove of apple trees, still looked the same.

Blandford School was almost two miles from the Jacques farm and harsh winters often made it very difficult, if not impossible, to get there.

The morning of September 15 was Mary's first day at school. From a distance she could see a large school bell on top of the cedar shingled roof. Clutching her old leather satchel with a broken strap, Annie's castoff, Mary arrived, breathless and filled with nervous anxiety. Blandford School S. S. No. 3 turned out to be a small, grey fieldstone building with two doors, one marked "Boys," the other "Girls."[2]

Once they'd left the city limits behind and were well into the country, Jim announced that he was starving. They stopped on the side of the road under the shade of a large oak tree. "What have we got in our basket?" he asked, spreading out the old plaid tablecloth. Mary had packed a picnic lunch of ham sandwiches, fresh tomatoes, and nippy old cheese. Mona was content to nibble on small chunks of cheese and the middle of a slice of white bread, already refusing to eat her crusts. She devoured a thermos of milk almost immediately. For dessert they had some large, juicy red apples that they'd stopped and picked along the deserted country road.

After lunch Jim took off his shoes, rolled his jacket up for a pillow, and stretched out against the base of the tree. He lit a cigarette and took in long, deliberate draws, savouring each one. Mary played with the baby in the sun, and every once in awhile turned to admire her handsome husband.

"Someday we're gonna strike gold, and when that day comes, my lady, you'll be wearing diamonds and fur. Our little girl will have the prettiest frock ever. As for me," he tapped himself on the chest, "I'll be behind the wheel of a shiny, brand new Russell."

While other men were building cars for the masses in the early 1900s, low-priced vehicles that almost anyone could afford, Thomas Russell had his eye set on the well-to-do. Though he used slogans like "A high-grade car at a wonderfully-low price" and "Made up to a standard, not down to a price," his namesake car, the Russell, was

> hundreds of dollars more than the competition — $450 more than Henry Ford's Model C, to be exact.[3]

With his cigarette dangling out of the corner of his mouth, he raised his arms slightly, curled his fingers, and wrapped them around an imaginary steering wheel. He looked at her, grinning the whole time like a young boy who'd been given a new toy, and said, "and it won't be black, it'll be cobalt blue. It'll have a ..." he paused as though he'd lost his train of thought or begun to feel foolish, took the cigarette out of his mouth and dropped his hands into his lap. "For sure, we'll be the envy of the neighbourhood someday when we strike gold."

"We already have," Mary replied, but Jim was too busy dreaming to hear her. Mona was growing restless, no longer content to sit on the blanket. After she took a few steps, Mary let go of her hand. She took a couple more, faltered, and tumbled gently into the long grass. She tired quickly, curled up on her mother's lap, put her thumb in her mouth and dozed off. This would have made a lovely family photo, if only they'd had a camera.

A light rain shower shortened their picnic and they ran to take cover in the car. By the time Jim had put the top up, the rain had stopped, but it was obvious that the best part of the day was gone. He was anxious to head home long before dark, so they packed up and left.

> Taking up the new fad — "the infernally combusting engine" — took courage. Patience and a spirit of adventure were as important as a well-stocked tool box. Early tires, for example, were flimsy affairs, and punctures (nobody called them flats then) were common. You had to know how to use the things in your trunk: patch kits, wrenches and the good old crank.[4]

The gentle motion of the car put Mona to sleep before they'd reached the first concession road. They only passed one garage on their way back to the city, but Jim was well prepared with his own gas can of extra fuel.

Mary had enjoyed their excursion in the country and knew the fresh air had been good for Mona. She wasn't in the habit of taking her to public places for fear she might catch something, but an outing such as this was ideal. For the longest time, she wouldn't even take her in the buggy to the market. She preferred to go to the park for some fresh air. Mary had become a fastidious housekeeper, convinced that dust and dirt were how diseases like tuberculosis and scarlet fever started. Doctors didn't have all the answers. Jim kept insisting that she was too protective. "Mona needs to get out more and do things like other children. And we should get out more too."

The first time they left the baby was to go downtown to the Savoy Theatre. Mary had only seen pictures of balconies and box seats in magazines before that evening. Sitting in the first balcony holding Jim's hand and watching her first real live theatre made it easy to forget her responsibilities as a mother for a few hours. Little did she know that one day she'd be returning to watch "moving pictures."

Once the warmer months arrived, they got in the habit of asking Mrs. Tolten to babysit in the evening. Sometimes they took the trolley, an open streetcar, down to the docks to sit and look out at the Royal Hamilton Yacht Club, one of the most elegant structures of its kind on the Great Lakes. They could easily hear the music that floated across the water from the second-floor ballroom.

"Someday we'll be dancing in that ballroom," said Jim, grabbing her hand and pointing, "dressed in our finest." It amazed Mary that he never tired of dreaming; in fact she believed he thrived on it.

"Let's just enjoy right now," she said quietly.

"Why are you so easily satisfied?"

"Because I'm happy." She was content to sit on the dock and watch from a distance. Like most home children, Mary had grown up in a world where she was an observer. Jim, on the other hand, was a doer, not a watcher. "I couldn't be happier," she reiterated, patting his leg affectionately.

Just when Mary had their place on Charles Street nicely decorated, Jim announced that they were moving to an apartment on Dundurn Street (Fortinos Plaza today), once again convinced it was a better location for his business. It was their third move in three years and she hoped that her curtains would fit the new windows.

About the same time, Mona entered the terrible twos. In spite of her tantrums and fussiness, the little girl continued to charm her mother. Mary started asking Mrs. Tolten, who absolutely adored Mona, to babysit so she could have a break and go downtown to window shop and browse. One of the most elegant stores in Hamilton was the Right House, on the corner of King and Hughson. The building, trimmed in Ohio freestone and steeped in a rich history all its own, stood out among the others because of its height and grandeur. So many plate glass windows faced both streets that it came to be known as the Crystal Palace.

The gilded gold lettering on the stone sign read, "1843. Thomas C. Watkins, 1893." The original dry goods store known as the Right House had been so successful that fifty years later Watkins decided to build a lavish, four-storey addition to the original structure. Painted on the side of the building in bold capital letters, the sign read:

THE RIGHT HOUSE
DRY GOODS
MILLINERY
MANTLES
CARPETS
THOMAS C. WATKINS

Mary could only imagine how wealthy this man must have been before he died three years ago. It was rumoured that his ghost lived in the store. According to the story that has remained unsubstantiated, the Otis elevator car was locked in the basement each night after the store closed. A key was required to move the elevator. Every morning it could be found on the fifth floor where Watkins' office was located.

Mary was reminded of this story as she approached the tall, stately building. She felt like she didn't belong here and knew better than to ask if there was bargain basement shopping. As she walked through the large doors, she kept telling herself that anyone was allowed to look. With a weakness for hats, she headed to the millinery department to admire the brimless wool cloches and veiled sateen pillboxes. She wandered through the dress goods, quickly past the mourning-goods counter, thankful to have no need for it. Mary would have liked to come home with a dress length of cashmere, crepe, or de laine, but instead just ran her fingers over the silk velvet as she walked through the dress and mantle trimmings.

Although there were several elevators, she climbed the beautiful hardwood staircase to the waiting gallery halfway between the ground and second level. It looked like a fancy sitting room complete with chairs and writing desks. The public were encouraged to sit and rest or arrange to meet a friend here. Mary enjoyed the view from the balcony. Somewhere she'd read that there were over 150 Canadian tungsten lamps on the main floor.

It was fascinating to watch people. Some hurried in to make a quick purchase, while others lingered and ended up buying nothing. Mary fell into the second category. She had another look from this vantage point before climbing to the second floor to see the beautiful damask tablecloths and curtains made of white linen lawn. The third and fourth storeys had carpets, linoleums, and other home-furnishing items. Offices occupied the fifth and sixth floors of the building. She'd also heard that there was an emergency ward complete with a bed.

Mary usually paid a visit to the washroom. The facilities were the prettiest, most impressive example of modern sanitation that she'd ever seen. Even if she had no need at that moment she went in and washed her hands. The polished Italian marble trim glistened like the sideboard in a rich man's dining room. And Mary would know since she'd worked for a number of well-to-do families.

On her way out, she had another look at the hats and bought five cents worth of yellow ribbon to make Mona a hair bow. As she made her purchase, the clerk stopped to answer the phone. It annoyed Mary because she thought a customer should have the salesclerk's undivided attention. At the same time she was impressed that the store hired females and had telephones in every department.

Mary hurried out the big doors, glanced up at the city hall clock tower, and was surprised that she'd been gone that long. She jumped on the streetcar, anxious to get home. As she walked in the house, Mona ran toward her with outstretched arms.

"How was my little girl?"

"A perfect angel," replied Mrs. Tolten. "And how was your shopping?"

"It was fine. I just browsed in the Right House," Mary said, sitting down on a kitchen chair with Mona on her lap. "They have such beautiful things."

"By any chance did you see Thomas Watkins's ghost?" she asked, sounding far from serious.

"I don't believe in ghosts," Mary said unconvincingly, handing her some change. Mrs. Tolten kissed Mona goodbye and was gone. Ghost story forgotten, she busied herself in the kitchen preparing supper.

By late August Mary had had enough of the hot, humid weather. The thermometer still registered in the high eighties. The chain of events that followed would always remind her never to become complacent and take things for granted.

She and Jim had taken Mona to Gore Park for the unveiling of the statue of Queen Victoria, their daughter's namesake, when suddenly the little girl became violently ill. They immediately went home and put her to bed. At first they thought Mona had catarrh because of the flu-like symptoms of fever and sore throat. When she hadn't improved after a few days Mary feared the worst, some dreadful incurable disease like typhoid or scarlet fever. She remembered giving Mona canned peas a couple of days earlier. Was it possible that she might have food poisoning and be dying from "summer complaint?"

She asked Dr. Storms to make a house call. He examined the feverish fretting child troubled by a stiff neck, muscle pain, and cramping spasms in her arms and legs. The doctor suggested that they come to his office the following day. The concern in his eyes would haunt Mary forever. She was convinced that Mona was dying. Jim was convinced his wife was overreacting.

TEN

Infantile Paralysis

> "The old name for the disease, infantile paralysis, recalls the time when it was primarily a disease of infants and very young children and its outcome was paralysis of the affected muscles. Both the little crippled boy who could not follow the Pied Piper of Hamelin and Tiny Tim in Charles Dickens' classic A Christmas Carol, were probably victims of infantile paralysis."[1]

August 1907

"I'm afraid Mona's suffering from something more serious than ague or catarrh," Dr. Storms paused, "but I've ruled out scarlet fever and meningitis."

Mary's heart raced as she anxiously waited for his diagnosis. She kept repeating "Please God, let my baby be alright" silently in her head as she twisted and knotted a sweaty handkerchief in her hands.

"I believe she has infantile paralysis … polio."

"Polio … how can that be?" Mary shouted. "It isn't possible. I've taken good care of her. She's never been to any public places where there might be germs and disease. There must be a mistake!" It was common knowledge that "Polio was associated with the poorest, dirtiest children, not affluent adults in the prime of life, and with immigrants in slums. Nor were there iron lungs or March of Dimes cans."[2]

"We don't know much about this disease. Most respiratory illnesses occur in winter but for some strange reason polio appears in the summer months. It may be airborne, found in contaminated milk, or unclean water, or transmitted by flies but we're not sure." The doctor tried to reassure them that he'd do whatever he could.

> Polio children were sometimes led to believe their illness was a God-given challenge. How else can we explain a disease that appeared to strike randomly, a disease that hit without warning, when you were healthy, and that you did nothing to bring it on? "God gives us only what we can handle," the saying goes: "God gives the heaviest crosses to the ones he loves the best," is another.[3]

Mary questioned why God would do such a thing to an innocent child. A few days later she went to the library in the public health building to learn more about polio, the disease that had many names; poliomyelitis, infantile paralysis, Heine-Medin disease and poliomyelopathy. Then she went next door to Centenary Methodist Church (Centenary United today).

She returned to Dr. Storm's office but this time she went without Jim. "What could I have done differently? I've never taken Mona to a public pool, she hardly ever plays with other children, and my home is spotless. I've never even let her have a drink from the fountain in the park."

"The idea that a clean, dust-free home prevents disease isn't true. No one knows for sure why some people get this virus and others don't. Sometimes it's better not to protect children too much so they can develop their immune systems. If they don't have strong immunities, they're more likely to get sick," Dr. Storm replied.

Mary thought of Jim's words, "Mona should be out more, stop babying her. She'll be fine." Perhaps this was all her fault.

"But you mustn't blame yourself. As I said before, we don't really understand viruses all that well. Thankfully it didn't attack her respiratory system or it would have left her with breathing problems."

By the time that it was diagnosed, Mona was over the worst. Her left side had been weakened. She had one smaller calf and foot, a shoe-size difference and walked with a limp. "In the medical world it was referred to as a 'foot drop' due to a weak anterior tibial."[4]

She was relieved that Mona didn't need a wheelchair. Mary had been seven when she'd first seen one and had no idea that Mrs. Jacques was confined to the chair with the large wheels because she couldn't walk. She remembered how unhappy the woman had been and didn't wish this fate on her daughter. She'd read about different therapies including baths, massage, blackberry brandy, castor oil, and enemas. The doctor was skeptical but never discouraged Mary from trying them. She was nervous when Mona was near the kitchen stove or the side reservoir where water constantly simmered, for fear she'd lose her balance and get burned.

When the weather was nice she put Mona in the stroller and headed for one of the parks nearby. She often took her Bible along, a gift from the rector at St. Paul's in Innerkip. She'd hung on to it all these years. A little card entitled "Bible Helps in Times of Difficulty" was tucked safely inside, suggesting different Bible passages when feeling discouraged, depressed, or out-of-sorts.

That fall Mary accepted Annie's invitation to come to Drumbo for a Christmas visit. She was anxious to show off Mona, who was doing much better. But for reasons never explained, Mary went without Jim.

By the end of the year Jim was ready to move again. He found a little clapboard house for rent on Railway Street between Cannon and Barton. Mary was happy to leave the apartment since they'd have more room and a fenced backyard for Mona. It was handy to everything and the nearest Carroll's was only a few blocks away.

Shortly after moving in, Jim brought home a hand-cranked wringer washing machine. He got an incredible bargain because appliances were beginning to go electric. Mary was aware of the latest gadgets. She'd seen pictures of the electric vacuum cleaner, sewing machine, and frying kettle in magazines in the library, knowing they couldn't afford them. She

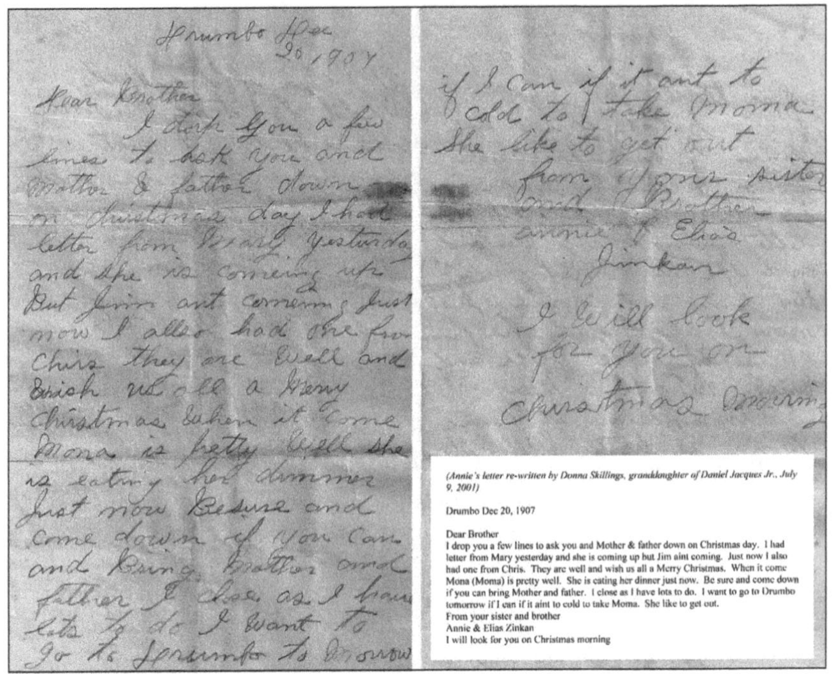

(Annie's letter re-written by Donna Skillings, granddaughter of Daniel Jacques Jr., July 9, 2001)

Drumbo Dec 20, 1907

Dear Brother
I drop you a few lines to ask you and Mother & father down on Christmas day. I had letter from Mary yesterday and she is coming up but Jim aint coming. Just now I also had one from Chris. They are well and wish us all a Merry Christmas. When it come Mona (Moma) is pretty well. She is eating her dinner just now. Be sure and come down if you can bring Mother and father. I close as I have lots to do. I want to go to Drumbo tomorrow if I can if it aint to cold to take Moma. She like to get out.
From your sister and brother
Annie & Elias Zinkan
I will look for you on Christmas morning

Courtesy of Donna Skillings, great-granddaughter of Daniel Jacques.

Annie (Jacques) Zinkan's letter to Daniel (see insert) told him about Mary's visit. She refers to her mother-in-law as Moma. It was common for aging parents to live with their children at that time.

The Pettit Collection.

The left side of a semi-detached house was 31 Railway Street, which today has been aluminium-sided. Called Railroad Street on city maps in the early 1900s, it was one block long and four blocks west of the streetcar line on James.

was delighted with her new washing machine, which would save time and be easier on her hands.

Mary hardy ever bought anything for herself, but that winter she purchased a pair of genuine patent-leather laced boots with Goodyear welt soles at J.D. Climie. They cost $2.68 and she hoped they'd last for the next twenty years. Mary was afraid to voice her concerns about money since Jim might interpret this as criticism that he wasn't a good provider. She realized that her life had been pretty good lately. She had a wonderful husband and a beautiful baby girl. The memory of her "home child" years was gradually fading. She smiled contentedly, glad that she hadn't told a soul the real reason why she came to Canada.

ELEVEN

Unexpected Visitors

"In 1908 the appalling death rate from cholera infantum among infants in City Hospital had led Dr. Roberts to ask city council for a grant to bottle, clean milk for bottle-fed babies. By using milk from a tuberculin-tested herd and sterilizing utensils and bottles (but not the milk itself) the death rate from cholera infantum in 1909 was reduced thirty per cent, a figure justifying continuation of the procedure."[1]

March 1908

Mary prepared beefsteak and kidney pie for Jim's twenty-fifth birthday. "It's just another day," he said, and plunked himself down in his favourite armchair to swill back a beer.

April marked the beginning of the rainy season. Mary leafed through Saturday's *Spec.* A cloudy overcast day had been predicted, yet the sun shining through her kitchen window made it difficult to read the paper. She was amazed how often the weatherman was wrong. Mr. Briggs, the elderly gentlemen next door, predicted bad weather by checking his sauerkraut barrel. His claim that there'd be a storm if the cabbage rose to the top of the brine was surprisingly accurate.

When Mary was on the farm Mr. Jacques was pretty good at predicting a change in weather: "He watched the sky each morning at sunrise to see what colour it was. According to the almanac, if the sky was red it meant plenty of rain was ahead. He also had noticed that Tiny, one of Daniel's dogs, had been eating grass lately, another sure sign that rain was on its way."[2] Perhaps the sauerkraut barrel and the *Farmer's Almanac* were as reliable as the *Spec*.

She skimmed through the rest of the paper. There was another ad for one of those new "electrified" sewing machines. The Right House had lace curtains on sale for $1.37 a pair and Home Outfitting Co. was advertising flannelette blankets for 79¢ or two for $1.35. Was it a misprint or were the blankets so thin they'd feel like tissue paper? Realizing she'd be late for church if she didn't catch the streetcar soon, she grabbed her hat and coat and hurried out the door.

Jim was waiting for her when she got home, anxious to spend the afternoon at the track. Mary found it hard to complain when he'd already fed Mona and settled her for an early afternoon nap. Reverend Whiting's sermon "The bread of life never gets stale" had reminded her that she was blessed. As she took off her hat in the front hall, she was startled by a loud knock on the door. It was probably Jim coming back for his pocketbook since they rarely had callers on Sunday. With a hatpin in her hand, she quickly turned to open the door. Two ladies, one quite tall, were standing on her tiny front porch. Mary's eyes darted from one to the other, noticing a striking resemblance between them.

"Mary?" She didn't recognize the voice, but she knew those eyes. Those dark, deep-set eyes belonged to her sister.

"Oh, dear God, Carrie?" she screamed, dropping the hatpin on the floor. She grabbed her and then turned to the other women, the smaller one, who had remained silent. "Emma … you must be Emma!"

She nodded shyly and Mary embraced her younger sister, for a brief moment letting go of Carrie. This had to be a dream, an illusion that she'd played out in her mind many times when she was feeling lonely. They stumbled into the front hall, hugging each other, and making utterances that would have been incoherent to a passer-by. Mary led them into her front room where they sat or rather clung to each other on her sofa. Outbursts of tears were followed by short periods of silence and then more tears.

"How did you find me?" Mary finally asked.

"I went to the Red Cross and they told me to contact the Salvation Army," Carrie said with a big sigh. "They asked me to put everything I knew in a letter. I had to prove I was searching for missing relatives, not just friends. I posted two notes even though I'd dreadfully little to go on, just what you and Willy looked like as children, the ages that you'd be now, and your married name. They put it in the missing person column in *The War Cry*.

> 5973. JANEWAY, WILLIAM: Age 25, brown hair and eyes, came to Canada in 1891 to Stratford (and Hamilton), sent to work on a farm in Ontario. May have gone to the States.
>
> 5974. CHURCH, MARY (JANEWAY): Age 23, brown hair, came to Canada in 1892 to Stratford, sent to work on a farm in Ontario, eventually moved to Woodstock.

"The Army," Carrie said, "that's what they call themselves, confirmed that you'd both been sent to Ontario. If you hadn't written to tell me that you got married, I doubt they'd ever have found you. They'd no luck tracking Willy down."

"I saw him twice when I was on the farm," Mary replied, having forgotten that he'd been called Willy as a young boy, "but he isn't there now."

"I use to lie awake at night wondering what happened to both of you. I heard different stories about what life was like for home children in Canada. One day I saw a picture of some children standing on a railway platform. I'll never forget it. The caption read 'Home Kids Waiting at the Station.' They had nametags around their necks, like ties on potato sacks. I stared at that picture of sad little faces, hoping I wouldn't find you or Willy. It worried me so, that we were all broke up," Carrie's voice quivered.

Mary had her own stories about home children. Back on the farm she'd heard that "two Home boys ran away on the eleventh line. They found them two days later, frozen solid. They carried them off like pieces of stove wood. And the year before that, a Home Boy ran away along the train lines in Peterborough, and the train squashed him flat. Nothing left but blood and ground-up bones."[3]

Carrie quickly changed the subject. In her soft-spoken voice and distinctive British accent she talked about the passage over. Mary learned that Emma, Carrie, her husband Frank, their two young children, along with Frank's brother and his family, had arrived in Saint John, New Brunswick, on March 20, eleven days after leaving Liverpool aboard the CPR steamship *Lake Erie*. They'd travelled across the country by train, arriving in Hamilton two days later.

Courtesy of Gail Horner, Emma Janeway's granddaughter.

Carrie (Janeway) Lunn had a photo taken Christmas 1907 with her two young sons before their arrival in Canada.

"Frank and I were sick for the entire passage. Thankfully, Emma didn't get ill and was able to take care of the boys." She dove into her purse and proudly handed her a photo. "Frank's three-and-a-half and Harvey's six months old. I don't know what I'd have done without her."

At that moment Emma decided to speak, surprising both of them. "If I had heard one more (making a baby voice) 'Auntie Emmy, Auntie Emmy,' I'd go stark raving mad." She laughed for the first time and Mary saw the face of a strikingly beautiful young woman.

"How long will you be staying?" Mary asked, turning from one to the other, dreading the answer.

"For good, Mary. We're here for good," Carrie replied. With that, the girls jumped up, grabbed each other's hands, and danced around the room in an uncontrollable frenzy of giggles. Anyone observing these antics might assume the trio had found the sherry bottle in the sideboard and imbibed in a few too many to help pass an otherwise quiet Sunday afternoon.

Suddenly Mary stopped. "I hear Mona stirring. That's my little girl. I can't wait for you to meet her," she said excitedly and quickly left the room. Carrie sat down again. Emma wandered around the room, looking at little trinkets. A pot-bellied milk glass bowl caught her eye. Little did she know that Jim had given that to his bride on their first anniversary. She picked up a china bud vase with a yellow silk rose in it. She noticed a framed picture on the wall that looked like a wedding photograph.

"That must be her husband. Handsome, isn't he?" Carrie nodded in agreement.

As soon as Mary returned, carrying a sleepy, dark-haired toddler wrapped in a pink blanket, Emma sat down again. Mona acted shy but soon was content to play while they chattered. Mary didn't say anything about the polio. They'd find out soon enough, once they saw her limp.

Emma got down on the floor to play with her. Mary had no idea that she'd worked as a nanny but it was obvious she liked young children. She was petite, about five feet tall, and probably weighed no more than a hundred pounds. Her dark hair, the colour of ebony, was swept up on top of her head in a bun.

"How old are you Emma?" Mary asked. Emma turned toward her but looked confused so Mary repeated the question.

Courtesy of Gail Horner.

This photo of Emma Janeway was taken in Lambeth, England, in 1888.

"I'm almost twenty."

"Do you remember Papa?"

"The only thing I remember was sitting on the step every afternoon waiting for him to come home. He'd always pick me up and give me a big hug. He took my picture with him wherever he went. I think he was afraid I'd grow up." She reached into her little crocheted handbag and produced a dog-eared picture of an angelic-looking child not more than six or eight months old. "I've kept it all these years."

"I remember you were a pretty baby, Emma," Mary replied.

"When I was older, he use to send me to the corner store for a pint," she hesitated as though she'd said too much. "Papa loved his beer. I quite liked going to the store because they'd give me a bag of candies, usually humbugs or toffees." Carrie frowned. "Carrie wasn't happy about me going but I quite liked it."

"You were too young and Papa shouldn't have asked you. It wasn't right," Carrie said. Emma's eyes dropped. To this day she couldn't bear to hear anything negative about her father. Carrie decided not to tell Mary that Emma use to sit on the steps outside the pub and wait for him because she was lonely.

Mary tried hard to picture Papa. She had little memory of what had happened after her mother died. Martha Janeway had suffered a fatal heart attack leaving six children motherless. Carrie was old enough to stay home and look after two-year old Emma while John, William and Mary were sent to orphanages. John ran away from the orphanage and left England to work in the coalmines in British Columbia. He was only twelve. William and Mary were sent to Canada as home children and placed on farms in rural Ontario.

Mary broke the silence. "What happened to the baby after Mama died?"

"Mama's sisters took him back to Glasgow. Ma had a feeling it would be a boy and couldn't decide whether to call him Thomas or Phillip. Papa decided on Thomas. The doctor warned him that he wasn't quite right, being born so early. We heard later that he only lived a year," Carrie replied sadly. "Things were never the same after Ma was gone."

"I loved getting your presents when I was on the farm," Mary said. "It was the only reason I looked forward to Christmas. Your letters made me homesick. I should have written back but I had no way to get to town to mail them." She also had no money for postage.

"I understand. It was my way of trying to keep us together after Mama died. I didn't know how to tell you about losing Papa, but I felt you should know. That was a hard letter to write. There was a small funeral and I kept the notice in my diary if you ever want to see it. He didn't want to go on without Mama." Mary nodded. "He blamed himself for her death because she wasn't strong and the doctors had told him they should go back to Scotland. Papa had refused."

"It must have been hard being the oldest."

"I'm not the oldest. Before Papa passed away, he told me we had an older sister named Martha, after Mama. I was too young to remember her. For some reason he wanted me to know this before he died. She's buried in Glasgow with Thomas."

"What happened to her?"

"Papa told me she died in the storm. That's all he said." Carrie decided it was time to change the subject. "He always favoured Emma. I think he felt most sorry for her, being just a baby and never knowing Mama. At least we have memories."

In 1877, William and Martha Janeway posed for a rare photo with their first-born child, Martha, named after her mother.

"I have trouble remembering what Mama looked like," Mary said, jumping up and going over to a small table. "But I've got a picture," she said, flipping right to the page. "There she is," she pointed, "with a little baby in her arms that I always thought was you."

"That was Martha, not me." Mary closed the photo album, setting it back on the table. Carrie explained how she put Emma in an orphanage after Papa died while she went into service as a maid for a well-to-do family.

"How long were you in the orphanage?" Mary asked.

"What?" Emma replied, turning to Mary. Carrie put a finger to her lips and shook her head just as Mary was about to repeat her question.

"Let's have tea and a biscuit," Mary said, and headed for the kitchen with Mona close at her heels.

Over a cup of tea, Carrie told Mary how her domestic job had paid for Emma's keep and it was where she met Frank Lunn, the gardener who became her husband. Carrie took a big breath. "Now it's your turn."

Mary admitted that she'd never told her husband about being a home child and they promised to keep her secret. She shared some of her experiences on the farm, omitting sad things like missing the Christmas sleigh ride as punishment for breaking a plate, and being called an orphan at school. She told them about Mustard, the cat she'd found in the barn, her best friend Josie Chesney, and how much she loved to go to school even though it was a two-mile walk in the country.

She told them about Reverend Ward, the minister who'd taken her to Holbrook to see Will. "Will, that's what he called himself, lived with the Lounsburys who were old but very nice. They didn't tell him I was coming because they wanted it to be a surprise. It was a surprise all right. I'll never forget the look on his face when he saw me."

"How old was Willy?" Carrie asked.

"Fifteen. He liked the farm work but didn't want to go to school. I could never understand that."

"He was shy, Mary. He might have been afraid he couldn't do the work and others would make fun." Carrie had heard rumours back in London that home children "would be sent to sit at the back of the classroom in the row saved for idiots and foreigners."[4]

"School was the best thing that happened to me. It's where I learned how to read," she paused. "I'm not sure if Will ever did." Mary felt she'd said enough about herself. "What made you come to Canada?"

"It was because of John," Carrie answered, wiping a crumb from her mouth with the corner of a napkin. "He was twenty-six when he came home for a visit and told us how wonderful life was in Canada. He'd done well for himself otherwise he couldn't have afforded the passage home."

"Having enough money seemed to dispel any skepticism of the advertisements in the newspapers concerning that land of 'milk and honey.'"[5]

"And then he went back?"

"It wasn't long before he headed to San Diego to work in the coal mines. He thought he'd get rich," she stopped, "working in those dark, dirty, god-forsaken coal mines. He wrote and told us how happy he was to be a trapper. I've still got his letter in my trunk."

"A trapper?"

"Pa told me the trapper opens and closes doors in the tunnels so the men and the coal can move through. And then he was promoted to a raker. He got to drive the rake of empty coal cars pulled by a horse, down into the mine. I remember him telling us his horse's name was Brandy."

"Did something happen to him?"

"John always wanted to be a driller, the man who bores a hole in the wall and puts the explosive in it. Pa warned him how dangerous it was but he wouldn't listen. Finally he got his wish."

> One of the mining dangers is that fire damp gas can be present in a hollow chamber in a coal bed and can burst out when the miner's drill reaches this cavity. After fire-damp burns, it leaves behind poisonous gasses such as after-damp and black-damp, both heavier than air, and the most dangerous of all, white damp: a gas without colour, taste, or odour, a gas lighter than air. A breath of it spells death.[6]

"Shortly before we set out for Canada, I got a telegram saying John had been killed in a mining accident." Mary was at a loss for words. "A letter came from the mining company saying they were sorry for what had happened. We never knew whether John died because of the falling rocks or the explosion but he was the only one killed. Pa always said you never hear about an accident when it's only one miner. The collieries had to do something if an accident took a lot of lives; otherwise it'd be forgotten. He said that cemeteries were full of the graves of miners, some of them mere boys as young as ten." Mary felt badly for Carrie, she'd been through so much.

"They sent us a photo of John. It broke my heart when I looked at him, knowing that he died alone. We were lucky they paid for the burial costs. I'm glad that Pa was gone by the time it happened," Carrie said quietly. "It would have been more than he could bear. He never got over losing Mama even though he tried to do his best. I don't doubt for a moment that he loved us," Carrie paused. "But that's when he started drinking."

This portrait of John Janeway was taken in the Bennette Studio on 5th Avenue, San Diego, California, 1907.

Courtesy of Gail Horner.

Mary was overwhelmed with the news of an older sister, deaths of three of her siblings, and Pa's drinking. She was thankful that Carrie and Emma had found her after so many years of separation, yet the passage of time had taken its toll on the Janeway family. The afternoon had a bittersweet taste. The girls rambled on in an attempt to make up for lost time. Eighteen years of living apart needed to be accounted for, an impossible task for one Sunday afternoon. They jumped from past to present and back to the past again. It was as though they were painting a mural, without the patience to wait for one colour to dry before dipping the brush in a new more vibrant one. The result was joyous turmoil.

Since it was a lovely sunny day, Mary suggested going outside. She scooped up Mona and they sat on the front stoop. Within minutes, the little girl squiggled out of her arms and ran under a tree in the yard. Carrie noticed her limp.

"She had polio," Mary said without waiting for her to ask. "The doctor said it was a mild case and she'd be all right." Mona started to wander, and just as Mary was about to get up, Emma ran down the street after her. Mary had been waiting for such an opportunity. "Why did you shush me earlier when I asked Emma about the orphanage? Did she have a bad experience?"

"She still has nightmares. I try not to bring it up in front of her. I felt terrible having to send her there but I'd no choice. Somehow Emma got the idea that Pa owned the pottery factory where he worked but it was his brother, Uncle Bill, who owned it. He was the one with all the money, not Papa. When he died, Emma couldn't understand where it had all gone. I didn't have the heart to tell her otherwise."

"I'm sure you meant well."

"I remember Emma wanting to change her name to Emaline because it sounded more distinguished. Little did she know that we had no money and I'd no means to take care of her. It was my nanny job that helped pay for her board at the orphanage, which is why I feel so badly about what happened."

"Did something happen at the orphanage?"

"Emma was given orders one day to clean the stairs. They were very strict and had ways of keeping close tabs on the children. When the matron came to check later, she found the two coins that she'd hidden under the edge of the carpet on one of the stairs. So she knew Emma had not done a thorough cleaning." Mary looked so sad that Carrie regretted telling her.

"What happened?" Mary asked in a whisper.

"She had her ears boxed. The women in charge use to box their ears on a regular basis. It was their method of punishment, no matter what the child might have done wrong. As a result of one of these bouts, Emma's eardrum was burst, leaving her deaf in that ear." Now Mary understood why she'd asked to have things repeated.

"We don't talk about it, there's no point. Emma's always been delicate and seems to catch things easily. A few years ago she was quite sick with catarrh and to this day she thinks that it caused her deafness. I'd like to believe that myself but I know what I was told by one of the older girls at the orphanage."

"You shouldn't blame yourself. You had no choice but to put her in a home. Just look at her now. See how happy she is."

Carrie looked protectively down the street in the direction of her younger sister. "It never should have happened Mary, it just never should have happened."

Emma's punishment in the orphanage reminded Mary of a time when she'd been hurt. "We all have things we'd like to forget," she said, glancing down at the scar on her right arm.

"Mommy, mommy," Mona squealed, running toward her with outstretched arms.

"And things we want to remember forever," Mary said, turning to Carrie as the little girl fell into her arms.

TWELVE

Life Goes On

> "Life was changing in the country, too — in October 1908 the first free rural mail delivery began, between Hamilton and Ancaster, Ontario."[1]

1908

Mary invited her sisters to stay with them but Carrie wouldn't hear of it. Frank and his brother got jobs on a dairy farm within a week, which meant they could stay in Hamilton.

That spring Mary treated herself to a new Easter hat trimmed with spring flowers — something she hadn't done in years. She debated whether to buy a pair of kid gloves on sale for seventy-nine cents but decided against it. One luxury at a time. She felt well-dressed sitting with her family in Centenary Methodist Church on Easter Sunday morning.

Mary went to a great deal of trouble to have a lovely family dinner. It was the first time in years that she'd been able to celebrate Easter with her sisters. She prepared a baked ham with mint sauce, glazed sweet potatoes, canned peas, yellow beans, and Queen's pudding. The dessert sounded fancy but was nothing more than a plain bread pudding, custard with some jelly spread on top, and garnished with meringue slightly browned in the oven.

After the holiday weekend Emma felt it was time for her to get a job. She sent letters to England asking for references, using Mary's address. She'd lived with this rich old lady named Mrs. Rough whom she felt certain would vouch for her. She also sent a note to Mrs. Sterling Saunder, a doctor's wife, but was less hopeful that this reference would be complimentary, as she had been let go. Carrie encouraged her to take a business course while she waited for letters from England. Emma took her advice and enrolled in a six-week course at the Hamilton Business College. Mary couldn't get over how much influence Carrie had over her younger sister. It could easily have been mistaken for a mother-daughter relationship.

Mary tried to see her sisters at least once a week. They always made plans to get together when they were with each other since no one had a telephone. If the arrangements had to be changed, they communicated through hastily written postcards. "I'll be there Tues at three instead of two" or "Sorry to hear Mona's not feeling well, how about the same time next week?" were the kind of scribbled messages that went back and forth. Mary wasn't surprised when the mailman asked how her daughter was feeling.

Sometimes they met downtown for an "ice," as Carrie and Emma would say, at Christopher's, the second door down from James, or at the Sugar Bowl on King. Both were popular candy stores and ice-cream parlours. Frank liked Turkish delight and sponge toffee and little Harvey always wanted whatever his brother chose. Mona's favourite was chocolate gingers. Once they had their treat in a bag, they'd head for the ice cream.

Mona would order a lemon soda, which consisted of vanilla ice cream and some sort of lemon pop. She'd sit on her mother's lap at the counter with her chubby legs hanging over the edge of the stool. Mary would hold the tall frosty glass while Mona took long, deliberate draws from the straw. It usually spoiled her appetite for supper but Mary didn't mind. She wanted her daughter to have the kind of childhood memories that she'd never had.

Depending on the weather, Mary and Jim often went on a family picnic on Sunday. They took the incline to the top of the mountain or a streetcar to the foot of Burlington Street and a boat over to La Salle

Park on the other side of the bay. It was quite a hike up a big hill to the park. There wasn't a lot there but green grass and a bathhouse, a place to change into a swimsuit.

The wool "bathing costume," with its collar and sleeves, became cumbersome when it got wet. Women were reticent to bare their legs in public, even in suits that fell to the knee. Some ladies wore stockings with their swimsuits and were more apt to sit by the water's edge than go for a dip. The majority of bathers were under the age of twelve. It wasn't until a few years later that the knit swimwear was introduced, which made swimming more practical and fun.

Mona spent hours playing in knee-deep water the temperature of warm pea soup and ignored her mother's suggestion to come out for a cheese sandwich and cold drink. The bay was always warmer than the lake and well worth the effort made to get there. Mona usually fell asleep in her father's arms long before they got on the streetcar heading home.

In early May Emma received several letters from her former employers. Mrs. Saunder provided a lovely recommendation written by her husband, a doctor, and a personal letter. Emma was disappointed that she wrote "Dear Nurse" rather than call her by name. Mrs. Rough, another employer, wrote that she'd been pleased with Emma but her comment "she has some notion of cooking" wasn't particularly complimentary. With references in hand, Emma began to look for a job. She moved in with Mary who was more centrally located than Carrie, which made job hunting easier.

The first time she travelled on the streetcar alone was quite an adventure. She boarded at the corner of Cannon and James, four blocks from Mary's house, found an empty window seat and sat down. When the conductor came around to collect the fare, Emma was too timid to ask about her stop. After a while she realized the streets were beginning to look familiar. She'd been on the streetcar long enough to see downtown Hamilton three times and had no choice but to head home before it got dark, no closer to finding a job. She was discouraged but within a few weeks was hired as a live-in nanny for a prominent Hamilton family.

Mary missed Emma but soon got back into her old routine. With only a little more than a month until Christmas, she planned to spend the day shopping. She'd already made Mona a dark-green sateen dress with puffed sleeves and a viyella shirt for Jim. She was used to sewing with wincey, a strong cotton-wool blend, not nearly as nice as viyella but much cheaper. Years ago he'd acquired a brown shirt made of this soft, cozy material. By now it was threadbare. She'd tried to throw it out several times but he wouldn't hear of it. "It's my favourite shirt, the only one that doesn't scratch. And I like this, too," he added, patting the pocket with the cigarette pack protruding. "Until it's in rags, I'm wearing it." She was convinced that he meant it, but a replacement might hasten its demise.

She'd also been busy knitting each of her nephews a cardigan. She felt badly that once little Harvey outgrew his sweater, he'd inherit his brother's in the same colour. The yarn had been on sale and the choice was burgundy or black. There was no way she was knitting a black sweater for a child.

Ever since her sisters had arrived, Mary had been extra careful with her grocery money, buying cheaper cuts of meat and doing less baking. She was saving to buy Christmas gifts for them. The only place she refused to scrimp was on her hair. She still went to the beauty parlour every three months.

Glancing at the kitchen clock, there was still time to read the paper and hunt for bargains before heading downtown. She'd been following the ongoing campaign for rural mail delivery. George Wilcox, a man from Woodstock, had written numerous articles because he thought if city folks could get home delivery at public expense, so should the farmers, who produced food for the nation. Mary wished there'd been mail delivery when she was living on the farm. News from her family back in England would have helped her get through some of those terrible, lonely winters in the country.

Realizing the time, she decided to take her chances on snagging a good deal, dropped Mona at the neighbours, and grabbed the streetcar. She went to both the Arcade and the Right House but couldn't find anything special enough within her price range so headed for Finch Bros. over on King West. They had real Brussels lace-border handkerchiefs ranging from $1.25 to $4.00. The most expensive ones were by far the prettiest but spending $4.00 on one gift was simply out of the question. Mary decided on a box that cost $1.50 and, to her surprise, the clerk gift-wrapped it.

She looked at blankets for Emma, who was always complaining about being cold. She wasn't used to the harsh Canadian winters. The blankets on sale were white with green borders. Mary picked one up and ran her fingers over it carefully.

"Can I help you ma'am?"

"I'm looking for a blanket for a gift, but these seem a bit thin," she said truthfully, putting it back down.

The clerk looked annoyed. "Perhaps you should consider a comforter. They're much thicker." Mary followed her to another table.

"How does this feel?" she asked, handing one to her.

"Very nice."

"It's genuine down."

"How much is it?" Mary asked timidly.

"It's our top of the line, $14."

"Do you have less expensive ones?"

"Of course," she said, circling the table and pointing. "I have them at $3.75, $4.50, $5.75, $6.50, and $7.00." Mary set the comforter down and started touching the others. They weren't cheap and still not much thicker than a blanket. "Perhaps you should look at some more blankets. You can buy a pair for a low as $3.69." Mary didn't appreciate the woman's comment and thought she should have been more tactful.

She had half a notion to return Carrie's gift but it was at a different counter and the girl had been very friendly. Mary slowly wandered around until the clerk was out of sight, then went back to the blankets to have another look and noticed one that she hadn't seen before. It was azure blue, the colour of a cloudless sky and felt quite puffy. She went up to the counter, having no choice but to deal with the same woman again.

"How much is this one?" she asked, handing it to her.

"$1.95," the clerk replied, with a clipped tongue. It was more than Mary had intended on spending, and, the woman, sensing her hesitation turned to walk away.

"I'll take it," she replied quickly. Mary wasn't surprised that the clerk didn't bother gift-wrapping it. Her shopping experience hadn't been as much fun as she'd anticipated, but she was happy with her purchases and hoped her sisters would like their gifts.

December arrived and, much to the disappointment of the children, was accompanied by very little snow. Mary invited the milkman, iceman/coalman, and mailman in for a Christmas drink. It was obvious that Earl, her mailman, had already accepted several invitations that day. A few years later the post office issued a booklet to its employees in an attempt to curtail such "social calls."

A week before Christmas Mary took Mona downtown to see Santa. The Santa Claus Reception in Stanley Mills had been advertised the day before in the Hamilton Herald. It stipulated that children must be accompanied by their parents and each child would be given a souvenir of his or her visit. They met Emma, Carrie, and her boys in Toyland. Frank had already found a spot at the railing of the toy train exhibit. With eyes as large as saucers, he watched the little black locomotive with real steam puffing out of its smokestack wind its way through a tunnel and chug-a-lug methodically over a bridge. The train route was one continuous figure eight but none of the children seemed to grow tired of watching.

Adjacent to the train was a mechanical monkey that flipped his hat with his tail to catch a coin that mysteriously popped out of his mouth. Rosy-cheeked porcelain dolls with ebony curls, pink satin gowns, and baby Jane shoes peaked through cellophane windows. A tall majestic Christmas tree, with its boughs laden with gold ornaments and candy canes, was surrounded by a picket fence covered in snow that looked surprisingly real. It wasn't hard for a young child to believe in the magic of Christmas.

Something far less obtrusive caught Mona's eye. She headed to the china dolls and porcelain dishes, safely displayed behind glass. Mary wished she could have afforded the dainty rosebud tea set and miniature dolls sitting on the tiny wicker furniture.

When they parted company Mona, Frank, and Harvey were clutching peppermint candy canes, the souvenir given to every child who came to see Santa. Mary bought a pound of shelled walnuts and some dates before getting on the streetcar to head home with a very tired little girl.

A light snowfall, almost sleet-like, fell on the city on Christmas Eve. Mona was thrilled that Santa would be able to pay her a visit. Jim sat in his favourite armchair and smoked while he watched Mary and Mona string cranberries and popcorn to decorate their tree. When they were finished a few ornaments hung from the thin, spindly branches, and a gift for Mona and each of her cousins sat underneath. The rest would be up to Santa.

It was a Christmas that had special meaning. The trip to Stanley Mill's Toyland to sit on Santa's knee, a light dusting of snow Christmas Eve, carollers huddled together under a street lamp, and a turkey dinner with all the trimmings meant so much more because a family could be together. Mary knew that Carrie and Emma were sharing her thoughts while Jim said grace. All their heads were bowed except the two youngest, Mona and Harvey, but even they were strangely quiet and watched with curiosity.

Carrie's gift to her sisters was a photograph of the three of them, taken earlier in the month at Shaw Studio. They had dressed in their finest after fussing with each other's hair. Mr. R.F. Shaw, the proprietor of the well-known photograph parlour, never rushed a family portrait even it meant other customers had to wait. The girls assumed that Mary, being

Courtesy of Gail Horner.

The Shaw Studio above the Treble Apartments at the corner of King and James was a popular photograph parlour in the city. Emma, Carrie, and Mary Janeway look very serious in this 1908 studio portrait.

the middle sister, would be in the centre, but Mr. Shaw had his own ideas. He patiently explained that Carrie's dress would nicely offset the darker tones that her sisters had worn and without further discussion, he positioned her between Emma and Mary.

With the exception of her wedding day, Mary could only remember having her picture taken on one other occasion — shortly after her arrival on the farm. She remembered because "everyone" had been included that day at school, even the home children.

Emma, still looking straight ahead at the photographer, gently tugged Mary's sleeve behind Carrie's back. Mary tried hard not to smile. Finally, Mr. Shaw put his head under the dark cloth, which meant he was satisfied. The girls remained motionless and silent. The photographer captured the moment, a beautiful family portrait that each of them would cherish for years. The photograph of the three girls was all that was left of the Janeway family, all except for Willy.

Courtesy of Joe Jacques.

Students at Blandford S.S. No. 3 posed for a photograph with the thrasher's gang lying down in the front row, 1892. Mary Janeway (fourth girl from the right in the third row) and Fred Cooper (third boy from the left in the second row) were the only home children in the school.

THIRTEEN

A Dream Comes True

"Henry Ford announced that he would produce only a single model: a simple, rugged, light, cheap car for 'the great multitude,' as he put it, to enjoy 'God's great open spaces.' Each car would be alike 'as one pin is like another pin' and any customer could have 'a car painted any colour that he wants so long as it is black.' In 1909 the first Model Ts came rolling off an 'assembly line.' Ford priced his car at $950."[1]

1909

The automobile, at one time only affordable to the very rich, was now within the grasp of everyday folks like Jim. He now had a steady job and had done well at the track. He headed to the Ford dealership in town and arrived home in a brand new Model T Ford. He honked the horn and waited. After a few minutes he honked again. Mary looked out the window and gasped. Wiping her hands on her pink cotton apron, she ran to the front door.

"What on earth have you done?"

"What you're looking at is our brand new automobile, Mrs. Church." He stepped aside, bowing slightly and sweeping his arm toward the car. "What you're listening to is the purr of an engine," he grinned. "What does the Missus think?"

"I think you've lost your mind! We can't afford this."

"Don't worry, I've got it all figured out." He jumped in and patted the seat beside him.

"What about Mona? She's still sleeping."

"We'll just go for a quick spin around the block. She'll never know we were gone." Jim reached over, opened the door, and, grabbing her sleeve, pulled Mary inside. He drove down the street waving to people he'd never met. "They made it so easy, you wouldn't believe it. Just signed a few papers and this baby was mine. At least I know how to drive. Last week they said a man took a car right out of their showroom, drove it down the road, and he'd never been behind the wheel a day in his life." Actually, "The average driver escaped licensing until 1927. When operator's licences were introduced — the only hardship was the $1.00 they cost. They were first issued without examination upon filling out an application form."[2]

Jim never told her what he'd paid for the car. Mary knew he couldn't afford to buy it outright, which meant that a portion of each pay was already spent. Jim had had quite a few different employers in the past, and when he was between jobs weeks would go by without any money coming in. But he had become a lot more responsible since his daughter had been born. She chose not to say anything that would take away from his excitement of the moment.

Mona celebrated her fourth birthday and three weeks later Emma turned twenty-one. Jim wasn't surprised when Carrie and Frank announced their plans to head west. He'd spent many hours with Carrie's husband on the front porch enjoying a cigarette after supper. Frank had talked about buying land and filing for a homestead.

"My doctor back in England told me I should be working outside. I used to be in an office and he said I needed fresh air. That's when I decided to come to Canada and try farming."

Courtesy of Gail Horner.

Emma looked mature and sophisticated in her high-neck eyelet shirtwaist with lace edging. She wore a gold locket engraved with her initials and Carrie's cameo, photo 1909.

Harvey Lunn's tunic, made from the same fabric as his older brother's, buttoned to the neck. Frank's jacket has been modelled after the masculine bicycling dress, worn at the turn of the century. Mona Church's empire-style dress, trimmed with frills, a rosette, and matching rosette headpiece, was reminiscent of an illustration by Kate Greenaway, the artist who brought about the revival of "empire" influence in the 1890s.

Courtesy of Gail Horner.

"It's back-breaking work, Frank. Are you sure?" asked Jim.

"Back home I heard that you could pick up gold right on the ground and I saw pictures of great big apples and oranges in store windows." When Jim heard him say this, he stopped blowing smoke rings into the still night air and shook his head in disbelief.

October arrived with two more birthdays: Frank's on the 4th, and his brother Harvey's on the 22nd. Carrie insisted on having a photograph taken of her boys and Mona to mark the occasion. Mary had been putting money aside to get Mona a Christmas dress and could see no reason not to buy it a little early. Five-year-old Frank looked so mature standing between his younger brother and Mona, both perched on stools.

A week later, the Lunns packed up and were gone. Mary had hoped they'd stay until after Christmas. She knew it was only a matter of time before Emma would follow her sister out west. Carrie sent word that they ended up in Fort Saskatchewan where both Frank and his brother got jobs at Featherstone's sawmill. Frank was happy living on a big farm with stables.

With the advent of spring, March brought some warm, balmy temperatures. At least three times a week Jim washed, buffed, and polished his car until he could see his own reflection in the chrome. Then he'd sit in the front room with a beer, content to look out the window and admire his work.

"If I'd have known how great it was to own a car, I'd have bought one sooner. Just look at that little beauty," he'd say, pointing out the window. Like others, Jim was convinced the motorized vehicle was here to stay. "Yesterday it was the plaything of the few," remarked one writer in 1907, "today it is the servant of many; tomorrow it will be the necessity of humanity."[3]

"Let's not forget that we don't own it. Until the payments are done, it isn't ours."

"There you go spoiling the moment, my practical little wife. If I thought like you, we'd never have anything. You have to think big."

"One of us has to think sensibly. I suppose that's me."

"Suit yourself. As for me, I'll continue to dream."

"If wishes were horses," Mary paused, raising her eyebrows, "beggars would ride."

"Call them what you want, they're what life's all about! The minute I stop dreaming, you better start worrying. Now, how'd you like to get your husband another beer?" he said, holding up his empty bottle.

By late April Jim was out of work and spending most days at the track. The inevitable happened — the car had to be sold. Mary never knew how much of a loss he took but felt badly, knowing how attached he'd become to the car. For weeks he was quiet and distant. Even Mona had trouble making her father smile.

"I'd like to talk to you about something," Mary said one evening, sitting down in the armchair across from Jim. He peered over the top of the *Spec* "The car," she said quietly.

He dropped the paper in his lap. "We don't own a car."

"We never did."

"Don't start on me."

"I was never angry with you for buying it. But I was afraid we were in over our heads."

"So you were right … is that what this is about?"

"No, it's about feeling badly because I know how much you loved that car."

Jim wasn't good at sharing his feelings and seldom let his guard down. Finally he spoke. "I'll have another one you know. It's just a matter of time."

"I know you will," she said and smiled. Convinced that the "old Jim" was back, she picked up one of her Eaton's catalogues and curled up on the sofa beside him. Mary never tired of looking at this big book of dreams and imagining what it would be like to have the things advertised on those glossy pages. "The most popular book in Canada, some said. Predictable as the snowfall, the new Eaton's catalogue arrived at the door to announce the change of season."[4] She'd almost forgotten where the out-dated "wishing book" had ended up on the farm. Mary had no idea that the Eaton's catalogue had been around for twenty-five years. It made its first appearance in 1884, the year she was born.

"There's no harm in dreaming, is there?" Jim asked.

"Of course not," she replied as something caught her eye. She shouldn't criticize her husband for dreaming; she did it too. The only difference was that her dreams didn't cost as much. But it didn't matter; they were equally unattainable. Mary was admiring a beautiful, fully lined lady's winter coat for $125. It seemed like a lot of money to keep warm. She sighed as she closed the book, knowing that they couldn't afford it.

That's when she realized she'd been looking at the Eaton's Fall & Winter Catalogue, 1902. The book was seven years out of date. She could only imagine what the coat really cost.

FOURTEEN

Hamilton: A City of Firsts

> "Hamilton is a city of firsts and inventions: the flashing turn signal, the center line on highways, the first telephone exchange in the British Empire, the first pay phones in Canada, the first sulphur matches, threshing machines, sewing machines and more."[1]

1910

Jim got another job, this time in the rail yard down at the docks. It was hard work but with steady hours and a regular pay envelope.

Hamilton's waterfront location on one of Canada's finest natural harbours attracted the attention of the steel industry. Leading steel companies in Montreal and Ontario, including the Hamilton Steel and Iron Company, merged to create the Steel Company of Canada (Stelco). Two years later the Sherman family founded Dominion Foundries, known as Dofasco.

By 1910, electric streetcars had replaced the horse-drawn trams in most cities. Urban centres were beginning to move at a much faster pace than they had in the first decade of the century. Controller Horatio Hocken's proposal to build a subway was considered a "harebrained" idea, one that would not be taken seriously for some fifty years, but Eaton's in Toronto had the first escalator in the country. Mary wished they could have afforded the trip to the big city to have a ride on the "moving staircase." Shoppers who were willing to try it out could enjoy a five-cent ice cream cone at the top.

Saving money was viewed less seriously. People were spending more and the number of cars on the road increased dramatically. In some cities there were as many auto agencies as livery stables. More homes began to install electric lights and telephones. The one-horsepower Brunswick refrigerator could make a pound of ice in an hour and the General Electric range had thirty switches and plugs. Movie-going was commonplace, but "talking pictures" were still a topic of gossip. The hottest dance craze, the tango, came all the way from South America and, although viewed as slightly naughty, it was extremely popular. A newfangled contraption called the radio was making its debut, which made it possible to listen to words and music from some faraway place in the comfort of your own home.

Mary saw Emma whenever her employer gave her time off. She hoped that her sister's British expressions would confuse Earl if he became inquisitive while delivering her postcards: "Missus gone a fortnight [two weeks], day off cancelled"; "Ran into a bad patch[rough time], sorry to cancel this week"; "Went to pay-box [box-office], got two for Saturday at 1."

The girls always met in front of Woolworth's. They'd go up and down each aisle in the five-and-dime for fear of missing an affordable treasure. Then they walked down to the Right House to admire the high-laced boots, narrow hobble skirts, beautiful chiffons, and satins in the window. Emma thought it would be difficult to walk in the new "vertical line" skirt. Mary was glad bustles were out and brassieres were in but whispered her thoughts for fear someone might overhear her. They usually ended up at Stanley Mill's millinery department before taking different streetcars to head home.

However, as the weeks passed by, Mary watched her sister grow weak and listless. "Emma, must you work so hard? You're not looking a bit well," she said, "and that cough of yours worries me too."

"You sound like Carrie."

Although Mary had no nursing training, she knew something was wrong and insisted that Emma go to the doctor. It didn't take Dr. Storms long to realize that Emma had tuberculosis, commonly referred to as TB. She'd had whooping cough as a young child, and he explained that TB often follows certain diseases, that being one of them.

"We have an excellent sanatorium that opened four years ago on the mountain. It's nicely removed from the city's congestion and air pollution," the doctor said. "It's not as bad as it sounds."

"I'm perfectly capable of looking after Emma. What can I do to help?"

The doctor walked her through the daily regime of things she'd need for a full recovery. "The important thing is cleanliness in everything that she touches. It's difficult to do this at home." But Mary insisted on looking after her sister.

Emma gave her notice and moved in with Mary. It meant there were changes that affected the whole family. Mona and Jim no longer had her undivided attention. The dining room became Emma's bedroom because it was quiet at the back of the house, one of the sunniest rooms, and she wouldn't have to climb stairs.

Mary prepared her a careful diet of wholesome, easily digested food, and washed Emma's plate, knife, fork, and spoon in boiling water and soda separately. She washed the floor in her room with soap and water regularly, boiling the duster after each use and made sure that Emma had lots of fresh air and sunshine. For the first six weeks she kept Mona apart even though the little girl didn't understand why she couldn't play with her aunt.

It was evident that Emma was getting better when she started to take an interest in food. One morning she asked for "buttered eggs," the ones that Carrie used to make. Mary looked confused. "It's very simple, she put two eggs in a bowl with a little water, beat them with a fork, and cooked them in a pan," explained Emma.

"Oh, you mean scrambled."

"Scrambled?" she repeated slowly. Mary laughed.

Emma flourished under her sister's care. They took short walks in the open air and ventured farther as she grew stronger. Mary took her temperature every few days and insisted she wear warm woollen underclothing and night garments to bed to help keep her comfortable as sweating was a common symptom in the later stages of the disease. Dr. Storms was pleased with her progress and the sanatorium was never mentioned again. All the time she was recuperating, Carrie had been asking her to come out west. By Christmas Emma was ready to go back to work and found a live-in nanny position with a family on Aberdeen Avenue.

That spring Carrie and Frank filed for a homestead in a small community near Waskatenau, sixty miles northeast of Edmonton. The Dominion was offering grants to land companies who sold land to homesteaders in an attempt to eliminate speculators, which meant they only had to pay a ten-dollar fee per quarter section.

The snowdrops and purple crocuses were popping out of the ground when Mary registered Mona for Kindergarten at King Edward School the first week of May. It cost twenty cents for two months, the remainder of the school year. Her teacher was Miss Allie Small, a spinster, or as some would say an "unclaimed treasure." At that time the board didn't hire married women.

Mona was supposed to return to school in September but came down with a severe cold that left her listless and lethargic for weeks. Mary didn't bother registering her that fall. Jim left his job at the rail yard to try earning a living as a painter and paperhanger once again. He struggled but wouldn't admit it. It didn't help that he missed getting a listing in the 1911 city directory. They were having difficulty paying the rent and had to move.

Their new home was an apartment in Treble Hall, a three-storey building at 8½ John Street North, where professionals, labourers, and merchants occupied space. Shops occupied the first floor, offices took up space on the second, and apartments were on the third, which previously had housed a large assembly hall. There was a fourth floor, barely detectable from the street. Mary noticed the tiny windows set into dormers peeking out above the roofline and hoped that no one had to live there.

During their eight-year occupancy, tenants came and went and businesses changed hands. When they first moved in, they lived above job printer J.A. Cox and Joyce & Wilson real estate. At one time they lived above the Capital Life Association Company, J.J. McAuliffe real estate,

The Pettit Collection.

In 1879, James Balfour, in depicting Renaissance Revival architecture, designed the flat brick walls of Treble Hall to complement the ornate sculptures of pressed metal decorating the window openings. In this contemporary photograph, the decorative ball finials that originally topped each window are no longer there and the road is paved.

and the City Dental Laboratory. Jim loved to make jokes about his neighbours. "Just think, we can get insurance, a house, or a set of choppers practically without leaving our apartment."

Jim liked being downtown because it was easier for him to find a card game or share a pint in one of the local bars. Mary found it hard to give up her house on a quiet street but at least she had a small back porch to hang out her clothes. And there had been no choice; they simply couldn't afford the rent on Railway Street.

Mary hardly ever heard from Carrie anymore. She realized that homesteading was hard work with little time or light left over at the end of the day for letter writing. That fall Carrie did post a letter with a picture of her youngest son, describing him as "quite the little man." Three-year-old Harvey, wearing a crisp white sailor suit and black high top boots, sat quietly for a studio photograph.

"They'll be all grown up before you know it," said Emma sadly. "They'll not remember me rocking them to sleep at night or how they clung to me during the passage over. I miss the boys and I miss Carrie too." Mary knew what was coming.

Emma headed west a month later with the hope of finding a job in Edmonton. Mary stood on the station platform and never shed a tear until she could no longer see her sister waving and the train was out of sight. A grey-haired, elderly gentlemen sitting on a bench nearby, looked up from his paper and asked if there was anything he could do to help. She shook her head and turned away.

Emma had become such an important part of her life and that was abruptly coming to a halt. Once again Mary found herself saying good-bye to someone that she loved, clinging to what was left — a collage of beautiful memories. At least this time she wasn't alone; she had a family of her own.

FIFTEEN

Missing Person

"Booze, sports and church — these were the opiates of the labouring poor. There were more saloons than there were downtown corners in most cities and towns. There, long after the banks were closed, a working man could dip into his hard-earned pay envelope and take home whatever was left some hours later. Liquor and beer were cheap."[1]

1911

Emma had been gone a little over a month when Mary received a letter. Wiping her hands on a towel and grabbing the letter opener from the windowsill, she sat down at the kitchen table eager to find out how her sister was doing.

Emma wrote the way she spoke, using short, clipped sentences but her choice of words reflected her gentle nature. Mary realized how much she missed her and struggled not to cry for fear Mona might hear.

October 23

Dear Mary,
Carrie got me in at the hospital where she works. I clean wards, do laundry, and housekeeping. I've acquired a bed-sitter at 2249 First Street. But I have to share the loo. I'm taking night classes at MacTavish College, a few blocks south of Jasper. I love shorthand. I hope to complete a secretarial course by this time next year.

How are your food prices? Round steak is 10¢ a pound, stewing beef 6¢. I'm thankful I drink tea, as coffee is more expensive. Most things are reasonable. It's just as well since wages are down.

Edmonton's a pretty city, but very crowded. Hotels and boarding houses are so costly that people are living outdoors in tent cities. The largest ones are by the CNR tracks and down in the Rossdale and Fraser flats.

Carrie's boys are growing like weeds, farm life agrees with them. She asked to be remembered to you. I miss you terribly. Must run to the post-box before class, hugs for Mona.

Your loving sister, Emma

Mary tucked the letter in her apron pocket. She felt an emptiness in her life that she attributed to missing her sister. That night Jim came home with a newspaper folded under his arm. Even before taking his coat off, he wanted her to see an ad.

"Have a look at this Mary. They've come out with a car made in Woodstock for $650. It comes fully equipped and can be driven year-round. Doesn't that beat all!" She wondered how anyone could drive it in the wintertime when it had no doors or windshield. "Good solid rubber tires and shaft-driven too," he added.

Mona came storming into the kitchen. She wanted to tell them about the Halloween party at school. Mary welcomed the distraction and hoped the car would be forgotten.

Christmas wasn't nearly as much fun without Emma. They did the usual family things, bought a tree at the corner lot, took Mona to Toyland at Stanley Mills, and went downtown after dark to see the electric decorations in Gore Park. Mary had hoped her feelings of emptiness would have been gone by then but the Christmas trappings seem to make it worse. This year she wouldn't be inviting the milkman, iceman/coalman, and mailman in for a Christmas drink. She didn't even know her mailman's name.

That evening, while sorting through Christmas decorations, Mary stumbled across a box of old photos. She felt more than a twinge of nostalgia when she saw Emma posing with her classmates at Hamilton Business College. It seemed longer than four years ago that women wore the high choker neckline. Mary was glad the short open V-neck and a deeper one filled in with a vestee had replaced it. The "pneumonia" neckline, as it was called, making reference to Canada's long bitter cold winters, was still modest but more feminine and flattering. Having completely forgotten about tree ornaments, Mary studied Emma's picture and thought about the day her sisters had appeared on her doorstep. If it hadn't been for Carrie's persistence and determination, they never would have found her. She couldn't help but wonder what happened to Will.

"Did you find the angel?" Mona asked, bursting into the room.

"I'm still looking," she said. Packing away the dusty photos, she decided to put an ad in *The War Cry* to try to find her brother. Mary wasn't overly optimistic about finding him but she kept telling herself that if enough people saw the paper, it just might work.

> 8295. JANEWAY, WILLIAM. Age 29, brown hair and eyes, came to Canada in 1891 to Stratford (and Hamilton), sent to work on a farm in Ontario. May have gone to the coalmines in San Diego or Western Canada.

Six weeks later the temperature dropped overnight and snow had crusted hard on the sill. Mary would have liked a little fresh air but knew those cold westerly winds would chill her to the bone. Ice strands like tangled shoelaces had formed across the windowpane, leaving cut-like designs on the glass. It reminded her of the patterns the kids use to make skating on Mr. Allenby's pond when she lived on the farm. She went downstairs to see if there was any mail, an excuse to take a break from ironing. There was a letter postmarked from British Columbia. Mary didn't know anyone who lived farther west than Edmonton. She ran upstairs to get her letter opener, and in her excitement forgot to shut the door tightly. Her hands were shaking as she opened the envelope, being careful not to tear the paper inside.

> February 18
>
> Dear Mary,
> I never spected to here from you. Fellas in town saw the papr and figured it was me you were talking about. Got a good job, stedy work, a cook at the coalmines in Nanimo. Its on Vancoover Islind. Nice place to live, not too cold. Ever bin here Mary? Right and tell me what your up to. Do you no where Carrie and Emma are? Sendin a pitchr. Don't spose I look like you remembr.
>
> Love Willy

Mary couldn't believe she'd found him. She wondered when he'd changed his name to Willy. She stared at his photo, remembering that Will's ... Willy's eyes had always looked sad. She smiled at his moustache and couldn't get over how old he looked.

The last time she saw him he was fourteen. He was coming down the dusty, county road in a small horse-drawn wagon and met her on her way home from school. He'd been given a job as an apprentice with a travelling peddler and didn't want to leave without saying say goodbye.

Mary had not seen her brother Willy since 1896. This photo was taken in Nanaimo, Vancouver Island, B.C., in 1911.

"Take me with you, please, Will," she begged, clinging to his arm. "I can help you."

"I can't do that. I'll be on the road for days. It's no life for a girl." Will paused, gently freeing himself from her grip. He lowered his voice as though someone might be listening. "I have a plan. As soon as I get settled, I'll come back for you. And we'll find John, we will." He added, "I promise. In the meantime I want you to take this," he said and handed her a small white envelope.

"What's this, Will?" she asked.

"It's money, not a lot … it's part of what I earned at the Lounsburys. I want you to keep it, Mary. If for some reason you can't wait for me to come and get you, you'll need some money. Hide it in a safe place and don't tell anyone!"

"When will I see you again?"

"I'm not sure, but I'll be back."[2]

Mary held his photo in her shaky hand. She was afraid it was a dream. Maybe Willy's letter and photo would disappear by morning. Jim arrived home and wondered why the door had been left ajar and their apartment was a chilly 63 degrees.

The next day Mary sent Willy a reply and wrote her sisters to share the good news. It would have to be a family reunion via the postal service, a little impersonal but no less exciting. Somehow she felt more secure, knowing where her brother was and that he was okay. Mary wrote to him on a regular basis but Willy's letters were sporadic.

Shocking news hit the papers in April 1912. "Wireless Played Noble Part in Saving of Lives." The article reported that ships nearby had answered a distress call from the *Titanic* and had averted a tragedy on the Atlantic. Mary had heard all sorts of glowing reports about the magnificent ship and wasn't surprised that no one had been hurt. But the next day, the headlines told a different story. The *Titanic*, which was supposedly indestructible, had sunk and over fifteen hundred people were dead. She'd made that same trip across the ocean twelve years earlier and could well imagine how frightening an experience it would have been, not only for those who died but also for the ones who survived. She was relieved that she didn't have any relatives aboard the fateful ship.

While she tried to absorb the magnitude of the tragedy at sea, she noticed a smaller headline on the front page: "Titanic Disaster Thrilled Hamilton." She thought it must have been a misprint. The *Spec*, known as "The Great Family Journal," explained that it had arranged for a special leased wire from New York, making it possible to issue a 6:00 a.m. extra that morning. They claimed that not only did it contain a more accurate account of the shipwreck but it was also the only paper on the street at such an early hour.

Mary realized that the headline meant Hamiltonians were thrilled with the impressive news coverage, not with the disaster. To say that this was poorly worded would be an understatement. But no one paid any attention to it. People were pre-occupied with checking the names of survivors listed in the paper, hoping their relatives or close friends were on it. Tragedies that claimed so many lives were hard to comprehend.

The last day in June Mona came home with her first report card. Mary was thrilled with her teacher's comment, "Mona is a polite, well-mannered child who follows the rules." Mona had already met her Junior I teacher (Grade 1) Miss Hazel I. Stephenson and was looking forward to returning in the fall.

"She has grey hair and glasses and she's very smart," she told her mother, "and her name starts with the letter 'S' just like my last teacher." Mona seemed so innocent and Mary didn't want that to change. She'd read an article in the *Hamilton Herald* about the risks of young girls growing up too quickly.

> The freakish fashions which shamelessly display the physical rather than the innocent charms of young girls, are a disgrace, and put their mothers in an equally bad light. With large and amazing hats, transparent shirt-waists, skirts reaching but a few inches below the knee, so tight that the figure is boldly displayed at every step, with stockings of the thinnest silk, our girls present a very improper spectacle. What has come to be a common street sight today would not have been tolerated ten years ago.[3]

Thankfully, Mona was content to go out for an ice cream, or a soda, or take the incline up the mountain with her family for a picnic. She loved going to the beach strip, the narrow strip of land that divided Lake Ontario from Burlington Bay, and the Canal Amusement Park to have a ride on the new Ferris wheel. Mary was mistrustful of the large, noisy contraption that resembled the waterwheel she'd seen at the gristmill in Innerkip. She preferred to take the eastbound radials to visit the orchards and small towns in the Niagara Peninsula. They stopped in Bartonville, Stoney Creek, Smith's, Winona, Grimsby, and Beamsville. It was nice to leave the city behind and enjoy the tranquillity of the countryside.

That summer Willy visited Emma and Carrie. Emma described how shy he'd acted when they met him. Mary could only imagine what might have taken place that day at the train station. According to her sister, Willy was soft-spoken and didn't talk much. He said that he'd never stayed put long enough to get married and he liked his job as a cook at the coal mines. He had had the chance to work underground but wasn't interested after what had happened to John. Somehow Willy must have found out about their brother's accident in the San Diego mines that cost him his life.

Willy stayed three days and headed back to Vancouver Island. He told Emma that he hoped to be able to afford a train ticket to Hamilton some day. Mary was sad to have missed the Janeway family reunion, but she was thankful her brother had been found.

SIXTEEN

Centennial Celebrations

> "Centennial week was ushered in with the worst electrical storm of the season. The storm broke in all its fury before midnight and continued unabated for nearly three hours. The rain simply came down in torrents, while the vivid lightning and terrific thunder made timid people quake with fear."[1]

1913

Mary lay awake listening to the windows rattle until the worst of the storm was over. She'd never outgrown her fear of lightning storms since that October day in 1889. Mary lost her mother the night of that terrible storm. She was five years old. As a child she'd always had trouble separating the two events, yet as an adult she knew they had absolutely nothing to do with each other. Mary was thankful that her daughter, sleeping soundly in the next room, did not share her fear as a lightning bolt momentarily lit up the sky.

A few hours prior to Hamilton's electrical storm, the Right House had run a huge ad in the paper. Shoppers were invited to enjoy the large, comfortable chairs on the balcony, use the telephone for city calls without charge, have their parcels checked in the basement at no cost, and visit the ever-popular tearoom during the Centennial Holiday. By Sunday morning everyone had forgotten about the "advertised extras" at the Right House.

Hamiltonians were bailing out their soggy basements and trying to salvage what hadn't been ruined. The *Spec* reported considerable flooding in areas where the sewers backed up as a result of the spectacular storm. The G.W. Robinson Co. had suffered heavy water damage, and for one day only, Wednesday, every piece of water-damaged stock would be half price. The following day, the Civic Holiday, everything would be closed.

Mary was in the crowd waiting outside Robinson's when the doors opened at 8:30 sharp. She came home with two cotton dresses, a purple sweater for Mona, and a slightly water-damaged shirt for Jim. She purchased several kitchen knives, an eggbeater, and some dress goods in the basement. Just before leaving the store, she bought herself a pale pink flannelette nightgown. Mary was satisfied that she'd made good, sound purchases — all half price!

As Hamilton prepared for its 100th anniversary, the storm and its destruction quickly became yesterday's news. In honour of the city's birthday, a house was built in twenty-six hours in Britannia Park, which Hamiltonians could inspect for a mere twenty-five-cent admission: "For more than 18 years, the house built in a day was a tourist attraction for visitors to the Ambitious City, especially after it was featured in Ripley's Believe It Or Not."[2]

Mary had never seen such crowds in Gore Park. Banners, buntings, and flags were draped across the storefronts. The Right House with its elaborate decorations gracing the six-storey building was positively breathtaking. The week-long celebrations reminded people of how proud they were to live in such a strong, bustling city that had not only survived one hundred years but also prospered.

Things quieted down soon after the celebrations. Mary was busy doing her preserves and getting Mona ready for school. She still hadn't answered Emma's last letter, the one that said she'd met a gentleman through Carrie who was very nice and had given her a diamond ring. Mary was concerned that Emma didn't sound very excited about her engagement. The arrival of another letter confused her even more.

September 7

Dear Mary,
I've met someone at the hospital. His name is Harry Robert Touchings and he's from Newfoundland. He's very handsome, has brown hair, a beard, and a moustache. He's terribly charming.

I must hurry to the post. He's coming at seven and we're going for a stroll in the park.

Lovingly, Emma

There was no doubt in Mary's mind that her sister had been swept off her feet. Emma never mentioned the fellow who'd given her the ring until two weeks later.

September 21

Dear Mary,
Harry and I have seen each other almost every other night. He had a twin brother, Henry Robert, who died as a baby. Harry taught himself to read and write because there were no schools on Pass Island. He has two older brothers, Joseph and William. Fancy that, we both have brothers named William.

Harry's people were fishermen but that wasn't for him. He worked in the coal mines in Sydney and Glace Bay, the nickel mines in Sudbury, and then went to Timmins. He heard about the boom in Alberta and headed west. He's a foreman on a construction crew in charge of pouring the cement for the High Level Bridge from Strathcona to Edmonton.

I wanted to return the other fellow's ring but couldn't muster up the courage. I asked my landlady to give it back when he arrived in his horse and buggy a fortnight ago. I know it wasn't the proper thing to do, but I was afraid. Last night Harry arrived with a basket of strawberries and cream and won me over. I wish you could meet him Mary.

Your loving sister, Emma

P.S. I've sent along a picture of Harry's bridge … hard to fathom anything worth two million dollars.

A month went by without a word from Emma and then a letter arrived from Carrie. Emma had come down with typhoid fever while working at the hospital and had been delirious for five days. The nurses rolled her in ice-cold sheets every three minutes to help break the fever. At one point they thought she wouldn't make it. Carrie said she was doing better but unfortunately her long, dark hair had fallen out in handfuls.

October 24

Dear Emma,
I wish you were closer so I could visit you. Carrie said you're getting good care and the nurses are kind. Do you remember how sick you were with TB? You pulled through and I know you can do it again.

Mona likes her new teacher Miss Stephenson but tells me the work is harder in Jr. I. We're reading a chapter of *The Wizard of Oz* every night before bedtime. Mona helps out with the easy words. You're in my prayers every night.

Love Mary

Emma replied within a few weeks:

November 29

Dear Mary,
I was very sick but the hospital has looked after me. I think they felt badly since I got sick working here. They did everything to try to keep the fever down. They gave me lots of water, milk, and ice cream. I'd have given anything for a cup of tea but I couldn't have it. The first time I tried to pick something up, I couldn't. I cried because I was so weak.

Harry brought me a dozen red roses. I stared at them every day for I don't know how long. It was all that I could do. The worst thing was losing my hair. It's slowly starting to grow back but it's almost perfectly straight. When I go out I wear a bonnet. It's hard when everybody else has long hair done up in a bun.

Lovingly, Emma

P.S. Harry is working on the flatiron building over on 95th. I don't see as much of him as I'd like.

Mary was relieved to hear that Emma was better. Glancing at the date on the letter reminded her that Christmas was less than a month away. That afternoon she went down to Stanley Mills in hopes of finding something for Mona. She saw enamelware dolls dishes, tubby dogs, teddy bears, and bright-eyed baby dolls with natural, life-like features, real hair, eyelashes, and eyebrows. But Mary wanted something special, something that would last forever.

She headed to Klein & Binkley on James Street North, next to the city hall and market. They'd been open since 1898 and had a very good reputation. She chose a fourteen-carat gold ring and had "Mother to

Mona Xmas 1913" engraved inside. It was an unusual present for a child, but Mona wasn't interested in the things most eight-year-olds liked. She preferred to read or do a jigsaw puzzle.

Mary had almost finished making Jim a plaid shirt and planned to buy him a wool scarf. She had secretly saved the coupons that came with his packs of Black Cat cigarettes and sent away for the Durham-Duplex Double-edge Safety razor. Luckily it arrived in time to go under the tree.

They stayed home New Years Eve. After supper Jim had his usual smoke while he leafed through the paper. Mary stood at the window and looked out on the snow-covered city street, which was virtually empty. It was still too early for partiers, anxious to ring in the New Year, to be heading to a dance hall or hotel downtown. She was tired, having spent the afternoon making scalloped potatoes with bacon, stuffed tomatoes, and a lemon meringue pie for New Year's Day. She quietly reflected on the year gone by.

Mona's health had been fair but she'd missed some school. Jim's business had done all right but it wasn't one of his better years. Emma had been engaged, unengaged, then swept off her feet by Harry Touchings while recovering from typhoid fever. Mary felt fortunate that she hadn't been sick the whole year, not even a head cold or a bout of catarrh.

Hamilton had finally got a Carnegie Library in its very own building. The HSR had a new bus route that everyone nicknamed the Belt Line since it made a circle around the middle of town. They'd had a huge electrical storm that summer just two days before the centennial celebrations. And for twenty-five cents she and Jim had gone through the house that had been built in a day to celebrate the city's 100th anniversary.

And finally Mary remembered making her first winter coat with a zipper instead of buttons. Mona had been fascinated with the little metal invention that had become so popular that fall.

"You're awful quiet," Jim said, heading to the liquor cabinet.

"Just thinking about the past year," Mary replied.

"What's there to say? We managed to keep out of debt and put food on the table. Sure do miss that Model T though. We'll get another one … for sure." The gramophone was softly playing "I'm Always Chasing Rainbows" as they clinked their sherry glasses and welcomed in the New Year.

SEVENTEEN

A Wedding and a War

> "When important news was expected — when war was imminent, when a king or queen was mortally ill, or on election nights — the latest available information would be scrawled across sheets of newsprint and posted in the windows of the newspaper offices. As each fresh bulletin was pasted up, those on the inner perimeter of the crowd would press eagerly forward, and pass back the news to those who swarmed behind."[1]

1914

People flocked to the beach strip to see the newly built merry-go-round that summer. Mary thought it looked far safer than the Ferris wheel, which had attracted the same kind of attention in the park two years earlier.

Hamiltonians were busy speculating on whether the world would go to war. Special editions of the *Herald* and the *Spec* explained the logistics, threats, and ultimatums being tossed between the major players at the time, Germany and France. Jim was excited about the prospects of Canada going to war.

"Do you think we will?" Mary asked.

"If the Germans refuse to leave Belgium, Britain won't back down. She'll declare war and so will we." And that's exactly what happened at midnight, August 4, two days after Mary turned thirty. Gramophones in parlours across the country played music reflecting this staunch support. "Every able-bodied Canadian male was expected to do his part, to join the colours, to serve king and country. The great majority of the youths and men of military age, at least in English Canada, simply assumed that they would be expected to enlist."[2]

Hamilton witnessed an exuberant crowd on their city streets the night that war was declared. Almost a year to the day they'd come out in droves to celebrate their one hundredth anniversary. Men enlisted on the spot as women cheered them on and the band of the 91st Highlanders played "Oh, Canada" and "God Save the King."

Jim went down to the drill hall to volunteer his services. Like most men, he thought the war would be short-lived. The number of Canadians that signed up far exceeded the quota, but unfortunately they lacked military experience. The first to go were a small group of veterans that had participated in the Boer War at the turn of the century. Once the initial excitement died down, life went back to normal. Jim was still hopeful that he would "get the call."

By late September there was already a chill in the air. Mary glanced out the window to watch Mona coming down the street. She seemed to like her Senior I (Grade 2) teacher, Miss Iona Clarke. As she drew nearer, her limp was more obvious. Mary wished she'd socialize more, but knew from her own experience what it was like to be different as a child. She remembered all too clearly her first day at Blandford School S.S. No. 3.

"Good morning, young lady. I'm Miss McGuire, and what is your name?"

"Good morning, Ma'am. I'm Mary."

"And your family name?"

> *Mary paused for a moment. "Jacques," she replied softly after biting her bottom lip.*
>
> *"No, it ain't," interjected Billy Skillings, a redheaded freckle-faced boy of about ten. The rest of the children were putting their belongings on their hooks but suddenly became very quiet. "She's the little orphan who come to stay at the Jacques's place. She ain't no real Jacques."*[3]

Mona came through the door, dropped her school bag, and went to the cupboard for a snack. She grabbed a handful of her favourite snack, Triscuits, the large whole-wheat wafers that came in the package with the lightning bolts on it to signify they'd been baked in electric ovens. She managed to eat and take off her coat at the same time. Mary hoped it wouldn't spoil her appetite for the beef stew simmering on the stove.

"How was school?"

"Okay," she replied with a mouthful of crackers. "Miss Clarke said my penmanship was perfect today so she let me hand out the readers. I like school, but I hate recess."

"You know how your dad feels about me writing notes to keep you in, and besides, the fresh air will do you a world of good." Mary gently patted the side of her face. "It'll put some colour in those cheeks. You're too pale."

"I can't keep up with the others. They run too fast," she complained.

"Then walk and be happy you're able to do that." Mary lifted the lid on the stew, had a peek, and gave it a stir. "It'll be ready in half an hour and I'm running behind. Be a dear and take the clothes off the line, then go wash for supper."

Mona reluctantly got up from the table, grabbed another handful of crackers, picked up the wicker laundry basket, and disappeared. Mary looked around her kitchen, wondering if there was time to do another chore before supper. She decided against it and put the kettle on for a cup of tea.

Mary and Jim celebrated their tenth wedding anniversary by going to the Savoy to see Charles E. Taylor's "Tango Girls," a "merry burlesque promising three laughs a minute throughout the performance," according to an ad in the *Hamilton Spectator*. The days were growing shorter, and by the end of October it was starting to get dark by suppertime. Once the dishes were in the drainer, Mary loved to relax in her cozy blue afghan with a book or magazine while Jim read the paper.

"Do they really think they'll stop men from drinking by passing this crazy law?" he asked. He was referring to the War Measures Act, legislation that closed hotel bars and liquor stores. "Why in time of war, that's when a fellow needs a drink most." Once he voiced an opinion, he was off on another subject.

"Remember when I worked for Bain Wagon back in Woodstock?" he asked. Mary nodded absentmindedly. "There were around two hundred of us. That was a big company in those days. Listen to this," he said, flicking the paper to make it rigid. "Bain Wagon responded to wartime military needs by quickly moving to two shifts, employing 950 men to make artillery shells, special wagons and ambulances for the army."[4] He peered over the top of the paper. "Ain't it too bad a guy can't get a decent job 'til the world goes to war?" Mary wasn't listening; she was thinking about Emma's last two letters.

October 12

Dear Mary,
I have the most exciting news. Harry asked me to marry him and I have accepted. I've just got enough time to choose a dress and my dear friend Isabel Stuart will stand up for me. The rector, Charles McKuin is going to marry us at Christ Church in Edmonton in four short weeks. Do wish you could be here. Think of me on Saturday, November 28th. I'll send you a photo.

Lovingly, Emma

P.S. My bouquet will be red roses, just like the ones Harry brought me in the hospital.

Mary wondered why Emma didn't mention Carrie in her letter. A week and a half later, another letter arrived that answered her question.

> October 23
>
> Dear Mary,
> Carrie is disappointed in my choice and won't be at my wedding. She preferred the other fellow that I was seeing. Willy doesn't want me to get married either because he wants me to go to San Diego with him.
>
> Even my landlady doesn't approve of Harry because her own nephew is sweet on me. She said, "Oh Emmy, you're not for him. He's not good enough for y'all." And I told her, "I liked him anyway. That's all there was to it. I don't care; I don't like anybody else better than him. He was a good change for me."[5]
>
> I miss you.
>
> Lovingly, Emma

These objections seemed to have made Emma more determined to get married. Mary wondered if Carrie's feelings had anything to do with the fact that Harry came from the east coast. She'd heard that "a lot of people who came to Canada from England had changed their status on the boat," claiming to be more prosperous and successful than they actually were and looking down on others.

"Have you heard anything I said?" Jim asked. Mary nodded, but he wasn't convinced.

It wasn't until the first week in December that she heard from Emma again. Willy must have had a change of heart because he appeared the night before her wedding, having taken the train up from Vancouver. It was a chilly 5 degrees Fahrenheit and he wasn't even wearing an overcoat. Emma couldn't help notice that he was rail thin and coughed a lot. He preferred the milder temperatures in British Columbia and headed back

On the day of her marriage to Harry Touchings, November 28, 1914, Emma wore a crisp, white, high-necked shirtwaist with lace detail on the bodice and sleeves.

Courtesy of Gail Horner.

to the island a few days later. Mary studied Emma's wedding portrait. She felt genuine sadness that she'd been at neither of her sister's weddings nor they at hers. At that moment Mona burst through the door.

"I have to make candy to take to school on Monday," she said breathlessly, "candy for the mite box. Miss Clarke said there are lots of kids who won't be getting anything from Santa. Isn't that horrible?" She paused. "That's why we're going to make candy for the mite box, the box for the poor, and we get to take it to the police station. I've never been in a police station."

The police at the East End Station believed that many kids living east of Sherman Avenue wouldn't likely be getting anything for Christmas. They had a "Santa Claus" box at the station to receive donations. "It is the intention," said the *Spectator*, "to supply each kiddie on the list with a pair of new stockings well filled with nuts and candies. Toys will also be handed the boys, with dolls for the girls, while the whole will be rounded out by the distribution of a large, well-filled basket of food to each family."[6]

"What kind of candy do you want to make?"

"Peanut brittle!" she said enthusiastically.

Mona's class delivered their homemade candy, individually wrapped and ready to be put in the children's stockings. Mary thought it was the best lesson that her daughter could be taught to explain the "true meaning of Christmas." A plea went out to the public asking for help in delivering the goodies to the poor. Cars, wagons, lorries, and handcarts lined up on Sherman Avenue waiting for baskets of food, toys, and old clothes. It was one time that Mary wished Jim still had a car.

In late February, Emma sent photos of their modest two-bedroom bungalow on 120th Street. Mary was envious that they could afford to buy. Although she'd never met Harry, she felt she knew him. Emma told her that he was hard working, very determined, liked to eat fish, and didn't believe in going to church. He knew the Bible well and would often quote it. Harry lived by the motto, "Your home is your cathedral, make it so and you will be happy with life." Emma, who'd been raised differently, continued to go to church every Sunday.

She wrote Mary that summer after her son Gordon was born. Along with her good news she was concerned about Harry. His job was contracted and the government was taking his men and sending them overseas. He didn't think he owed England a damn thing and wasn't going. He'd decided to sell his business and file on a homestead. It didn't sound like Emma was happy about leaving Edmonton. She was a city girl who was accustomed to being a nanny in a proper English home and serving afternoon tea with crumpets. Mary suspected that the prospect of living in a log house in dense woods was not what little one-hundred-pound Emma had envisioned.

Mona's health had deteriorated and she struggled through August but was much stronger when the cooler September temperatures arrived. She was in Junior II (Grade 3) with Miss Stephenson who'd already taught her in Junior I. Mona liked her and didn't mind having the same teacher again.

Fires were a common occurrence in Hamilton and it was a familiar sight to see the horse-drawn wagons pull out of the Sophia Fire Hall on Sophia Street, originally called Princess Street. The Royal Hamilton

Yacht Club, considered one of the most prestigious structures on the Great Lakes, burned to the ground less than a week after it had been closed for the season. It happened just after midnight on September 18th. A short circuit in the wiring was blamed for the $25,000 damage. Huge fireballs lit up the night sky as the curious got out of bed and rushed to the bay front. Dark clouds of smoke tangled with the orange flames to further blacken the sky in the harbour. In no time, the lake was dotted with rowboats, skiffs, and yachts so onlookers could have a better vantage point. Jim went down to watch but Mary stayed home. Her fear of fires was not unlike her fear of storms, another example of Mother Nature out of control.

Unable to sleep, she sat at the table and waited patiently for the kettle to boil. She reminisced about the times that they used to take the trolley down to the docks to sit and look across the canal. Colourful flags and bunting fluttered in the summer breeze on the magnificent balconies that wrapped themselves around the three-tier building. Only the rich could afford a membership but anyone could enjoy the music that wafted across the water from the second floor ballroom.

"Someday we'll be the ones dancing in the ballroom," Jim had said, squeezing her hand. The whistling teakettle brought her back to her tiny kitchen in their walk-up on John Street. Her husband was such a dreamer. Mary had never believed that they'd be dancing at the Yacht Club.

That fall the Arcade department store was enlarged. An additional storey was added to make it level with what had once been the Griffin Theatre. Along with numerous others, Mary and Jim were curious to see how a huge auditorium full of theatre seats could possibly be transformed into one of the largest shopping palaces in this part of the country. It was nicknamed the "Daylight Shopping Palace" because of the huge plate-glass windows across the front of the store.

The newly completed Arcade had a checking room in the basement — a place to leave parcels while shopping in the store. The packages could be sent anywhere in the city or to the terminal in time to be picked up before catching a streetcar. Telephones had been installed on every floor for public use, free of charge. The Arcade would do well until it closed its doors in 1927 and the first Eaton's in Hamilton took over the same location. As far as Mary was concerned, it would always be called the Arcade.

Emma's Christmas letter arrived, explaining that Harry had gone ahead to build their new home in Elbridge. Since there were no roads or transportation, he went by foot to clear and break their land as required by the Homestead Act. With the help of three local Norwegians who'd already filed, he built a modest log cabin. Emma had fond memories of their honeymoon home in Edmonton and was sad to be leaving.

The war was starting to affect the economy and Jim's business slowed down. But in many ways life went on as normal. Occasionally an incident would be reported that acted as a reminder that war was more than a series of battles and lists of casualties. A photo of a local boy who wasn't coming home, a story about a soldier in the trenches, or a widow and her fatherless children brought the reality of war into people's homes:

> A father of three from Hamilton, Ontario, a man who had never been lucky enough to have a steady job in civilian life, dug trenches in a cold, relentless rain. Every now and then he had to cut through the decomposing body of a weeks-dead French soldier. He vomited the first time it happened, but after a while he came to accept the fact that corpses were part of life on the western front; in fact they were easier to shovel than the thick, clinging mud.[7]

Mary thought about the young man. Did his family live across town or the next street over? Would he be lucky enough to come home? And if he did, would he be right in the head? She could never understand why a man would volunteer to go to war for a dollar a day. And if he didn't return, his widow would get a mere thirty cents a day, a little more if she had children.

Yet war still remained remote and distant for Canadians at home and affected them little in their daily lives. Prohibition was a different matter. When the government passed the Ontario Temperance Act, it was mainly folks in the country and the middle class that supported the new law:

> Hamilton, with its large working class and non-Anglo-Saxon population, was a centre of opposition to the legislation. Soon, there was a thriving illegal trade in liquor and beer, much of it centred in the North End of the city. A number of "blind pigs" (illegal drinking houses) were established close to the factories in the East End. At the "House of Nonsense," on Ferguson Avenue North, workers could drink, play cards, and shoot craps. The most notorious Hamilton bootlegger was Rocco Perri. He and his wife owned a grocery store on Hess Street North and sold whiskey for 50 cents a shot.[8]

Jim bemoaned the new drinking law and openly ignored it. Mary began to worry as she watched him spend more time drinking and gambling than working. But when Emma's letter arrived, it made her realize that her sister's life wasn't easy either.

Courtesy of Gail Horner.

Harry Touchings spent several years clearing the land by hand after his family moved into the log cabin at Thorhild, Alberta.

March 13

Dear Mary,

Our log house is small but well built. Harry put down a vinyl floor with big red poppies. I could have wept I hated it so much, but when I saw the look on his face, I didn't have the heart to tell him.

Yesterday he walked eight miles to the Anton Lake Store and returned with a hundred pounds of flour on his back. There are days when I long to be any place else but I'm afraid to loose sight of the log house for fear of getting lost. I've thought about running away but there's no place to go. Dense trees surround us and the only sky I can see is straight up above the house.

Our closest neighbours, the Lindsays, live a mile and a half cross-country through heavy bush. I hope to meet them some day. I'm told that winters are bad with heavy snowfalls. I guess I'll find out soon enough.

Lovingly, Emma

P.S. We hear the wild coyotes at night.

Her next letter was more cheerful since she'd had an unexpected visit from Willy. He had no idea that there'd be so many miles to cover on foot. Emma thought his coughing seemed worse. He didn't stay long and headed back to Edmonton to catch the train to British Columbia.

On Saturday, April 8, Mary received a special delivery in the mail. It was a registration of death notice. Willy had died of tuberculosis in an Edmonton hospital at the age of thirty-three. She was listed as his next of kin and asked to sign and return the document. Mary remembered Jimmy Chesney, a boy back on the farm who'd died of the same disease twenty years ago.

She was sorry that Willy had never married or had children. It was a reminder to her of how fortunate she was. She deeply regretted not seeing her brother after she'd found him. Looking at Willy's picture only made it worse. She tucked it away in a drawer, hoping that time would make her feel differently. Mary wrote her sisters the same day, finding it difficult to put her thoughts into words. She wished she could have afforded a headstone to mark his grave.

The war orders had come into the factories and there was a serious shortage of labour. Women were being hired to work in the steel mills and factories, jobs that had previously been for men only. It was not uncommon to see a woman drive a streetcar. It didn't hit home until Mary saw her first female bank teller. Although Jim's business was in a slump, he didn't want her to work.

Mary decided to volunteer several mornings a week, folding bandages and packing parcels to be sent to the troops overseas. Getting out of the apartment made her aware of how women's roles were changing. Skirts were shorter, modestly falling just below the knee, and more women were wearing lipstick and cosmetics. She was shocked by a couple of ladies actually smoking in public.

The city was getting a facelift as well. While the Arcade was being renovated, the Waldorf Hotel was torn down to make room for a new one. The million-dollar hotel, the Royal Connaught, got its name from a young boy who entered his suggestion in a school contest. The Duke of Connaught, Canada's Governor General, happened to be on tour at the time.

The official opening of the Royal Connaught Hotel was one of the great social events that year. On June 5 at 3:00 p.m., the doors were open to the public. According to a *Times* reporter, who observed the event, "until five, a continual stream of people, several thousand in all, roamed through the spacious corridors, lounging rotunda, bedrooms, kitchen, everywhere. No restrictions were placed on their movements, though plain clothes men and detectives were present to see that nothing out of the way took place."[9]

Mary and Jim were among the curious. As they were being ushered down one of the grand halls from the impressive main foyer, Jim bumped into his cousin Walter Church. Walter told him that his brother Arnold had died two years earlier in a drowning accident and that he'd recently married. Mary thought it was a strange place for a family reunion but it was brief, as the men seemed more interested in seeing the new hotel than re-kindling family ties.

A letter was waiting for Mary when she arrived home. Emma was excited that Harry had raised the ceiling in their log house, even though it meant losing the stairs and having to climb a ladder outside to reach the bedroom. It sounded strange to Mary who had just seen the inside of a million dollar hotel. She was convinced that her sister was no longer a city girl.

That spring Mona only attended fifty-four school days out of ninety-three. She missed the entire month of May. The doctor said it was a respiratory illness, which left her weak and without much of an appetite. Mary worried that she wasn't getting enough milk, fruits, and vegetables … the "protective" foods. She'd read in her cookbook that exercising teeth increases circulation and helps to distribute nutrients, so she encouraged Mona to nibble on carrot sticks.

Mary prepared her daughter's favourites: moulded steamed rice, toast points, and brown hash, which was basically shepherd's pie fried like an omelette and served with hot tomato sauce. Strangely enough, Mona wouldn't eat shepherd's pie. She'd have been content to live on caramel junket and fruit roly poly, a tea biscuit dough covered in jam, rolled, dredged in flour, steamed, and served with sugar and cream. Mona still couldn't resist her mother's apple charlotte when it came out of the oven, piled high with toasted buttered crumbs.

By September she seemed better and went back to school. At first she didn't take to her Senior II (Grade 4) teacher, Miss Nellie Stuart. "Would you believe I have another teacher with an S name?" she asked. But Miss Stuart quickly won her over and she never missed a day of school that fall.

On Christmas Eve Mona put out a bottle of Coca-Cola with her cookies for Santa. She'd been taken with the shape of the new bottle that had come out earlier that year. It was curvy to resemble the shape of a cola nut, one of the secret ingredients in the popular fizzy drink. At eleven-and-a-half, Mona no longer believed in Santa Claus, but pretended she did because it made her mother happy.

EIGHTEEN

A Bitter Cold Winter

"The bitter cold of Canadian winters imposed a particular burden on the working classes, the unemployed, the sick and the elderly. From October to May each year there was the constant, nagging need to find something to burn to keep warm — or at least warm enough to ward off colds, the 'flu, grippe, croup, catarrh' and similar respiratory ailments from which many died each winter."[1]

1917

Jim wasn't home when the city enumerator came around. Mary confirmed that John Bizley and Alex Selkirk still lived at the other end of the hall. She wasn't certain what Jim wanted as his occupation in the directory but said he was a "painter."

"It doesn't matter what I call myself," Jim said later that evening. "There's no work out there for a guy who wants to earn an honest living. Everything's been affected by this damn war. Sure hope it's over soon."

Mary was glad that Mona hadn't been within earshot to hear her father use blasphemous language. She understood his frustration, but things could have been worse. Many husbands, sons, fathers, and brothers had said goodbye to loved ones at railway stations across the country and many of them wouldn't be coming home.

That year parliament passed a law that required all eligible single men between twenty and thirty-four years of age to serve in the army after completing a fitness test. Mary felt relief that Jim had been spared, guilt for feeling that way, and empathy for those who had to sign up. As a home child, she knew what it was like to be separated from her family and sent to a strange country with feelings of uncertainty about the future. How was that any different than a soldier having to saying goodbye to his loved ones and heading overseas? Almost three years had passed since the world had gone to war. Planting victory gardens, rolling bandages, organizing knitting clubs, card games, and dances helped raise money to send cigarettes and candy overseas. On Sunday afternoons local marching bands played patriotic music in the city parks.

Mary joined the local knitting club. The soldiers overseas needed gloves, sweaters, scarves, and socks. Socks became an important commodity when the men spent so much time knee-deep in mud holes. The colour or whether they matched wasn't important, as long as they were warm and had no holes. A new pair of socks was considered a prized possession to a man in the trenches. It became a challenge for the women to see who could make the most interesting pair.

Letters from her sister helped Mary forget about the realities of wartime. Emma kept busy helping Harry pile brush, prepare a garden, and milk the cow. Mary was shocked when she saw a photo of her sister standing on top of a hay wagon holding a pitchfork. It was a far different image than Emma sipping a cup of tea in the parlour.

When Mona met her new Junior III (Grade 5) teacher, Miss Lavinia Truscott, she couldn't wait to get home to tell her mother the good news. "My teacher's name is Miss Truscott … that's Truscott, spelled with a T!"

That fall Mary helped wrap the "Overseas Christmas Boxes" organized through the Red Cross Nursing Services for the men in the trenches and training camps not expected home for Christmas. The volunteers

Courtesy of Gail Horner.

There was no time for idleness on the homestead. Emma (girl on the left) worked on the hay wagon, but her son, two-year-old Gordon, was too young to help.

filled each tin container with a pack of cigarettes, tobacco, pipe, pipe cleaners, cigarette paper, matches, soap, chocolate, playing cards, writing paper, envelopes, a pencil, return postcard, and a pair of heavy shoelaces. After a morning of volunteering, Mary felt like she'd done her part to help "keep the home fires burning."

One day as she sorted through a box of second hand books, Mary came across Stephen Leacock's *Literary Lapses* and *Sunshine Sketches of a Little Town*, and her leather-bound copy of *Anne of Green Gables*. She also had several books written by the British poet Robert W. Service, who'd spent his childhood in Glasgow, not far from Rutherglen where she'd been born. She remembered reading that "the novelist took leave of a tearful mother at the docks in Glasgow to sail to the New World. He was a 'steerage emigrant' on a tramp steamer."[2] She'd made that same journey across the ocean, but at a much younger age.

Her favourite Robert Service poem, "The Cremation of Sam McGee," was one he'd written about dying and yet it was very funny. He'd also written poetry about young boys going to war:

Young Fellow My Lad

"Where are you going, Young Fellow My Lad,
On this glittering morn of May?"
"I'm going to join the Colours, Dad;
They're looking for men, they say."
"But you're only a boy, Young Fellow My Lad;
You aren't obliged to go."
"I'm seventeen and a quarter, Dad,
And ever so strong, you know."[3]

Mary thought about Tessie Paterson, her neighbour who had all three of her boys fighting overseas. She watched the poor woman worry sick every time the postman came to her door, for fear he might be bringing bad news from the warfront.

Amidst all the war efforts, the city continued to grow and prosper. Hamilton acquired its own Loew's theatre with a seating capacity of 2,900 and opened its doors to the public that New Years' Eve. It was Marcus Loew's 218th theatre, but a first for Hamilton. Tickets cost ten to fifteen cents during the day, fifteen to twenty cents for evening performances, and a box seat could be reserved for fifty cents. Several hundred people were disappointed after waiting in line to buy tickets at the box office.

According to the *Hamilton Times* it was the largest theatre on the continent in proportion to the population. With its impressive size and comfortable dark-green leather seats, it became known as "the palace of enchantment." Mary Pickford in *Rebecca of Sunny Brook Farm* and Andrew Kelly in *The Man With the Brogue* were advertised as two of the more popular vaudeville shows.

January and February brought frigid temperatures and howling winds, typical of an Ontario winter. Wood became scarce and very expensive. Long underwear and woollen sweaters would only keep you so warm without the comfort of a fire burning in the wood stove. Mary worried that soon they wouldn't be able to afford a cord of wood.

By mid-February Jim looked listless and tired but continued to work, play cards in the evening, and go to the racetrack every Saturday. Mary grew concerned when he came home from work and started going to bed shortly after supper.

"Shouldn't you be seeing the doctor?"

"I'm fine," he replied curtly.

"You look a little peaked."

"I told you, I'm fine."

It was obvious to Mary that he was anything but fine. The following Monday Jim came home from work and went right to bed. She took him some chicken broth and dry toast, which he hardly touched.

By morning he was coughing and his breathing was laboured. His face was colourless, almost ashen. Mary went down to the dental lab and asked to use their phone. Dr. Storms seemed confident that what Jim had was a bad winter cold that only bed rest and lots of fluids would cure. He didn't see any need to venture out in the cold unless his condition grew worse. Mary decided it was time for a good old mustard plaster and Jim was too sick to object.

Mona watched with curiosity while Mary prepared this strange concoction in the kitchen and then put it on his chest. She sat at the foot of her father's bed and waited for his reaction.

Jim stirred a bit and tried to turn on his side. Mary held the mustard plaster in place. "Ahhh … Mary, I swear I'm dying. If this is what it's like, please let it be over soon. I feel like I'm on fire! I'm burning up inside," he complained and weakly raised his right arm to his chest. Mona turned pale.

"Your dad needs his sleep. Remember Dr. Storms said he needs plenty of bed rest and it's our job to see that that happens. I'll stay for a while. You run along dear," Mary said kindly.

Mona stood in the doorway. Her eyes, filled with tears, were fixated on her father. "Mama, is it true?" her voice quivered. "Is he going to die?"

Mary had been two years older than her daughter when Josie Chesney's brother died. She remembered overhearing adults say that Jimmy had "passed on, passed away, met his maker, gone to his eternal resting place, or gone to the other side." She'd been frightened, confused, and left with the feeling that death was a dark, foreboding, and mysterious thing.

Mary walked over and put her arm around Mona. "We're doing everything we can for your father. You need to include him in your prayers and I'll do the same," she said softly. "Only God can decide when someone's time on this earth is finished. If this is His will, then in time we'll learn to accept this. It's not right to question God." Mary felt that she'd given her little hope. She added, "I believe he'll be okay. Your father is a strong man and I don't think it's his time yet."

Mary sat by his bedside for three days and three nights with her Bible on her lap. She was afraid that Jim might be contagious but Mona was so concerned that it was difficult to separate them. He seemed to brighten up when she was in the room. Mary continued to reapply a mustard plaster every six hours. Each time, he was visibly in pain at first, but once it subsided he fell into a deep, unnatural sleep. Home remedies were often harsh, inflicting a great deal of discomfort on the patient. For years people had believed that without experiencing some pain and suffering, an illness could not be eradicated.

The third night Mary made Jim a tent-bed to help him breathe. She'd seen it done on the farm. With her clotheshorse and Tessie Patterson's dressing screen around his bed, she draped several sheets over the screens to form a roof and left an opening at one side for the spout of the kettle. By morning, the fever broke. He'd finally sweated it out of his body.

"Am I back in the land of the living?" he asked weakly.

"You actually never left. It probably just felt like it."

"Mary, I've never come so close to dying before in my life. I can't remember when I've been in such pain. I don't mind admitting that I was scared."

"Well you don't have to be afraid anymore. I knew you'd make it. I put my faith in God and asked for His help. We have so many things to be thankful for," she said, clutching his hand, her Bible in the other. "I must find Mona, she'll be so happy." Mary kissed him on the forehead and hurried off to share her good news.

After a few days Jim was able to stay up several hours at a time. It took him a couple of weeks to fully recover. Mary enjoyed having him home, and every day after school Mona went to his room with a deck of cards, a board game, or a crossword puzzle to entertain him until supper was ready.

He missed three weeks of work, which meant Mary had to be extra careful with her grocery money. He'd also missed going to the track and playing cards at the Connaught in the evenings. But when he returned to work, life went back to the way it had been before he got sick. Unfortunately, Jim's drinking and gambling habits hadn't changed.

In Mary's letters to Emma, she rarely mentioned her husband. She talked about Mona and interesting things that were happening in the city, like the opening of the Loew's Theatre on New Years Eve. She intended to send the clipping but decided to leave it on the table in hopes that it might give Jim the idea of taking her out for a night on the town. She couldn't think of anything more exciting than sitting in the balcony of the new vaudeville house and catching a glimpse of her idol, Mary Pickford.

NINETEEN

Armistice

"In the last three months of 1918, Canada, along with most of the world, was hit by the worst epidemic since the Black Death of the Middle Ages, an invasion of the dreaded influenza virus known as the Spanish 'flu. By the time the Armistice was signed, the whole country was in its grasp. And it was at least as deadly, and as chillingly impersonal, as shrapnel fire. Hospitals, their wards filled to overflowing, had to turn thousands away. Undertakers and casket-makers could not keep up with the demand. Something like one in every four people in Canada contracted the disease."[1]

1918

Mary woke early the morning of October 5. She looked over at her sleeping husband and wondered if he'd remember their anniversary. Where had fourteen years gone? She thought about their first ride on the incline railway, strolls through Gore Park on warm summer evenings, the catarrh and fatigue that turned out to be a baby, Jim's numerous jobs, the summer Mona was stricken with polio, her sisters appearing on their doorstep, the Model T they'd owned less than a year, finding her brother, six address changes, the nights Jim came home late from the racetrack, and last winter when she nearly lost him.

She tiptoed out of the bedroom, put the kettle on, and went downstairs to get the *Spec*. Whenever Jim questioned the cost, she reminded him that they'd won a good set of china dishes because of a contest she'd seen in the paper. Mary had correctly paired a cartoon with a matching proverb published a week later. Only a regular reader could have been that lucky. She smiled, remembering her good fortune.

The headline in the morning paper, "Spanish Influenza Epidemic Is Serious," quickly altered her mood. The flu had swept across the country like a forest fire out of control, exhausted doctors and nurses were getting sick, schools were closed, and streetcars had to be disinfected daily. Public gatherings had been cancelled and people were encouraged to stay home to stop the spread of the disease.

Mary's previous experience as a nanny had taught her some basic nursing skills. Within a few days she decided to volunteer twice a week at the Scott Park Barracks due to the overcrowded hospitals. Some schools were converted into hospitals as a temporary measure to meet the demands of the afflicted. As the influenza continued in its destructive path across the country, the war was coming to an end.

November 11 was an exceptionally warm Monday morning, a washday she'd never forget. After hanging out the clothes, she went down to check the mailbox, hoping there might be something from Emma.

> November 3
>
> Dear Mary,
> Just when I think I'm getting use to farming, something happens. Yesterday Harry cut his leg using a double-bladed axe to clear bush. He wanted me to stitch him up with a needle and thread. I couldn't do it so he did it himself and went right back to work.

The weather has turned cold and I fear we're in for another long winter. There's so much talk that the war is almost over. I do hope they're right.

I read in yesterday's paper that two student nurses in Calgary were fired for cutting their hair. Did you ever hear such rubbish? I find the short bob a delightful style. I'm considering cutting my hair off. What do you think?

Lovingly, Emma

P.S. My neighbours are envious that I have white flour for my bread. Most everyone has cracked wheat or barley.

Mary was always amazed at how many topics her sister could cover in one letter. While she made her second cup of coffee, she turned on the radio. The announcer interrupted the music program with an important bulletin. Although there was some static on the airwaves, she couldn't believe what she heard:

> Formal surrender terms were signed and Canadian Brigade Headquarters received a message, which began: Hostilities will cease at 11 A.M., November 11th, 1918.... Just after eight o'clock, when the breakfast tea was being brewed and the early winter sun was beginning to slant across the battle fields, the long-awaited word spread throughout the Canadian trenches like a prairie grass fire. People laughed, cried, shouted, danced, and kissed strangers. There was an incredible feeling of relief. There were prayers of gratitude. There was swelling pride. And, for many, there was the bittersweet awareness that their boy would never be coming home.[2]

She shrieked with joy and startled Mona, who came running into the kitchen. Mary grabbed her hands and almost swept the blue gingham cloth right off the table as she twirled her daughter around. "I can't believe it, the war is finally over."

Hamilton celebrated the end of the First World War by releasing twenty-two prisoners without sentencing and doctors gave prescriptions to anyone who requested them "so that everyone might celebrate fittingly in spite of William Hearst."[3] Jim was among the onlookers who went downtown at noon to watch a man from Washington who was known as the Human Fly climb the Bank of Hamilton Building, the city's tallest building, to celebrate the end of the war.

Just when Hamiltonians were beginning to feel a sense of reprieve, the world around them was collapsing once again. The influenza continued to take its toll in their city. Desperate attempts were made to contain the epidemic: "Anyone coughing, sneezing or spitting in public was liable to a $50 fine. In Hamilton a department store announced that there would be no Santa Claus that year."[4]

Mary accepted her neighbour's invitation to tea that Christmas, anxious to get out of her apartment. "Come on in," Tessie said taking her by the arm. "It's been awhile since we've seen each other. Take your flu mask off, we're all fine here. Did you notice that the Campanellas three doors down have a placard in their window? I heard their youngest one, little Hannah, has come down with it."

"I'm sorry to hear that," she said, removing her mask cautiously.

"How much longer can this go on? You can't take a streetcar or shake somebody's hand and I read something in the paper that said most have sworn off kissing."

"We can't be too careful," Mary replied. "I heard that eating raw onions and garlic is supposed to help. I know a woman in the country that swears by wearing a poultice of cooked onions around her neck. Dr. Storms says there's no medical reason any of that should work."

Tessie leaned on her elbows, moved closer to Mary and whispered, "I've even heard of people inhaling fumes from hot water and turpentine. If you ask me, that's just plain crazy! But I've got the answer and I'm happy to share it with you." She grabbed the back of an envelope and jotted down her secret recipe:

½ pt. warm milk (pint)
1 egg
¼ T. ginger (teaspoon)
¼ T. soda
pinch of sugar
f.g. black pepper (few grains)

"Nothing farfetched about any of these things," she said, handing her the list. "Simply mix them together and drink it fast. It was my grandma who told me about this and she lived to be sixty-eight. She claimed it was the best thing to ward off infection and disease," she said emphatically. "Oh I almost forgot. Take it before bed. It's more effective while you sleep." Mary found it was humorous that Tessie assumed she'd try it. She was glad Tessie hadn't talked about her boys being overseas since Mary never knew what to say to ease her mind.

Jim and Mona weren't as enthusiastic as Mary when they tasted their neighbour's concoction. But no one in either household came down with the flu and no amount of discussion would ever have convinced Tessie it wasn't due to her grandmother's special potion. Doctors continued to be baffled by the outbreak and mass devastation of the disease:

> The epidemic continued its inexorable rampage through that Christmas, the winter months that followed, and into the first days of spring when, according to some mysterious pattern, it began to peter out. Hamilton was not the only city to be hit hard. The entire country had fallen to her knees in a little over two months. By March 1919, the Spanish "flu" had killed almost 65,000 Canadians.[5]

With so many returnees from overseas, Jim worried about having a job. With the price of food escalating, Mary worried about being able to afford coffee, which had doubled in price. What they didn't know was that the twenties would bring excitement and prosperity that neither of them had ever experienced in their lifetime.

TWENTY

The Roaring Twenties

> "In the 'Roaring Twenties' the City of Hamilton suffered a series of blows that left her hanging on the ropes. In 1922, an epidemic of 747 cases of diphtheria claimed 32 lives and weakened others. The City's debenture debt skyrocketed from ten million dollars in 1919 to seventeen million dollars in 1924. The wheels of progress began to ride rough shod over Hamilton life. The familiar electric radial cars were scrapped, in favour of the upstart motor cars."[1]

1920

In early January, they moved to 167 Ottawa Street North (Laidlaw Memorial Church today) just in time for Jim to get his usual listing in the city directory as a "painter" along with their new address. Emma didn't write as often since she'd had her second child, Lois Eileen, but it was just as well — Mary was busy with her own family. Since Mona hadn't been at school for over a year she decided to keep her home. Mary was happy to be moving to the east end of the city, but had concerns that they'd only be a few blocks from the Hamilton Jockey Club track. She feared Jim's weakness: "In the early years of the twentieth century horse racing was blatantly, often almost comically, corrupt. In 1910 the Canadian parliament ruled bookies off the tracks and substituted pari-mutuel betting, administered by the jockey clubs."[2]

Mary didn't approve of Jim's gambling. Sometimes he'd split his winnings with her in an attempt to appease her. She took the money reluctantly and salted it away in a shoebox at the back of her closet. Occasionally, when he was unemployed, it had helped to buy groceries. She still had a fair bit saved, hopefully enough for an electric sewing machine some day.

Unfortunately, the re-location to Ottawa Street didn't help Jim's decorating business. The city was in political chaos. In last year's election he'd supported the Independent Labour Party headed by Walter Rollo, a

Courtesy of Gail Horner.

Fourteen-year-old Mona Church had inherited her father's dark, mysterious eyes.

broom-maker who became the first workingman in Ontario to hold a cabinet position. They joined in coalition with the United Farmers to form the government, but there were too many split beliefs in fundamentals such as tariffs and prohibition.

Following the First World War, inflation was blamed for the labour unrest. Who would have thought that unemployment would reach an all-time high at 15 percent in the city and that the housing situation would be so bad that ex-servicemen and their families would be living in tents?

The fashion industry was also changing dramatically. One style magazine claimed that a women's hair and skin colour should be matched to her clothing. Women grew more conscious of their figures and weight became a popular subject. They were encouraged to exercise and avoid eating certain foods such as white bread, cream sauces, small fruits and berries, and anything with sugar in it. Mary had been watching her weight since she'd turned twenty. It was difficult to hide a few extra pounds when you're only five feet, two inches tall. Her weakness was "pudding," as Emma would say, the British expression for desserts.

Advertising promoted the idea that beauty was more important than brains. Everything from face creams to fashionable clothing was available to help women catch and keep a man. Mary was shocked to read that one of the latest trends was for a woman to swell her lips with bee stings for fuller lips. However, even she'd started to wear a little eye make-up and a pale lipstick for special occasions. Mary loved going to the beauty parlour, but it was a luxury she couldn't afford more than once every three months. She'd heard about the new apparatus for permanent waves in Eaton's beauty salon and was anxious to try it. Unfortunately, they didn't have an Eaton's in Hamilton.

That summer, Jim's mood changed. He was optimistic about everything from the weather to his business. When he started to bring gifts home for "his girls," Mary knew that it could only mean one thing — he'd fallen into a winning streak at the track. She was tempted to remind him that his luck could change as suddenly as the wind from the lake effects surrounding their city. Instead she decided to enjoy his good fortune.

Sunday became a family day. They took the ferry across the bay to Wabasso Park (later renamed La Salle Park), owned by the city of Hamilton but situated in Burlington along the harbour shoreline. Mona was thrilled with the amusement park. Regular outings included a trip to the beach strip, a picnic on the mountain, or a streetcar ride downtown to the drug store's soda shop. Nothing was more enjoyable than some homemade ice cream, a fountain-mixed soda, or a chocolate milkshake on a hot summer day. Mary would look back on that summer with fondness.

Their anniversary fell on a Wednesday that year, her lucky day of the week. At dusk they took a stroll along the shoreline down at the lake. Jim asked a passer-by to take their picture with his brand new camera.

Courtesy of Gail Horner.

Strong winds caused by the lake effects would often appear and change the temperature dramatically without warning.

Mary waited until after Christmas before buying a sewing machine. Her new Singer came with a customer satisfaction guarantee and she couldn't wait to make her first scoop-necked chemise, which was all the rage that spring. She made Mona several outfits, but knew she'd want something store-bought for her sixteenth birthday.

She went back to the jeweller where she'd bought Mona's gold ring eight years earlier. Mary thought there was nothing more beautiful than fine gold jewellery. She wished someone had felt that way when she'd turned sixteen.

The Pettit Collection.

Mary gave Mona an eighteen-carat gold brooch, monogrammed with her name, in May 1921.

It was no surprise when Jim started talking about buying another car. Prices had come down considerably and the idea of buying on credit was catching on. The auto industry boasted that there was one car for every twenty-two Canadians that year. People were enamoured with the new motorized vehicle and impressed with how quickly they could get downtown, head to the lake for a picnic, or take a scenic tour of the countryside. Some of them still had to be hand-cranked to start and had no heaters. Luxuries such as foot pedals for acceleration, adjustable seats, and brake lights were a thing of the future.

A loud squawking noise alerted Mary to peek through the lace curtains in the front room. Her husband was sitting in a dark brown 1919 McLaughlin Buick. Wiping her floured hands on her apron, she ran out outside. Jim was grinning like a little boy who'd just been given a chocolate-fudge, double-decker ice-cream cone.

"I got the deal of a life time. You won't believe it. The salesman practically gave it away."

TWENTY-ONE

Mr. Jacques's Funeral

"Twenty years after the first models appeared on the roads, almost everyone was buying a motor car. The days of 'getting out and getting under' were gone. The electric starter was replacing the crank; the 'closed car' was making travel on dusty, rural roads more bearable; tires became more durable; and the pump and patch kit were put in the trunk. Somebody invented windshield wipers, someone else the heater. Cars were no longer available only in black, but in almost any colour of the rainbow. At $900, even low-cost cars were expensive — about a worker's yearly earnings."[1]

1921

Jim's painting business was doing so well that he hired Ernie to help out. Mary still had to be careful with money, but was able to enjoy the occasional luxury like an Easter bonnet or a sixty-nine cent imitation goat handbag. She liked living on Ottawa Street. They had good neighbours and it was handy to the streetcar. When the enumerator came around,

Mary was pleased that they'd had no change of address. Jim got a separate listing for his business at the corner of Cannon and Oak Avenue.

Occasionally Mary reaped the benefit of a slow day at the store. Jim would arrange for Ernie to come to their house to do some decorating. She had her front room papered in her favourite floral pattern, the gumwood trim in the hall refinished, and a fresh coat of paint in Mona's room. She was happy to take advantage of the situation since Jim never seemed to get around to sprucing things up. She smiled to herself, thinking it was a bit like the local dentist whose own children had crooked teeth. Mary was pondering the next decorating project while she washed the supper dishes. She was debating what colour to have her kitchen cupboards painted when her thoughts were interrupted by a sharp knock at the door.

Mr. Armstrong, their neighbour, said she had a phone call from George Mundy regarding a family matter. George and his brother Dan, Mrs. Jacques's nephews, lived in Hamilton and Mary had given them her neighbour's phone number in case of an emergency. Even though some of her childhood memories were painful, she'd never completely severed her ties with the Jacques family. She hadn't forgotten that they'd taken her in when she needed a place to call home.

If she hadn't bumped into George occasionally at the market, she would never have known that Daniel Jr., the youngest Jacques boy, had married his childhood sweetheart Jane Chesney and had a son named Joseph. She also learned that Annie had five children, Gordon, Mary Elizabeth, who only lived a short time, Clara May, Ruby Pearl, and Doris Irene. George was the one that told her Mrs. Jacques had passed away the summer of 1912. Mary had thought about going to the funeral, but her memories were still too vivid and she decided against it.

Wiping her soapy hands on a towel, she hurried next door, wondering what had prompted this unexpected phone call. With sadness George told her that Mr. Jacques, Daniel's father, had passed away the day before. He was eighty-five. According to the doctor the cause of death was quite simply that "he wore out."[2]

Mary had been very fond of Mr. Jacques and never doubted for one moment whether to go to his funeral. She was glad that Jim's business was going well and they had an automobile. She made sure that her family was well dressed before heading to Innerkip for the funeral. Annie invited them to drop in en route. After a brief visit, they continued on to the Jacques farm following behind Annie and her husband Elias.

Mary found it eerie as they travelled down the 7th Concession that ran all the way from Drumbo to Innerkip. Twenty-one years had passed since she'd seen the farm. It gave her a strange feeling as they crossed the sixteenth line, a stone's throw from the Chesney farm. She wondered if her childhood friend Josie still lived around there. Jim couldn't possibly understand the way she felt about returning to the Jacques farm since he had no idea that she'd been their domestic servant, not a relative. That little secret was the reason she and Mona had gone alone to visit Annie one Christmas. That was a long time ago and Mary could see no reason why the subject would come up now.

They were fast approaching the farm on the 6th Concession, Blandford Township, on the outskirts of Innerkip. She caught a glimpse of the house beyond the trees that were in full leaf. As they approached the lane, the barn and shed looked exactly the same as she'd remembered but her eye caught something different: "It was a shiny, galvanized steel mailbox with D. Jacques stencilled on the side."[3]

A large, shaggy collie greeted them as they pulled into the lane. It reminded Mary of the two dogs they'd had when she was there. Tiny was a scrawny hound that Daniel had found in a field dying of starvation, and Ben, a brown-and-white-spotted beagle, had been given to him on his ninth birthday. She looked again and the dog was gone. Her eye went to the dinner bell on a pole that she'd used to call Mr. Jacques and his sons in from the field at meal times. When she rang the bell at unusual times of the day, it alerted Mr. Jacques that she needed his help because his wife was suffering from a seizure.

Then she spotted the two pumps, one for the cistern and one for the well. How vividly she recalled having to fill the reservoir in the stove with water from the rain barrel and the kitchen pail with well water morning and night. Daniel and a young boy appeared at the door. She approached the house alone, leaving Jim to help Mona out of the car.

"Hello, Mary," Daniel said as he reached out and gently squeezed her hand for a moment. His mannerism, however fleeting, reminded her of his father.

"Hello Daniel. It's been a lot of years."

"I want you to meet my boy, Joe. He's ten." Joe nodded. He'd watched them come down the lane and had been quite taken with their fancy automobile. Cars were still a rarity out in the country.

Seeing the tall, lanky boy reminded Mary of one of Annie's letter that described Joe's operation.

August 20

Dear Mary,
It's a hot summer. Gordon is nine. He's a big help on the farm. Clara May helps out but Ruby and Doris are too little.

Daniel's boy Joe had an operation. He could not breathe from his nose. He had his tonsils and adnoyds out. I'm not sure how to write that. Dr. Hossack and Dr. Hotson come to the farm. They did it on the kitchen table they moved to the front room by the window for some light.

They never told the boy 'til that morning when he couldn't have no breakfast. He must have been scared. He's seven … same age as my Clara May. Joe is fine but it took him a whole day to get over the sedation. Daniel said it cost $7.

From Annie Zinkan

"Thanks for coming," Daniel said quietly. "My father always had a soft spot for you."

"Things haven't changed much," she said, scanning the yard in an attempt to hide her emotions.

"Did you notice our mailbox on your way in?" Mary nodded.

"Got that in the spring of 1916. Sat right on the kitchen table for weeks 'til I found the time to put it on a post. I guess part of me didn't mind going to the station to pick up the mail," he said wistfully.[4]

Mary knew from living on the farm that a visit to the post office was as important as attending church on Sunday. Without telephones, it was the only way a curious neighbour could find out the latest gossip in town, get the local paper, news from a distant relative, and the long-awaited mail-order catalogue.

Mr. Jacques, who never learned to read, enjoyed leafing through the farm implement section of the Eaton's catalogue. He claimed that "the three bestsellers" in the book were the cream separator, bicycle, and sewing machine. When Mr. Skillings picked up the big box with a shiny new red bicycle in it, everyone in the community knew what his boy was getting for Christmas. And once the catalogue became outdated, the pages were used to light a fire in the wood stove or found their way to the privy.

"Change isn't always easy," Mary replied, glancing down the lane in the direction of the shiny new mailbox. She turned back to Daniel. "I'm awfully sorry about your father. I haven't forgotten how kind he was to me."

"He had a good life. He was proud of his hundred-acre farm and apple orchard. And he got his way, he wanted to die here," he said as the collie reappeared from behind the barn and ran up on the porch. "I suppose you already met Rover in the laneway. He always comes out to greet the company and then disappears. He's Joe's dog."

"Daniel, this is Jim and my daughter Mona," Mary said. The two men nodded respectfully but said nothing.

Joe noticed that the girl walked with a limp. Later he overheard Mary say to his dad, "Mona's fine, as long as she takes her medication. If she didn't, it would be curtains."[5] He wondered what ailment a young girl could have that would be so terrible.

They filed into the kitchen with the dog leading the way. When Mary had lived there, animals weren't allowed in the house because Mrs. Jacques had allergies to animal fur. Daniel introduced his wife Jane, a pretty woman with dark hair, and his daughter Mary Maria (pronounced Ma-rye-a). The little girl looked about two. The family had just finished eating a big dinner when they arrived. Mary looked around the table, recognizing Thomas immediately. He stood up and shook her hand. "Hello Mary. You're looking well enough," he said politely.

"Hello, Thomas. How are you?" she answered with the same politeness. She had no ill feeling toward the Jacques's boys.

"Folks around here just call me Tom. This here's my wife Edith." He turned to the woman beside him. "This is Mary, the young girl who came to live with us on the farm when our ma needed extra help," he explained. Mary was relieved that Jim was talking to Daniel and hadn't heard that last comment. "And these two are our boys, Earl and Bev."

Mary learned that Tom and his family lived in Burgessville, a small town south of Innerkip, and he worked as a linesman on the telephones. Chris, the only family member who wasn't there, was living in Jamestown, North Dakota, with his wife Eva and son Elmer. He was a millwright by trade and unable to come home for his father's funeral.

Mary stood awkwardly beside the table. Daniel, sensing this hesitation, took her by the arm and ushered her into the front room. Daniel's father, Daniel Sr., was lying in a shiny oak casket at one end of the room. Mary didn't feel that Mr. Jacques had changed much over the years except he looked frail. She remembered him as a soft-spoken, gentle man with an even disposition. He had often been silent in her company, not unlike today. The only thing that seemed strange was Mrs. Jacques's absence.

Reverend Shields, Innerkip's Anglican Church minister conducted the service while the hearse waited outside. For all the years that Mary had lived in this house, she'd only been in the parlour on three occasions. The first time was when Mrs. Jacques was having a work bee with some neighbours and Mary's job was to serve tea and biscuits.

"Ladies, this is Mary, the new girl I told you about," Mrs. Jacques announced with a sweep of her hand. Mary smiled and nodded her head.

Mrs. Graves turned to Mrs. Jacques as if Mary were either deaf or invisible. "She's awful scrawny and thin, May. Will she be strong enough to be of help to you?"

> *"There wasn't a lot of choice in younger girls. It was the best we could do," Mrs. Jacques replied.*[6]

On the second occasion that she'd been summoned into the parlour, Mrs. Jacques expressed concern with her behaviour:

> *"No child living under my roof is going to fly off the handle like that. You best be reminded that we took you in when you had no one that cared about you and nowhere to live. We've made a home for you here and we're doing the best we can. Remember where you came from," she said, pointing her index finger at Mary. "And you can certainly be sent back."*[7]

The last time Mary recalled being there was to draw the window blinds in the middle of the day:

> *As Mary approached the window in the parlour she saw a strange sight. A black horse-drawn wagon, carrying an enormous wooden box, was followed by a buggy and several men on horseback. It looked like the Chesney's buggy. An odd sensation came over Mary as she drew the blinds down and blackened the room.*
>
> *Nothing more was said until ten minutes later when she was instructed to open them again.*
>
> *Once back at school Monday morning, Mary learned from the teacher that Jimmy Chesney had died of consumption the previous Friday.*[8]

The room held little in the way of positive memories. But today she was here to say goodbye to Mr. Jacques, a man who'd treated her with kindness a long time ago. She recognized the pink and green hurricane lamp sitting on the side table in front of the window. The braided rug and oval framed black-and-white photograph of Queen Victoria were in the same spot that she'd remembered.

She glanced over at her daughter who'd been named after the lady in the portrait. Mona was sixteen, the same age that Mary had been when she ran away. She couldn't imagine her daughter doing such a thing. Of course, Mona had no reason to run away. She had a devoted mother who loved her unconditionally. The minister's words brought her back to the present.

"Daniel Jacques, born February 5, 1836, died on July 14, 1921. He was an honest man who worked hard all his life. He lived off the labour of the land, some years more prosperous than others. He is predeceased by his wife, Mary Elizabeth, who passed on the 7th of this same month in 1912. He leaves four grown children, Annie Marie, Thomas, Christopher, and Daniel Jr., and nine grandchildren to mourn his passing." He paused. "Let us bow our heads in prayer."

Mary closed her eyes while the minister began to recite one of her favourite Psalms. "The Lord is my shepherd; I shall not want…." His voice grew dim as the memories took over.

> *"Wheelchair? You mean she doesn't get out of that chair?" Mary asked innocently.*
>
> *"She hasn't been out of that chair for over a year except when Pa lifts her into bed at night or if she decides to go to church."*
>
> *"She … she can't walk?" replied a stunned Mary.*
>
> *"Why do you think you're here?" retorted Annie.*[9]

Annie coughed. "He leadeth me in the paths of …" The memories were strong and took over again.

> *"And what do you think Mother will say about this, Daniel?" The laughter came to an abrupt halt. "Playing with a girl, and the help at that!"*
>
> *In Annie's mind, Mary was different. Her clothes were not as nice as hers and she spoke with a slight accent. Mary was not part of her family and never would be. She was a servant girl, needed here on the farm to help her*

invalid mother. Her brother should not play with a servant — it wasn't proper.[10]

"The valley of the shadow of death…." Mary heard the word "death" and it reminded her that she was here to say goodbye to Mr. Jacques. On her eighth birthday, he'd given her a piece of real chocolate: *"You're a hard worker and a good girl, Mary" he said with a smile. Mary cherished those words for he was a quiet man and rarely spoke to her.*[11]

"Surely goodness and mercy shall follow me all the days of my life, and I will dwell in the house of the Lord forever." Mary looked around the room. What she saw was a family grieving the loss of a father and a grandfather. Her eyes went to the coffin. Mr. Jacques looked serene and dignified. It was how she would always remember him and was glad she came.

The service didn't take long and the family waited outside for the funeral procession to begin. Jim went around to the side of the house, lit up a cigarette, took a long draw, and blew smoke rings. He was growing restless. Mary overheard him say to Daniel, "Time and tide wait for no man, Dan."[12]

Jim lived by that motto. He was a man who lived for the present, not the future. At times it concerned Mary, but she knew better than try to change the man who she'd fallen in love with almost eighteen years ago. She reflected on how different he was than Daniel, who like his father believed that all things come in due course to those who are willing to wait.

The families followed the hearse through town down Main Street to the cemetery where Daniel Jacques made his final resting place beside his wife, May. Mary said goodbye to everyone, hugging Daniel a little longer than the others, and left Innerkip for the last time.

Years later, she heard from George Mundy again: "Daniel Jr. had lost his battle with pernicious anaemia. There was no cure for this condition in 1932. The only medical advice was to eat half a pound of liver a week."[13]

He died at the age of fifty.

TWENTY-TWO

A Child Is Born, a Child Is Lost

"In 1922, a serious depression and high unemployment cut spending to buying essentials. On butcher's shop windows they advertised the following; Minced Steak — 15 cents a lb., Beef Brisket — 8 cents a lb., Old Cheese 30 cents a lb., Ontario Eggs 43 cents a dozen."[1]

1921

Small independent businessmen struggled to survive in the early aftermath of the war and the world-wide flu epidemic. High unemployment cut people's spending drastically. Home decorating was a topic that people hardly discussed and Jim's paint business suffered terribly. Some days he never left the house. He started to drink a little more, a little more often. He had to let Ernie go and close the store. It was back to doing business from home. Two weeks later he sold the car.

Mary found it difficult to write Emma when things weren't going well at home. She never mentioned Jim's business or that they were having trouble making ends meet. At Christmas she sent her usual presents out west. She had a little cash squirreled away and had been saving some of her grocery money.

She bought Emma's son Gordon a plush wind-up toy and a doll with a porcelain face for three-year old Lois. Mary was too superstitious to send a gift for the new baby that her sister was expecting. Emma gave birth to her third child, Robert Harry, on New Year's Day.

The second week in January the enumerator, a tall, rakish woman in her mid-forties, knocked on their door. "Good morning Ma'am," she said, glancing down at her notes. "Does James Church live here?"

"Yes," Mary replied.

"Is he still a painter?"

"Yes," she said, even though Jim hadn't had a paintbrush in his hand for almost a month.

"Is there anyone else living here, besides you and your husband?"

"My daughter," she replied, smiling to herself. She wasn't about to tell a stranger that she was "in a maternal way," expecting another child that summer.

"And her name and birthdate?" she asked impatiently.

"Mona, that's what we call her, but her real name is Gloria. She was born May 24, 1905. It's hard to believe she's that old."

"Thank you, ma'am. Have a good day," and off she went next door. When the directory came out in June, in error Mona had been given a separate listing. No one was to be listed unless eighteen years of age or older, and she was only seventeen. It was never a problem since no one knew a "Gloria" Church.

At thirty-seven, Mary thought her chances of having another baby were unlikely. She was shocked by the doctor's news. Surprisingly, Jim was pleased but that was because he still wanted a son. Babies and birth control weren't discussed among husbands and wives in the early 1920s. Magazine ads tried to educate women on these little-understood and very taboo subjects: "In response to such demands, the 'feminine hygiene' industry became a multimillion-dollar business … the advertisements for such products as Lysol and Dettol intimated that they could be turned to contraceptive purposes."[2]

As Mary blossomed, Mona was becoming a growing concern. She languished around the house, complaining of pain in her legs and the light hurting her eyes. Mary knew she wasn't well when beating her father at checkers was no longer important. Mary prepared some of Mona's favourite foods and encouraged her to play outside, but in spite of her attempts, she continued to languish. The doctor didn't have any solutions either.

By early July Mary thought it was time to start preparing for the baby's arrival. She'd already decided to go to the hospital so she'd have the option of "twilight sleep" medication for the pain. Although she was superstitious about making clothes beforehand, she thought it was all right to have a bed ready. Mary found the oval-shaped wicker basket buried at the back of her closet.

"Can you believe that you slept in such a little thing?" she asked. Mona, who was curled up on the sofa, lifted her head slightly. "Well you did for almost three months. I'm sure glad I kept this little basket," she said, cradling it above her swollen belly. "What colour should I make the blanket?"

"Pink. I think it's going to be a girl," said Mona, smiling.

Mary hoped she was wrong for her husband's sake. "Why don't I make it white, just in case it isn't."

"How about blue? A girl can have blue."

Mary hurried off to buy some pale blue flannel and matching satin to edge the border. She also picked up some Sun-Maid seedless raisins for Mona. The treat in the little red box was full of iron and only cost a nickel.

The *Spec* had forecast fair and cooler weather the Friday Mary's son was born at the Hamilton General Hospital, formerly known as City Hospital. July 28 turned out to be a fine summer day with moderately warm temperatures. James Ross, named after his father, would be called Ross. At the time "James" was one of the top five most popular names for a boy according to the baby book of names that Mary had found in the library.

Jim was ecstatic. He headed downtown for some Helmars, imported Turkish cigarettes, to celebrate, and grabbed a bite to eat at the Arbor Cafeteria while he read the paper. For $2.50 admission, including tax, the Jockey Club was having seven races on Monday, including a steeplechase. Jim hoped that the birth of his son would bring him luck at the track. Unfortunately, he lost twenty-four dollars while his wife was in the hospital recuperating.

The day Mary turned thirty-eight she arrived home with a healthy six-and-a-half pound baby boy. She had a surprise waiting for her. Jim had replaced her dingy, cracked kitchen floor with a new product on the market called linoleum. The black-and-white checkerboard floor sparkled with a high gloss finish that Mary could easily keep clean with a damp mop. She thought about poor Emma who had big red poppies on her floor.

Once the baby was asleep, Mary settled down with a cup of tea and the paper. The death of Alexander Graham Bell and an article about the recent outbreak of infantile paralysis made the headlines that day. Mary was more convinced than ever that Ross should be nurtured on Borden's eagle brand milk. It was difficult for a new mother to ignore the warning that "safe milk is a matter of life or death in Hamilton today." Infantile paralysis and tuberculosis had hit the city hard and pasteurized milk was thought to be the only answer.

Ross was baptized on Sunday, August 27, at Centenary Methodist Church. Even though they couldn't really afford it, Mary insisted that Jim buy a suit for the occasion. She reminded him that he hadn't had a new one in almost twenty years.

"I guess a man's got to have a suit to baptize and bury," he said jokingly. He came home with a navy blue pinstripe suit, and a belt and trouser hanger, which were given away with every suit sold at Fralick's that weekend. It cost him fifteen dollars. Jim also had a first-class union shave in the barbershop at Carroll's Cigar Store to celebrate his son's baptism.

The summer of 1922 turned out to be bittersweet. Mary watched her fair-haired, blue-eyed baby plump up and flourish. Ross was the spitting image of his father except for his colouring. She did her late summer pickling and enjoyed the strong, heady smells that emanated from her bubbling pots on the stove. The aroma that escaped her open kitchen window wafted down the street. Mrs. Wetham always knew when Mary's preserves were being "done down" for the coming winter. This year she'd filled sterilized sealer jars with her spicy chilli sauce, pepper relish, vinegar pickles, and diced tomatoes. Every other year she did sweet jams, jellies, and tangy marmalade, and capped them with a layer of melted wax.

The last week of August was warm, with light showers and thunderstorms almost every day. September brought more of the same warm unsettled weather. Mona continued to complain about muscle weakness and joint pain. She'd also lost interest in food. Mary had always tried to limit Mona's desserts since there'd been a great deal written on the ill effects of too much sugar. She'd been shocked to learn that the average child had five rotting teeth. But since her daughter's appetite was so poor, in desperation she made her lemon jelly, chocolate sponge, and fingers of toast dipped in corn syrup.

She even bought Mona Chiclets, the bite-size candy-coated chewing gum that was so popular. Mona's favourite flavours were peppermint, tutti-frutti, and spearmint. If she felt strong enough, they went downtown for a Laura Secord ice-cream cone.

Mary longed for the cool temperatures that September usually brought, hoping that Mona would regain her strength just as she'd done every other year. Unfortunately, September brought no such good news.

On Thursday, September 14, Mary was awakened in the night by a strange sound. She listened carefully. It was hard to hear anything but the rain, which was pelting the windowpane. She tried to go back to sleep but heard the sound again. It was coming from her daughter's bedroom. Mona was burning up with fever and shaking uncontrollably. Jim ran next door and called Dr. Storms. He was there within the hour. He told them Mona was having convulsions and her high fever was the result of inflammation on the brain. There was nothing that he could give her, but she mustn't be left alone for fear of injuring herself or biting her tongue.

Mary sat by her bed through the night, putting cool cloths on her forehead to keep the fever down. Thoughts ran through her head like a millrace, the wild current that drives the waterwheel to operate a gristmill … an image still so vivid and easily recalled from her time spent on the farm. She remembered a conversation she'd had with Daniel Jacques at his father's funeral. He'd asked about Mona's limp. She'd told him "Mona was fine as long as she took her medication. If she didn't it would be curtains." The medicine was nothing more than a tonic Mary had concocted that she believed made her daughter stronger. Now she began to question herself. Could she have done more?

Mona died on Friday morning. The rain had stopped just before dawn. There was no evidence of the previous night's turbulence. Dr. Storms said

Mona had died of an infection that had gone to her brain and nothing could have been done to save her. Mary and Jim were numb with shock.

The funeral took place the following Monday afternoon in their home. Jim wore the same suit that he'd worn three weeks earlier at his son's baptism. By the time friends had gathered, the living room was crowded and stuffy. At Mary's request, the service was brief. Reverend Whiting did his best to explain why God would take such a young child.

Mary found it hard to comprehend that six weeks earlier she'd given birth to her son and today she was losing her daughter. Jim grieved silently. As they left the cemetery, he turned and quietly said to her, "We have a son to raise now."

The obituary appeared in Tuesday's *Spectator*, a day after the funeral. Unfortunately, there was a misprint, referring to Mona as "Flora Victoria" instead of "Gloria Victoria." Mary was too tired and too sad to bother notifying the paper. A stone marker was placed on Mona's grave a few weeks later.

Mona made claim to a part of her mother the day she passed away. Mary's life was changed forever and she would never be the same.

The Pettit Collection.

Mona Church was buried in the Hamilton Cemetery in 1922.

TWENTY-THREE

Picking up the Pieces

"A Saturday evening programme called 'Hockey Night in Canada' began on March 22, 1923, when Foster Hewitt, a broadcaster with the Toronto Daily Star's radio station, climbed inside a tiny, noise-proof glass box in Toronto's Mutual Street Arena and described the play on ice. A Canadian tradition was launched."[1]

1923

In early February the enumerator came around, but neither Mary nor Jim were home. She was finding her job quite tedious that day since a light snowfall and temperatures hovering around zero had made the sidewalks icy and slippery. She went next door and, after getting an update on Mrs. Wetham's listing, asked if she'd mind answering a few questions about her neighbours.

"Not at all," she replied.

"Does James Church live there?" she said, pointing next door. Mrs. Wetham nodded. "Is he still a painter?"

"When he can find work he is."

"Does Gloria Church still live there?"

"Who?" Mrs. Wetham asked. She repeated the question. "I don't know any Gloria Church. They had a daughter who died but her name was Mona. Poor thing was only seventeen." The enumerator crossed out the name on the listing, thanked her for her help, and moved gingerly down the walk.

It was just as well Mary hadn't been home to answer those questions. She was trying very hard to go on with her life, but missed Mona terribly. Taking Ross for a walk, wandering through the market, and having afternoon tea with a neighbour were things she did to keep busy. She found evenings were the worst time of day, the time when she felt the loneliest. Mary would try to relax on the sofa with one of Mrs. Armstrong's old *Maclean's*, but her interest in the world around her had diminished. She longed for her daughter and lived for her son. Jim spent more time at the track and had gotten into the habit of dropping in on the neighbours in the evening to listen to their brand new radio.

"It's the prettiest darn thing set right in a walnut cabinet. It has tubes, tuning dials, and speakers. It was so clear last night, I felt like I was at the game," he said, referring to the senior league match between Toronto and Kitchener, the first radio broadcast of "Hockey Night in Canada." Mary knew it wouldn't be long before Jim traded in their old crystal set for a fancy new one. The Armstrongs were the first on the block to heat their home with oil, buy an electric washing machine, and get a telephone. Jim claimed they owned nothing, all they'd done was put a little money down.

She watched Ross playing on the floor. It was hard to believe the little fellow was already eight months old. He was amusing himself with one of her kitchen pots and a large wooden spoon, so she grabbed the opportunity to read yesterday's *Spectator*. Carroll's had home-grown cabbage for 5¢ per pound, a twenty-pound bag of Redpath's granulated sugar for $2.30, and two packages of shredded wheat for a quarter. She couldn't beat those prices elsewhere.

By mid-May Jim was so busy that he had to hire some help again. For the first time in four years prosperity was returning to the city as new technologies sped up work and the number of non-unionized workers increased. Hamiltonians were leaving the farm/labour government and turning to the Conservative Party. The country appeared ready for social revolution. One of the most significant changes was the fact that women could go to the polls and exercise their franchise.

"It's about time women got a say during an election, don't you think?" Mary asked.

Jim paused, looking up from the newspaper. "I guess so. I've never given it much thought."

"I'm glad people are starting to realize we can do more than cook and clean. Why shouldn't a woman work in an office, a bank, or even go to medical school or law school if she can afford it?"

"I wouldn't go that far. I say let them vote and work in an office if they want but there's no way I'd go to a woman doctor. And I sure wouldn't trust a lady lawyer to look after my money." Mary knew that Jim wasn't alone in his thinking — lots of men thought that a woman's place was at home.

At about the same time that women's rights were changing, so was the fashion industry. Tight-fitting garments and the waist in women's wear was gone, and the boyish, flat-chested look became popular. A shorter hairstyle called the "bob" was all the rage. It was a time for flappers and dance crazes like jazz, the Charleston, and the Black Bottom. Hemlines continued to rise, but it wasn't until around 1925 that skirts were worn above the knee and women began to shave their legs. Mary enjoyed leafing through the glossy pages of the *Canadian Home Journal* or *The Canadian*, but when she closed the magazines her world was still the same. It consisted of housedresses and aprons, not plunging necklines and fur coats.

However, she never needed to be reminded of how fortunate she was to have a husband, a child, and a home. She'd read bits of *Emily Post's Etiquette: The Blue Book of Social Usage*, which covered every topic imaginable in its seven hundred and seven pages. Mary agreed that a housewife should change her dress and fix her hair before her husband came home from work: "The wife who smears her face with cream and rolls her hair in curlers before going to bed is not a sight that many husbands can endure. With a handy portable drier, there is no reason that hair cannot be dried while doing chores."[2]

Mary took Ross downtown on the streetcar for an "ice" to celebrate his first birthday. She treated him to an Arctic Sweetheart, a dainty little cup of Neilson's ice cream with a layer of crushed fruit and its own handy little spoon. Sitting on her lap in Christopher's Ice-cream Parlour, Ross held the spoon like a shovel and insisted on feeding himself. By the time he was done, his face was covered with vanilla ice cream and crushed strawberries, making him appear as if he'd been into a can of red paint. Mary had brought Mona here when she was three and remembered teaching her how to use a straw to drink her soda.

Jim came home from work that night in an exceptionally good mood. Several customers had finally paid their long outstanding bills. It was money he thought he'd never see so he planned to go to the track but, first, gave Mary half.

"You've got a birthday coming up, my love. Monday morning I want you to head downtown, buy yourself a new dress, and get your hair done up. Buy a fancy pair of shoes, too. Something to go dancing in," he said, thumbing off a wad of bills that he took out of his pocket.

"What about Ross?"

"I'm taking the day off to spend it with my son."

"But I don't need fancy things."

"I say you do. Don't come home until you've spent it all on yourself, not the baby, and not the house. And phone Mrs. Wetham to mind Ross on Thursday night. I'm taking you out on the town for your birthday."

Mary couldn't remember the last time she'd had a store-bought dress. She was used to hunting for a bargain or simply window-shopping and hardly knew where to start. First she went to the beauty salon and asked for a haircut, something a little more up-to-date. Twenty minutes later the hairstylist held up a hand mirror so Mary could see the back. She had no idea the woman would cut it that short. It was the new cropped off "boyish bob."

After peering in the window of the Right House, she went to the dress department to find the soft peach chemise with the simple, elongated bodice and scooped neckline that had caught her eye. The mid-calf skirt length made her feel positively elegant as she studied herself in the mirror. She felt like she was looking at a stranger. Was it the new hairstyle, the dress, or both?

"Do you think I'm too old to wear this?" she asked the salesgirl, who was probably ten years her junior.

"Absolutely not, Ma'am. I think the new straight-cut is most flattering on you, not being so tall." She put her hands gently on Mary's shoulders and turned her to the side so she could get a better look in the three-way mirror. "I'm sure your husband will like it."

"How will it stand up to washing?"

"It's 100 percent cotton voile, completely washable and colour safe. It's guaranteed."

After paying the clerk, Mary headed down King Street to Hamilton Slater and J.D. Climie, two well-known shoe stores, side by side. Years ago she'd bought a pair of genuine patent-leather laced boots with Goodyear welt soles for $2.68 at Climie's.

Slater's had quite a large selection in their window so she went there first. Mary liked the white tiled walls and the store's stock box system. The owner, Mr. J.W. Bridgett, appeared from the back and offered her a seat. In no time, strappy shoes, shoes with buckles or bows, as well as plain, serviceable pumps, surrounded her. She settled on a sleek little leather pair with a Louis heel and a buttoned strap that would look perfect with her new dress. She completely forgot about going next door.

Mary saved the best for last — shopping for a hat. She headed to Sam's, a very friendly Jewish man that owned at least half a dozen millinery stores in the city. She tried on seven or eight but didn't feel guilty because today she was a paying customer. "Have you got that one in peach?" she asked, pointing to a navy cloche in his window.

"I'll go and see if I have one, Ma'am." Mary waited the longest time and knew what was happening. If Sam didn't have what you wanted, he'd run out the back, down the alley to one of his other stores, and a few minutes later would appear with the exact hat that had been requested.

Sam seemed a bit winded when he returned with a peach bowler-shaped cloche, practically brimless like the one in his window. It had a soft, creamy bow that draped just above Mary's left eye as she pulled it down over her newly coifed bob. She watched him wrap it in tissue but was disappointed when he put it in a bag. The ones that came with hat-boxes were the European imports that cost quite a bit more. She still had enough money for a pair of flesh-coloured rayon stockings. They were a bit shiny but at a quick glance could be mistaken for genuine silk, at less than half the price. She hopped on the streetcar feeling very excited about her new outfit.

Mary felt like royalty as she and Jim boarded the Moonlight de Luxe and took a cruise to Grimsby Beach. They danced the night away on the steamer "Corona." Tickets were seventy-five cents per person, but when Jim decided to do something, he did it right. He regretted not owning a car so they could have driven down to the Burlington piers to catch the boat. However, he told her that that would likely be changing soon.

Two orchestras with special feature attractions, W. Norman Black, lyric tenor, and J. Rowcroft, tenor, entertained the guests at the front and rear of the boat. After they danced to the last waltz, "You Tell Me Your Dream, I'll Tell You Mine," they got on the streetcar and headed home. Mary had a feeling that life was slowly returning to the way it had been.

Jim's business continued to flourish and he was happy. She wasn't surprised when he arrived home behind the wheel of a grey 1920 Chevrolet Sedan. He'd left the morning paper on the table with several automobiles circled in the used car ads. Mary knew how lucky she was to have a hard working husband, a healthy happy baby, and realized it was time to accept her daughter's death. She'd never "get over it," as one of her neighbours had so callously suggested, but she was ready to deal with it. She put some of Mona's pictures and things that she'd made at school in a large cardboard box. When the time was right, she'd show them to her brother.

They'd talked about getting a telephone in the past, but other things always got in the way. Now Jim felt it was a necessity for his business. Everyone had a party line and the Bell telephone operators' assistance was required for each call. It was understood that you had to wait your turn and the entire community might be listening in. Party-line eavesdropping, or "rubbernecking," as it was called, was becoming a popular pastime. It was rumoured that sometimes a mother, at a loss as to how to deal with a naughty child, would suggest that her son or daughter pick up the phone and listen in for a while. It's doubtful whether Dr. Spock would ever have recommended this as a solution for misbehaviour.

It was a red-letter day in the Church household when their shiny, new black telephone was delivered and they were given their very first phone number — Garfield 1752. Mary couldn't wait to have a two-way conversation with her friends instead of waiting for a reply to her hastily written postcard.

Jim showed her how the "big black box" worked, even though it wasn't necessary. "First you turn the crank this way." He briskly turned the handle clockwise. "Then take the receiver off the hook and put it on your ear, like this." As he did it, the hook immediately sprang up. "You have to wait until you're connected to your party. When you're done, ring off by turning the crank just like you did before. Sound easy?"

"Let's call somebody," she said, impatiently.

"Don't forget we got the phone mainly for my business. I don't want you tying up the line so customers can't get through."

"Don't worry, I won't," she replied absentmindedly as she tried to decide who to call first: Affie and Vi or Tessie Patterson?

"When I get home from work, I don't want you on the phone. I expect my supper to be ready." Mary nodded again. She couldn't wait to try out what was being referred to as the world's "ninth wonder."

It seemed that the more money Jim had, the more he spent. He knew where to go for the cheapest whisky, some camaraderie, and a fast card game. While it was illegal to manufacture or sell alcohol, it wasn't illegal to drink it. He insisted that he couldn't be arrested for having bootleg alcohol in his home, after all it was so easy to get.

> By the 1920s, the Perri Gang ran the biggest bootlegging operation in Hamilton, Guelph, Brantford, and the Niagara Peninsula. Some think the gang's operation was the biggest in Canada. Through much of prohibition, they handled up to 1,000 cases of 60-proof whiskey a day, bought for $18 a case and sold for $80.[3]

In January, Jim requested a bold business listing in the city directory. For ten dollars he could have his name in bold print as well as own a copy of the directory. For a mere fifty cents he could have his name in bold

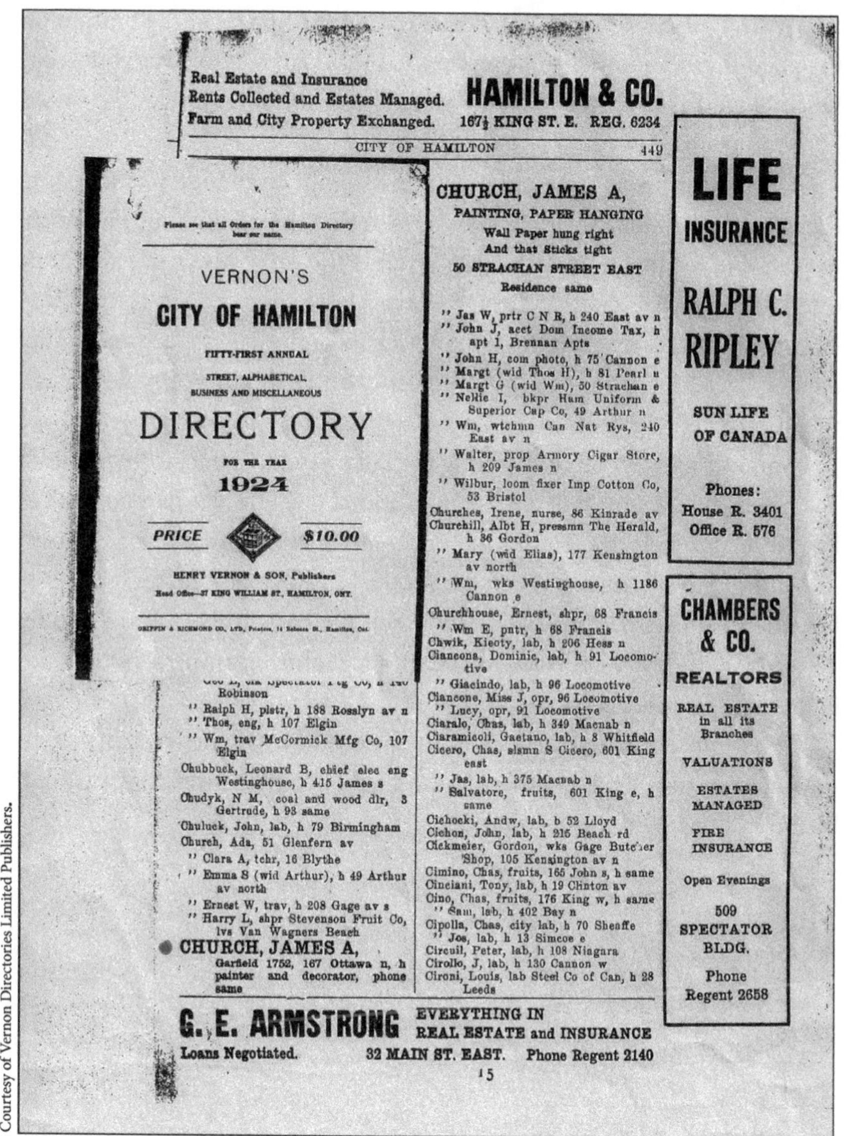

Real Estate and Insurance
Rents Collected and Estates Managed. **HAMILTON & CO.**
Farm and City Property Exchanged. 167½ KING ST. E. REG. 6234

CITY OF HAMILTON 449

Please see that all Orders for the Hamilton Directory bear our name.

VERNON'S

CITY OF HAMILTON

FIFTY-FIRST ANNUAL

STREET, ALPHABETICAL, BUSINESS AND MISCELLANEOUS

DIRECTORY

FOR THE YEAR

1924

PRICE $10.00

HENRY VERNON & SON, Publishers
Head Office—37 KING WILLIAM ST., HAMILTON, ONT.

GRIFFIN & RICHMOND CO., LTD., Printers, 14 Rebecca St., Hamilton, Ont.

Robinson
" Ralph H, plstr, h 188 Rosslyn av n
" Thos, eng, h 107 Elgin
" Wm, trav McCormick Mfg Co, 107 Elgin
Chubbuck, Leonard B, chief elec eng Westinghouse, h 415 James s
Chudyk, N M, coal and wood dlr, 3 Gertrude, h 93 same
Chuluck, John, lab, h 79 Birmingham
Church, Ada, 51 Glenfern av
" Clara A, tchr, 16 Blythe
" Emma S (wid Arthur), h 49 Arthur av north
" Ernest W, trav, h 208 Gage av s
" Harry L, shpr Stevenson Fruit Co, lvs Van Wagners Beach
CHURCH, JAMES A, Garfield 1752, 167 Ottawa n, h painter and decorator, phone same

CHURCH, JAMES A,
PAINTING, PAPER HANGING
Wall Paper hung right
And that Sticks tight
50 STRACHAN STREET EAST
Residence same

" Jas W, prtr C N R, h 240 East av n
" John J, acct Dom Income Tax, h apt 1, Brennan Apts
" John H, com photo, h 75 Cannon e
" Margt (wid Thos H), h 81 Pearl n
" Margt G (wid Wm), 50 Strachan e
" Nellie I, bkpr Ham Uniform & Superior Cap Co, 49 Arthur n
" Wm, wtchmn Can Nat Rys, 240 East av n
" Walter, prop Armory Cigar Store, h 209 James n
" Wilbur, loom fixer Imp Cotton Co, 53 Bristol
Churches, Irene, nurse, 86 Kinrade av
Churchill, Albt H, pressmn The Herald, h 36 Gordon
" Mary (wid Elias), 177 Kensington av north
" Wm, wks Westinghouse, h 1186 Cannon e
Churchhouse, Ernest, shpr, 68 Francis
" Wm E, pntr, h 68 Francis
Chwik, Kieoty, lab, h 206 Hess n
Ciancona, Dominic, lab, h 91 Locomotive
" Giacindo, lab, h 96 Locomotive
Ciancone, Miss J, opr, 96 Locomotive
" Lucy, opr, 91 Locomotive
Ciaralo, Chas, lab, h 349 Macnab n
Ciaramicoli, Gaetano, lab, h 8 Whitfield
Cicero, Chas, slsmn S Cicero, 601 King east
" Jas, lab, h 375 Macnab n
" Salvatore, fruits, 601 King e, h same
Cichocki, Andw, lab, h 52 Lloyd
Cichon, John, lab, h 215 Beach rd
Cickmeier, Gordon, wks Gage Butcher Shop, 105 Kensington av n
Cimino, Chas, fruits, 165 John s, h same
Cinciani, Tony, lab, h 19 Clinton av
Cino, Chas, fruits, 176 King w, h same
" Sam, lab, h 402 Bay n
Cipolla, Chas, city lab, h 70 Sheaffe
" Jos, lab, h 13 Simcoe e
Circuil, Peter, lab, h 108 Niagara
Cirollo, J, lab, h 130 Cannon w
Cironi, Louis, lab Steel Co of Can, h 28 Leeds

LIFE INSURANCE
RALPH C. RIPLEY
SUN LIFE OF CANADA
Phones:
House R. 3401
Office R. 576

CHAMBERS & CO.
REALTORS
REAL ESTATE in all its Branches
VALUATIONS
ESTATES MANAGED
FIRE INSURANCE
Open Evenings
509 SPECTATOR BLDG.
Phone Regent 2658

G. E. ARMSTRONG EVERYTHING IN REAL ESTATE and INSURANCE
Loans Negotiated. 32 MAIN ST. EAST. Phone Regent 2140

15

Courtesy of Vernon Directories Limited Publishers.

The Vernon City Directory, *first published in Hamilton in 1901, came out annually and provided street addresses. Only a successful businessman could afford a bold business listing, representing status in his community.*

print. Jim chose the latter. Unfortunately his listing was at the bottom of the page and his competitor, a painter with the same name was at the top. Jim was glad that at least he had a telephone number, unlike the other James Church.

That year a bylaw was passed in an attempt to reduce accidents on the city streets. Mary was shocked to learn that the automobile had been responsible for five deaths and 125 injuries the previous year. Hamilton, often called a "five-cent tin lizzie" town, was the first city to try out the stop-street bylaw approved by the Ontario highways department. The curious came out to witness this milestone, which dramatically decreased the number of accidents.

Something went terribly wrong the fall of 1924. The majority of Jim's customers had been using credit and couldn't pay him. He had no choice but to let his help go. He fell behind with his bills and started drinking and gambling more. When he showed up for work late, customers became dissatisfied. He was forced to sell the car and have their phone disconnected. Mary found a job working nights cleaning schools and churches. She hired a young girl to mind Ross.

When the enumerator came to their door, Jim said he wouldn't need the bold business listing in the city directory. What he didn't say was that he did not have fifty cents to waste.

TWENTY-FOUR

A Knock on the Door

> "The well-to-do invested in stocks and bonds, expecting to make a killing in radio, or steel or nickel through their brokers in Toronto, Montreal or Wall Street. Ordinary working men and women pursued theirs pots of gold at the ends of cheaper but no less gaudy rainbows. At race tracks across the country the thoroughbreds might be owned by the rich, but most of the two dollar bets were placed by the poor."[1]

February 1925

Mary was far more tired since she'd taken on a part-time job. It had been a long day and Ross had tried her patience, as only a two-and-a-half-year old knows how to do. She was preparing supper while he played underfoot with his building blocks. Setting the table was a challenge as she sidestepped and dodged the tall stack of blocks that resembled a pyramid.

There was a knock at the door and Mary quickly went to answer, hoping Jim hadn't been disturbed. She opened the door. A tall moustached police officer was standing there.

"I'm looking for James Church," he said briskly.

The tone of his voice frightened her. "Just a minute, I'll get him," she said, closing the door and leaving the policeman standing on the front porch. She ran to the bedroom and woke her sleeping husband. "Jim, there's a policeman at the door and he wants to see you," she said nervously.

Jim was groggy from having been awakened from a deep sleep. He got up and threw on his trousers, his suspenders hanging down. Barefoot and shirtless, he went to the door. "Officer, what can I do for you?" he asked.

"Are you James Church?"

"Yes."

"You're under arrest. I'm taking you down to the station."

"There must be a mistake," he said raising his voice. "What have I done?"

"Get your coat, you're coming with me."

Mary watched in silence as Jim grabbed his shirt hanging on the back of the bedroom door and put on his socks and shoes. He turned to his wife. "I'll be home in a couple of hours. There's nothing to worry about," he said quietly. Ross started to follow his father and Mary intercepted him, scooping up the squirmy toddler. She held him tightly as Jim threw on his coat and closed the door behind him.

Mary fed Ross, read him "Jack and the Beanstalk," and tucked him into bed. She put their untouched dinner away and waited for Jim to come home. In later years she was unable to recall the sequence of events that unfolded which changed her life forever.

Mary went to visit Jim the next day, but had trouble finding a babysitter. The girl who usually minded Ross refused to come and her mother acted strange when she spoke to her. She finally had to take him next door to her neighbour.

The Barton Street jail is a stately three-storey, white brick building that she had passed many times taking the streetcar downtown. The building could have housed government offices or been a well-maintained boarding house. A black wrought-iron fence surrounded the premises and it hardly looked like a place to confine criminals. Behind closed doors Mary was told that her husband had been charged with carnal knowledge, sexual intercourse with someone under the age of consent or mentally disabled and therefore prohibited by law. Mary was so horrified that she almost went into a state of shock. Jim assured her that there'd been a terrible mistake and his lawyer would clear it up.

In the days that followed, Mary moved through her daily routines as though she had been swept into a bad dream. She held her head high, continued to work, and asked her friend Mrs. Harkness to help with Ross, assuring her that these arrangements would be temporary. Mary visited Jim as often as she could. He maintained his innocence and she believed him.

Two months went by in a blur. On Tuesday, April 14, Jim had his day in court. Mary remembered feeling so alone, so overwhelmed as she climbed the steps of the Wentworth County Court House. The main courtroom was on the second floor and Mary sat in the back row. The room was huge and the ceiling was probably thirty feet high. Large windows on two sides of the building lit the room, as well as a dome skylight in the centre of the ceiling.

Two guards led Jim into the courtroom. He was in restraints and looked tired and drawn. Mary wanted to shout out that somebody had made a mistake. He was a good man, a husband, and a father, and he needed to come home. The judge came in and asked Jim to stand for sentencing. He explained that any crime committed and deemed punishable by more than two years must be served in a federal institution. Mary couldn't understand why he was saying this and was so frightened she was holding her breath. She would never forget the judge's words as long as she lived.

"James Allan Church, you have been found guilty of carnal knowledge." Her husband was convicted of a crime that he claimed he did not commit and was sentenced to five years in a federal penitentiary. Mary was devastated. How could this have happened? It made no sense to her. How could her husband have such little regard for himself, if not for his family?

Everyone was asked to rise. Mary remembered leaning on the back of the chair in front of her, her legs buckling as she watched two policemen lead Jim out, handcuffed and shackled. As he past her, he reached out and she drew back. Mary looked him squarely in the eye as he mouthed the words "I love you." Then he was gone.

Mary felt so betrayed. All along she'd believed in his innocence. How could she question the decision of a respected judge in a court of law? Jim had convinced her that he wasn't guilty but after what she heard that day, she would never trust him again. Inside was a hollow, empty feeling like the one she had when Mona died. Mary ran out. Everything was a blur. The future had seemed so promising when they married in the Woodstock County Courthouse twenty years ago. Now it had been shredded apart in another courthouse.

Mary couldn't remember taking the streetcar home or picking up her son. She had no one to turn to and no one to tell her that everything would be all right. Her emotions swung back and forth from tears to anger, and she finally cried herself to sleep, being careful not to wake Ross.

The next morning Mary sat at the kitchen table, wrapped in a frayed blue housecoat, her fingers laced around her coffee cup for warmth. She watched Ross innocently play on the floor at her feet. Her coffee grew cold and she poured it down the sink. Nervously twisting her wedding band, she looked out the window at the cloudless sky, as if hoping it might provide some answers. She'd vowed never to take her wedding ring off and somehow could not bring herself to break that promise. Although the laws had changed and it was easier for a woman to divorce her husband, Mary never considered it.

In her mind she was a forty-year old widow with a young son to raise. There was no point in looking back on what *could have been* or what *should have been.* She'd already lost her daughter and now her husband. In barely an audible whisper she said, "Who will be next?

TWENTY-FIVE

Kingston Penitentiary

> "The K.P. is surrounded by four great limestone walls, twenty-five feet in height, surmounted by four observation towers, one at each corner, manned by armed guards around the clock to ensure perimeter security. It was conceived in 1833 as an impregnable fortress for the captive society, built to withstand the winds of the lake — and of time."[1]

1925

Jim was sent to the Kingston Penitentiary, one of the oldest federal penitentiaries in Canada. His personal information was recorded in *The Convict Register & Description Book*, his street clothes were exchanged for a grey prison uniform, and his belongings were placed in a vault. He was issued a personal identity code. Jim never heard his name again or saw it in writing until his release. He became known as "K939."

> The "K" in the inmate number did not refer to Kingston. They were using an alphanumeric system in those days

From *The Convict Register & Description Book – Kingston Pen.:*

When Received:	April 15, 1925
Registration #:	K939
Name:	James Church
State:	Married
Age:	43
Height:	5' 5 1/4"
Weight:	159 lbs.
Complexion:	Dark
Eyes:	Grey
Hair:	Greyish
Religion:	Baptist
Where Born:	Bright P.O., Oxford Co., Ont.
Special Marks:	No marks
Occupation:	Painter
Read:	Yes
Write:	Yes
Use of Tobacco:	Yes
Intemperate:	
Moderate:	Yes
Abstainer:	
Crime:	Carnal Knowledge
Where Tried:	Hamilton, ON
When Sentenced:	April 14, 1925
Term of Sentence:	5 years
Discharged:	
Remarks:	

Canada's Penitentiary Museum, Kingston, Ontario.

Every prisoner had his identity condensed to a one-page summary.

> starting with A001–A999, then B001–B999, and so on. It helped to avoid the repetition that occasionally happened in the older numeric system. That system ran from 1 to 9999 and then repeated. If someone was here on a life sentence, and if admissions were high enough, it was possible that two individuals would have the same number.[2]

K939 was inscribed on his trousers, underwear, shirt, socks, boots, coat, and cap. His bedding consisted of a sheet, pillow, mattress, and a towel changed twice a month. Summer and winter blankets were issued according to the season.

In the early 1920s, prison life reflected ideas that had been established almost a hundred years ago and little had changed. Prisons initially had housed soldiers who'd shown disrespect for officers, civilians convicted of crimes varying from stealing a loaf of bread to taking a life, and lunatics who had no other place to go. Banishment and hanging had become obsolete by the mid-1800s. In their place was a new theory, the idea that severe punishment would act as a deterrent for others.

Jim was allowed to write one letter a month, which had to be scrutinized by the guards, and incoming mail was subject to the same rules. After a while he didn't bother since his unopened letters came back with "return to sender" written across the front in Mary's distinctive handwriting. He could have one visitor, a family member every three months. No one came.

At 6:00 every morning the bell rang and the lights came on. Jim had half an hour to wash, dress, put his bunk and table up against the wall, and stand at his door waiting for the tapper (sometimes called turnkey or guard) to run down the tier and "tap him out." "To think of Kingston Penitentiary you have to think of the infamous bell. You lived and breathed by the bell. It told you when to eat, when to sleep, when to think: it was just incredible. It drove some people literally crazy."[3]

Jim figured his cell was about five-and-a-half feet across, seven-feet long, and nine-feet high. He could almost touch his fingers from one wall to the other by stretching out his arms and walk the length of his cell with three strides before he bumped into the back wall. The metal bars he faced every morning were set in a stone door frame. The dull slate-grey bricks in his cell had been repainted a number of times, but years of accumulated graffiti could still be seen.

Prisoners seemed to have an obsession with dates, numbers, and symbols but never words. Jim scanned his walls. He was able to make out "1911–1919," no doubt the length of one man's sentence. A good chance that the "54" higher up was months and even higher still he read "12 … 7 … 28." Could someone have lived here for twelve years, seven months, and twenty-eight days?

Over in the corner to the right of his bunk he saw some stick-like symbols in groups of four with slashes through them, the age-old system of counting by fives, but five what? It couldn't have been "months" since no prisoner's stay would have been less than two years. He concluded that some poor fellow had stayed in this very cell for twenty-one God-forsaken years.

The food was as monotonous as everything else. A man never went hungry but often felt empty. Every meal was ladled into a badly chipped or cracked white soup bowl and set on a food tray. Cornbread was served with most meals. It didn't take long for Jim to memorize the week's menu:

Monday: beef stew and boiled carrots
Tuesday: boiled mutton and baked beans
Wednesday: mutton soup and boiled potatoes
Thursday: boiled pork and turnips
Friday: brown beans and cabbage
Saturday: boiled pork and parsnips
Sunday: rolled brisket, swiss chard, and turnip

Jim was assigned duty in the mailbag manufacture and repair shop. He followed the rules, avoided confrontation, and kept his distance from certain inmates. He noticed something on the wall in the Keeper's Hall adjacent to the Main Dome area. In time he learned that it was an intricate count board, which had been invented by Deputy-Warden Tucker to keep track of all the prisoners.

> On this board is a hole corresponding to every cell in the place arranged according to location in tiers and ranges. An empty hole means, at a glance, an occupied cell. A red plug means a man in hospital. A blue plug means a man undergoing punishment. And so on. Every cell in the penitentiary must be checked by the guards on this board and totals made to tally before the all-clear signal rings at night and the prison is sealed tight as the tomb of Tutankhamen.[4]

Jim was allowed two library books a week, hand-delivered Monday morning by one of the prisoners under the watchful eye of a guard. He'd never been much of a reader except for the paper, but now found that it helped to pass the time. Often he was more amused with what the prisoners had written, usually inside the book cover, than with the actual story. Sometimes he requested the same book again to see if any new comments had been added. His favourite was scrawled inside the back cover of a book of poems:

> Here I sit in mustard vaper
> This dam shithouse has no paper
> The boss is comin', I must not linger
> Look out asshole, here comes finger.[5]

Jim had no way of knowing that this "literary ditty" had been hand scrawled by the convict in the next cell. Little things like this helped him get through another day at the Kingston Pen.

TWENTY-SIX

Ottawa Street

> "When a couple separates, it is never publicly announced, although the news generally spread quickly. Because they are legally married, the woman continues to use her husband's name and wears her wedding ring."[1]

April 1925

Mary put an ad in the *Spectator* looking for a house-keeping position and donated Jim's clothes to the Salvation Army. When she finished boxing everything up, there was no evidence that a man had ever lived there. As she carried them out along with a pile of old papers, a picture of Jim's dream car, a $1,400 black Overland Six, fell on the floor.

The weather predicted showers, and it was starting to drizzle. Her mood matched the weather. She found her ad in the classifieds, directly above one that began "coloured lady wishes cleaning," and was thankful that her neighbour Mrs. Armstrong had offered her the use of her phone number. Mary's main concern was Ross, who would be turning three in a couple of months. The chubby little boy with a tumble of blond hair asked the same question over and over again: "pappa gone?" Sometimes she'd nod or repeat his words without the voice inflexion at the end, for there was no question in her mind. As time went on, he stopped asking.

Mary had one response to her ad. An elderly gentleman wanted a housekeeper, but unfortunately it was only for three mornings a week. She started to read the want ads, but most were looking for live-in help. It would be difficult to find an employer who'd hire someone with a young child. Mrs. Harkness, a long-time neighbour who lived on Wilson Street not far from West Avenue, offered to take Ross if Mary couldn't manage.

Several months went by, Mary's savings were dwindling, and she was frightened. At least she owned a sewing machine and could make Ross's clothing. She was adamant that her son would not go without.

Her sister's letters were a welcome distraction from the realities of her own sad life. Emma described how she washed and bleached flour sacks by laying them outside on the grass in summer or on the snow in winter so her children wouldn't be wearing clothing with "Five Roses" or "Robin Hood" stamped on them. She baked bread six days a week, dried kindling nightly on the oven door for the morning fire, and acted as a midwife for her neighbours. It reminded Mary that even though her own life wasn't easy, neither was Emma's.

July 12

Dear Emma,

I can imagine how busy you are with Gordon, Lois, and Bob. Is Harry still working as hard as ever?

We had some excitement in Hamilton yesterday. People lined the street to see the automatic traffic lights installed at the Delta, that's where King and Main Street cross. Even Toronto doesn't have any yet.

Ross is growing like a weed. Jim's business is not going well and I'm looking for a job.

Love, Mary

She felt badly saying Jim's business wasn't good and knew the day would come when she'd have to tell Emma that he was gone. For now she had other things on her mind, like looking after Ross and finding a job.

Mary had heard that Mr. Meakins over at the basket factory was hiring. She'd never worked in a factory before but she was getting desperate. Mrs. Wetham took Ross and she jumped on the streetcar, thankful that the Hamilton Street Railway had guaranteed the five-cent bus fare for the next three years. She'd passed the three-storey building on the corner of King and West Avenue many times on her way downtown, never thinking that she'd ever be going there looking for a job.

Mr. Meakins was a nice enough man. He'd been in business twenty-five years manufacturing brushes, brooms, woodenware, baskets, and mats. Her starting salary was $8.50 a week cash in a manila envelope, handed out every Friday. She made arrangements for several of her neighbours to take turns minding Ross. Mary would have preferred a job as a live-in housekeeper, had it not been for her son. The pay would be about the same as the basket factory, but without living expenses she'd be far better off. After a few weeks it was obvious that she was still having trouble making ends meet, so she went back to Mrs. Harkness in desperation.

"Whatever will I do? How can I possibly look after Ross if I take on a housekeeping job and have to live in?"

"I'll take him … to help you. He can have a bedroom in the attic. You can visit him whenever you want." Mary had hoped she'd say that, but still didn't know if she could give up her son. She said she'd think about it.

In late January the enumerator came knocking at her door. Mary requested an "r" in front of her address since it was a residence and no longer a business. It was the last year that Jim's name would appear in the directory.

When she could no longer afford to pay her rent, she went back to Mrs. Harkness. It made Mary sad to think that she needed help to raise her own child, but she wanted what was best for him. She found a job as a live-in housekeeper, gave her notice at the basket factory, and Ross moved in with Mrs. Harkness. Mary paid her a small sum for his keep. Ross was delighted to have two "big brothers" but struggled to say goodbye to his mother, which made it even harder to leave him. She took comfort in knowing that he was being raised in a loving Christian home, but she never intended it to last fifteen years. She often wondered if she'd done the right thing and asked herself the same questions over and over again.

"How could you do this to your own flesh and blood? Hasn't he been through enough already, having lost both his sister and his father? Doesn't he need you now more than ever?" Her answer was always the same: "I had no choice in the matter."

Mary moved from one job to another when conditions became intolerable. She was surprised that Emma never questioned her address changes and could only assume it was because her sister was busy with her own life. She stayed the longest with Mrs. Ryckman, a lady in her early seventies. She was kind and not overly demanding. Her favourite meal

Courtesy of Gail Horner.

Mary, like her sister Emma, was an animal lover. Taking Blacky for a walk was one of the more pleasurable aspects of her housekeeping position.

was chicken fricassee — chicken rolled in flour, fried in bacon drippings, and served in brown gravy. She insisted on having dessert every night with her evening meal, and Mary became quite good at making tapioca custard, cottage pudding, and raisin pie. Mrs. Ryckman had the cutest little black dog, appropriately named "Blacky," that Mary simply adored.

She visited Ross after church every Sunday, her day off. She got in the habit of taking him a treat, usually some Liquorice Allsorts, a Sweet Marie, or a Milky Way. At the end of each visit before Mary said good-bye, she'd remind him of one thing. "Don't forget who your real mama is. She's just your paid mama."

When Ross was thirteen, he wanted to know what had happened to his father. Mary told him that he was sent to prison for gambling. Mrs. Harkness told him the truth.

TWENTY-SEVEN

Stony Mountain

"Eaton's catalogues advertised electric washing machines and the first electric refrigerators appeared — although the ice truck would remain a familiar sight on most streets for another decade or more."[1]

1926

Mary took a picture of Ross hanging on to the iron railing around the fountain in Gore Park. He was anxious to get home to play with the toy train that she'd bought him at Woolworth's that afternoon.

About the same time that she was taking the photo, Jim was taking the train to Winnipeg. An increase in theft and robberies had resulted in overcrowded conditions in prisons across the country and prisoners were being relocated. Jim was one of eighty inmates from Kingston Penitentiary being transferred to Stony Mountain Institution, a medium-security prison in Manitoba.

The penitentiary was built at the top of a sizable hill overlooking the flat prairie landscape, in the middle of nowhere. Underground cells had been built a long time ago for "very bad" convicts, which had weakened

Ross Church was warmly dressed in his navy blue double-breasted wool coat for an outing downtown on a chilly day in early March 1926.

Courtesy of Gail Horner.

the main walls and accounted for the obvious sag in the building. It was a reminder to inmates of how much worse conditions had been at one time.

Warden Meighen made every attempt to find a prisoner work in the trade he'd been in before being incarcerated. Jim was put in the paint gang and sent to paint fence posts, then joined the farm gang to repair wagons, and help re-shingle the tailor shop. He also did a stint down at the stone quarry, which was observed by guards on twenty-four hour duty from the tower on Target Hill. Like the others, he was given a wage sufficient enough to buy tobacco and a few personal things, and he was allowed an hour a day in the exercise yard, just north of the wall. Stony Mountain had a good library and a brand new fireproof moving-picture machine for the talking pictures that were starting to replace the silent films. Jim was happier here than at the Kingston Pen.

Time seemed to pass quickly that year. Mary thought that Ross looked taller and more grown up each time she saw him. She regretted missing out on so much of his childhood, but he seemed happy and healthy. It was obvious that Mrs. Harkness was taking good care of him.

Emma's Christmas letter was full of news. Mary realized how content her sister was on the homestead, looking after her husband and three children:

> December 15
>
> Dear Mary,
> I hope you're enjoying the Christmas season. No doubt Ross is excited about Santa Claus. I can't believe that Bob will be four on New Year's Day. Where has the time gone?
>
> Harry's relatives from Newfoundland sent us some rum in a big, strange-looking, flat bottle. It's very thick and strong tasting. Harry said if I warm it it'd taste like a hot toddy. I don't fancy it. He dug another hole in our dirt crawl space to store the bottle.
>
> He has prepared dried salt cod and hardtack for Christmas Eve. He soaked and washed the fish until it swelled up and the salt came out of it. Then he cooked it. Hardtack is nothing more than hard bread that has been soaked in salt water with the cod. These certainly aren't English traditions. Perhaps I'll acquire a taste for it.
>
> I'll never get use to pickled herring though. Harry eats it right out of the barrel. It's quite a sight to see the fish go in one side and the bones come out the other. He's a true Newfoundlander.
>
> I've rambled on terribly Mary, please forgive me. I miss you so.
>
> Lovingly, Emma

Christmas wasn't nearly as exciting for Mary. She spent the day with Ross and Mrs. Harkness invited her to stay for dinner. Mary bought him one of the most expensive wind-ups in the toy department at the Arcade, a sniffing dog made of tin, covered in plush. Ross ran to the kitchen to try out his new toy on the linoleum floor. Mary watched him repeatedly turn the key on the dog's back and squeal with delight as it walked along sniffing the ground. With each little step, his nose moved in and out, his ears rose up and down, and his tail went around in circles. She was glad she hadn't scrimped.

By spring Mary was feeling a little better about her son's "living arrangement." She managed to see him mid-week when she went grocery shopping for Mrs. Lockwood, her new employer. She'd found a room in a boarding house downtown since it wasn't a live-in position. Mary wished that Ross, about to turn five that summer, could move in with her, but he couldn't be left alone all day while she was at work.

That summer Hamilton got its own civic bathing beach, known as Hamilton's Sunnyside, at the foot of Bay Street. Sand had been trucked in and placed along the shoreline to improve the beach. The city provided a public dressing room, a lavatory, and a float for children to jump or dive from, anchored in the bay. Every Sunday Mary and Ross took the streetcar down to the bay front for a swim and a picnic. On sunny days it was usually crowded by noon. She didn't go to church that summer so she could spend the whole day with him. He got use to the routine of seeing his mother twice a week.

September arrived and Mary registered Ross in kindergarten. He was eager to go to school, but it meant that she'd only be able to see him once a week. His first piece of artwork was a blue and yellow woven bookmark, which she carefully tucked in her Bible.

Two weeks before Christmas, Mary took him downtown to Eaton's Toyland. The man dressed in red had a Santa Claus button for every little person who visited him. With reluctance Ross sat on Santa's knee, tightly fisting a peppermint candy cane.

That year Mary gave him his first Hardy Boys book, *Tower Treasure.* It was one of the first three published in a book series that became popular for young boys.

> In 1926 ghost writer Leslie McFarlane began hammering out a host of books that were read across the continent. Under the pseudonym of Franklin W. Dixon, he wrote twenty-one books in the Hardy Boys series — avidly followed by young boys although condemned by teachers and librarians for their low level literary quality.[2]

Mary planned to read Ross a chapter every Sunday until he was able to read by himself. If he liked the book, she'd give him one every birthday and Christmas until he had the complete series.

Emma had her last child, a little boy named Walter, in late February. Mary couldn't imagine the cost of raising four children when she was struggling with just one. The following winter Emma sent her a picture of Lois pulling her younger brothers through the snow in an orange crate attached to a runner sleigh. Mary was surprised how much they'd grown in one year and felt badly she hadn't kept in touch with her sister more often.

Mary had been saving part of her weekly earnings and wanted to give Ross something extra special that Christmas. She'd been looking at the bicycles in the window of the CCM Joycycle Store on James Street next to the Armories. They were expensive but she didn't want him to have second-hand. She knew what that was like, first-hand.

The look of surprise on his face when he saw the shiny, new red bicycle was worth all her scrimping and saving. Somehow the little things helped to make up for the big things that were lacking, like Mary's desire to live under the same roof as her son.

TWENTY-EIGHT

Freedom at Last

"During the first nine months of 1929, the great boom just kept rolling along, and people saw no reason to think that it would ever end. Public confidence was at an all-time high and manifested itself in a growing wave of installment buying. Why wait to buy a washing machine, or one of the new batteryless radios when you could have it now with a small down-payment? And the department stores and other retail outlets, sharing this belief in tomorrow, encouraged their customers to 'buy now, pay later.'"[1]

April 1929

Mary found Mondays hard since she wouldn't get to see Ross for six more days. Yesterday's visit was fresh in her mind. They'd spent the whole afternoon together, ending up in Gore Park. Ross loved taking the streetcar and Mary enjoyed having him all to herself. She'd never get use to him calling Mrs. Harkness "Mama." When Mary reminded him that she was his "real" mama, Ross would nod but she wondered if he truly understood.

So far her morning hadn't gone smoothly. Mrs. Lockwood had been late eating her breakfast and Mary was already behind. She hurried to finish the dishes so she could start the laundry. The sun was peeking out from behind a cloud and it looked like she'd be able to hang the clothes out on the line to dry.

That same Monday, April 8, K939 was discharged from Stony Mountain, a free man after serving four years less a week of his five-year sentence. His prison garb was exchanged for a white shirt with cuffs a little on the short side, a brown serge suit with dated lapels, a striped beige tie, dark socks, and a pair of size 8½ ill-fitting black shoes. It felt strange to be wearing street clothes. Jim had no idea what he looked like, but it didn't matter.

The clerk emptied the contents of a manila envelope labelled K939, which included an old black leather pocketbook, one key, a monogrammed handkerchief, and a gold pocket watch. He was told to put them in his trouser pockets. The clerk unlocked a cash box, handed him a ten-dollar bill, and recorded the date in the convict register and description book.

Warden Meighen shook his hand and said, "You're a free man now. I hope you learned something in here. Work hard. I never want to see you again."

Jim was escorted to the CNR station in Winnipeg and handed a second-class ticket to Hamilton. "Change trains in Toronto," were the only words spoken. He boarded, turned back, and the escort was gone. Jim was on his own for the first time in four years. He took a window seat at the rear. When the train pulled out of Union Station in Winnipeg, Jim thought it was probably around five o'clock, suppertime at Stony Mountain. He'd forgotten that he had a watch.

The CNR had two routes from Winnipeg to Capreol, a major connection point about twenty-five miles north of Sudbury Junction. The Longlac-Nakima trek headed in a northerly direction, making a stop at Sioux Lookout. The other route, the one Jim was on, headed east across the country. The train would thread its way around a series of tiny inland finger lakes and rivers, like a string of black ants playing follow-the-leader around puddles the day after a rainstorm. It was slightly longer but far more scenic.

He watched out the window as they crossed Rainy River, passed through St. Boniface, and entered a heavily wooded area surrounding the Lake of the Woods. The train left behind the open rolling countryside that was so unique to the Prairies. Jim's pocketbook was empty except for a card with his name and address on it and the ten-dollar bill. The key was for the front door at 167 Ottawa Street. His grandfather's pocket watch was still running, but he doubted it was three-thirty.

The train lurched forward and went into a bend. Jim, glad to have a window seat, watched black smoke from the locomotive curl upward and dissipate into the grey-blue sky. He caught a glimpse of the club car, two ahead of him — the car that only travelling salesmen, elderly widows, and nannies could afford to ride in. Looking over his shoulder, he saw a string of coach cars like the one he was in and several baggage cars pulling up the rear.

Once the train straightened out again, he guessed they were going about sixty miles an hour. It had been ages since he'd had a real conversation with anyone. Jim asked the conductor for the time to set his pocket watch. It worked like a charm. He'd grown accustomed to not knowing the time of day, the day of the week, or the date. Basic routines like guard changes had only provided an approximation.

> In the absence of calendars and clocks, the prisoner devised his own measure of time. The setting of the sun and the tolling of the bell marked another day. The fullness of the moon, a month. The slick of morning dampness on the walls of his cell meant autumn had returned. And when the water in his basin froze, he would know that winter had come.[2]

The railway crossed to the American side and ran through the state of Minnesota for about forty-five miles. Jim looked at the last of his belongings. He ran his fingers over the raised initials, *JC*, on his linen handkerchief like a blind man reading Braille, folded it, and put it in the breast pocket of his newly acquired suit. It seemed strange not to see K939 stamped on it.

They stopped in Minnesota long enough to pick up passengers at about half a dozen stations before crossing back to Canadian soil at Rainy River and heading to Fort Frances where the train filled its tanks from the waterspouts at the station. Jim could see the paper mill in the distance.

At four o'clock Tuesday morning they arrived in the "twin cities" of Port Arthur and Fort Williams (Thunder Bay today). He'd slept for a good portion of the last three hundred miles but woke up as soon as the gentle swaying of the train stopped. Jim was confused and uncertain where he was. There was no cell, bars, or graffiti on the walls, just brakemen in raincoats waving lanterns back and forth in the darkness, and then he remembered.

The train followed the shoreline past Black Bay and Nipigon Bay, skirting Lake Helen heading north toward Lake Nipigon and inland to the Longlac Station. From here they struck out in a southeastern direction. Jim began counting the number of stops as they were announced. "Hornepayne, Oba, Peterbell, and Gogama." After a while he lost count, but he figured once they got to Capreol, he was over halfway.

It was dusk by the time the train arrived in Capreol, an important divisional point on the CNR. The stop was longer in order to take on fuel and water as well as accommodate a number of passengers. They made a brief stop at the Sudbury Junction, at which point Jim dozed off. He vaguely remembered stopping at Parry Sound and Orillia.

The train lumbered into Toronto Union Station, a grey, ominous, tunnel-like structure at four o'clock Wednesday morning. "Last Stop! Union Station! Downtown Toronto! Union Station!" Jim began to feel anxious as he got off the train and found a bench near the empty depot marked "Hamilton." People seemed to be in a great hurry as indistinguishable announcements boomed over the loudspeakers.

The train arrived shortly and Jim boarded, along with a handful of others. It was the last leg of his journey. He found another window seat near the back. The train slowly crawled out of Union Station. It skirted around the grounds of the Canadian National Exhibition and crossed the Humber River. Just before Port Credit, Jim could see the rifle ranges used by the military forces of Toronto, immediately to the left of the railway. The tracks followed Lake Ontario's shoreline, a route that was remarkably flat yet very fertile, judging by the number of fruit-bearing orchards that flanked the railway. They made stops at Clarkson, Oakville, the fishing village of Bronte, and Burlington. As the sun came up, he noticed several fine looking golf links and clubhouses.

The choppy blue water of the Burlington Bay came into view. A freighter was in the harbour, probably full of coal from the Appalachian areas of Pennsylvania or delivering a load of iron ore. His surroundings were starting to look familiar. Jim knew that he was less than fifteen minutes from home when he saw the blast furnaces of the Steel Company. Home … what a strange sounding word.

He stared out the window, trying to take in as much as he could as the train quickly approached the steel city. It looked bigger than he'd remembered. A very tall building caught his eye. Jim had no idea that it was the Pigott Building, the newest, most impressive acquisition in the city, and Hamilton's first skyscraper. The train slowed down, seeming to be in no hurry. It made him feel impatient. He'd waited so long for this day to arrive. At 7:00 a.m. it sluggishly pulled into the Hamilton Station, braked several times, and finally came to a halt. There was a loud, steamy hissing sound, followed by silence.

Mary woke from a fitful broken sleep. She had relived the past three decades of her life, condensing them into the time frame of one night. It wasn't any wonder she still felt tired. She glanced at the clock, concerned that she'd overslept. Mrs. Lockwood wouldn't be very understanding if she arrived late and her morning routines were broken. She claimed that it put her "out of kilter" for the rest of the day.

Mary pushed back her comforter and leaned over to close the window. Mr. Morton was already tinkering in his garage and it was only just seven. The sky looked overcast and cloudy so she decided to take her umbrella to be on the safe side. With any luck she'd catch a streetcar right away. Mrs. Lockwood liked her to be there no later than eight o'clock to serve breakfast.

Every Wednesday the ironing had to be done before picking up groceries. She insisted on everything being fresh, which meant shopping three times a week. Mary didn't mind at all. When she was downtown she'd look for something for Ross. She had three more days, not counting today, until she got to see him again. She used to buy him socks or underwear, but he preferred a toy or a sweet. His favourite was "Bertie," a character made entirely from the individual candy pieces found in a bag of Bassett's Liquorice Allsorts. Mary tried not to take candy every week, sometimes choosing an inexpensive little toy at Woolworth's instead. He'd be seven this summer and she didn't want to ruin his permanent teeth.

It was one of those mornings that she had trouble getting out of bed. If she got behind with her chores, she'd be rushed all day. Mrs. Lockwood's evening meal had to be on the table at five o'clock sharp. Mary could never understand why ten minutes either way was so important.

Already running late, she dragged herself out of bed. Mary didn't have a good feeling about those dark clouds and wondered what the day would bring.

Jim gazed out the train window but all he could see was his own reflection in the glass. It was the first time he'd seen himself in four years. He took a good hard look, touching his unshaven face and wondered if she'd think he looked older. He quietly whispered, "I'm coming home Mary, I'm finally coming home."

It didn't take long for Jim to find out where she lived. For weeks he waited at Mary's bus stop when she returned home from work and begged her to take him back. She never did. After awhile he gave up hope and stopped waiting.

TWENTY-NINE

The Great Crash

> "During the summer and early fall of 1929 wheat prices on the Winnipeg Grain Exchange dropped off gradually. Then came Black Thursday, October 24, 1929, greatly influenced by the events of the preceding few days on New York's Wall Street. The following Monday saw the slide continue at an accelerating rate … and then came Tuesday, October 29, 1929 — the day of the Great Crash, the day the twenties flew apart."[1]

1930

The prosperity of the twenties contributed to a strange mix of technical advancements and financial ruin, which came to be known as "the dirty thirties." In later years, those who'd lived through the Great Depression criticized anyone who spent recklessly or refused to save for a rainy day.

Hamiltonians, like the rest of the world, lost their jobs without any warning or severance pay and had little security to fall back on. Some never worked the entire decade. Young people full of boundless energy and enthusiasm, having just graduated from school, were lucky to find jobs at the local soda shop or selling encyclopedias door-to-door.

More women found themselves in the workforce as the divorce rate increased. Although people tolerated this trend, a fair degree of scorn went along with it. Work camps were established in the country by the Department of National Defence to provide jobs for unemployed single men in an attempt to alleviate the growing number of transients and panhandlers in the big cities. Families who in the past would have been too proud to ask for handouts or second-hand clothes were grateful for them. People improvised with flour-sack lingerie and cardboard insoles. Soup kitchens, bread lines, and penny cigarettes were commonplace on the street.

The Depression didn't affect Mary as much as some. She was no stranger to hand-me-downs and doing without. Her prettiest dress, one of the few store bought that she owned, was the one Jim had insisted she buy almost a decade earlier. Her cotton voile peach chemise with the scooped neckline hadn't been worn for five years. Neither had the leather shoes with buttoned straps or bowler-shaped brimless cloche at the back of her closet. Women were starting to wear slacks and smoke in public but covered their bathing suits with short skirts. Mary never felt comfortable in pants and considered smoking a man's pastime. Men wore short pants called "plus fours" for golf and other casual occasions but it was still illegal for them to go topless in most places.

Mary continued to correspond with Emma, whose letters were mostly about her children and homesteading. Mary's were about Ross. Since she still wore her wedding band and hadn't gone back to her maiden name, she saw no reason to tell Emma the truth about her marriage. She longed to see her sister and hoped she'd keep her promise to come east for a visit someday.

The birth of the Dionne quintuplets near North Bay was timely since the world was eager for a distraction amidst the financial turmoil in 1934. No quints in the history of the world had ever survived for more than a few minutes. The girls became the world's youngest celebrities and a bigger tourist attraction than Niagara Falls. Advertisers grabbed the story of the "million dollar babies" and used it to their advantage to sell toothpaste, corn syrup, soap, and baby products. Even the Life Saver Company used the quints to promote their five famous flavours in one package.

Advertising in the thirties had to be dramatic and gimmicky to attract attention when money was so scarce. Mary looked longingly in a shop window at the new $125 refrigerator, an appliance slowly replacing the icebox. She knew others who were worse off. At least she could afford canned soup and the new wonder wrap called cellophane.

While people were forced to live hand-to-mouth, technology continued to forge ahead. Greater distances could be travelled by car and airplane, the telephone made it easier to communicate with families separated by many miles, and more houses were equipped with electricity. By the mid-thirties radio had come into its own and kept folks informed as well as entertained. The noisy crackly crystal sets were being replaced with more modern New Westinghouse Pilots and Stromberg-Carlsons. Not everyone could afford one, but there was

Mary posed for a photo beside the petunias in full bloom outside the Woods brothers' house at 265 James Street South, September 1934.

The Hewson Collection.

usually someone in the neighbourhood who could. When something big hit the news, people crowded around the little gadget that brought the world into their living room.

Mary would never forget listening to snippets of the 1936 Moose River Mine Disaster in Nova Scotia. She was working as a maid and cook for two bachelors and had a room at the back of their large house. During the live broadcast she happened to be in the dining room polishing silver, and when she was finished she decided to dust the tiny crystal droplets on the huge chandelier to stay within earshot.

J. Frank Willis from the Canadian Radio Broadcasting Commission had been sent to the site and was granted five minutes of airtime every half hour to broadcast the news. It meant that almost everyone in North America who could get to a radio could hear what was going on at the exact moment it happened. The Canadian Broadcasting Corporation (CBC) was born six months later. While few realized the political significance of broadcasting the mining disaster, everyone understood the power of radio.

Three years later, Mary, along with hundreds of others, got hooked on "The Happy Gang," a noon-day program full of music, banter, and jokes sent in by the public. The infamous knock on a door, someone answering, "Who's there?" and the predictable reply, "It's the Happy Gang!" gained unprecedented popularity. And her British roots were stirred as she fondly remembered the CBC broadcast covering the entire six-week royal tour of King George VI and Queen Elizabeth to Canada in 1939. She'd caught a glimpse of the royal couple during their tour when they paid an official visit to Hamilton's Market Square.

Mary worked for the Woods brothers until ill health forced them to sell their house and move into an old folks home. She had a number of domestic positions after that, but none were as fulfilling. Invariably, she had to move on when conditions became intolerable. Ross continued to live with Mrs. Harkness, and when he was old enough, got a job as a delivery boy. His father stayed in Hamilton and carried a note in his pocket: "If anything happens to me, contact Ross Church at Tamblyn's Drug Store, 753 King E." Mary never knew if Jim ever made any attempt to locate his son.

Jim died of heart problems in January 1939 and was buried beside Mona in the Hamilton Cemetery. For some strange reason Mary felt more alone after his death, even though she hadn't lived with him for almost fourteen years. Years later, Jim's uncle, Walter Church, was buried in the last family plot, which meant there'd be no room for her.

That fall Canada went to war. Six days after the British Prime Minister Neville Chamberlain admitted that he'd been unsuccessful in keeping his country out of war, Canada joined the fight against Germany. Canadians panicked just as they had during the First World War and stockpiled things like sugar and flour. Women took up the cause and began to knit, as young men hungry for employment poured into the cities to enlist. With a decade of high unemployment, the promise of clothes, boots, shelter, pay, and medical care led to over-crowded recruiting stations.

The Depression had left Canadians tired and desperate, but once the country was at war it seemed to make people feel more determined and less victimized. Prairie wheat prices rose and textile mills prepared themselves for the inevitable demand for an endless supply of uniforms and wearing apparel. Employment soared as Canada braced itself for the war. Hamilton's armouries downtown quickly filled with people willing to enlist — in the first ten days of the war 1,500 Hamiltonians enlisted. Orders for war materials such as guns, shells, and tank and airplane parts poured into Stelco and Dofasco.

At fifty-five, Mary didn't have the same energy that she'd had during the Great War and was struggling to make ends meet. This time she didn't join the local knitting club but helped the Red Cross wrap Christmas boxes to send overseas. Ross, now eighteen years old, joined the Air Force and was sent to England as a pilot and a gunner for the Air Sea Rescue. Mary was extremely proud of him and her letters out west invariably included tidbits about her son.

By the fall of 1941 the cost of living had risen considerably and Mary was finding it difficult to pay bills on time. Sales and excise taxes on phonographs, radios, cameras, cigarettes, and liquor were increased, which didn't affect her at all. But she was disappointed when the price of soda pop went from a nickel to six cents because carbonic acid gas was taxed more heavily. She loved the occasional ginger ale when she tired of her usual tea.

Ration booklets were issued for sugar, butter, tea, coffee, and meat. She was thankful the butter ration never fell below six ounces a week per person and the meat ration never less than two and a half pounds of the cheaper cuts. It helped that she knew the owner of the corner grocery store, and sometimes Mrs. Reynolds offered to sell her a tin of salmon from under the counter. This particular day she'd done just that. As Mary hurried home with her small brown bag, she was thinking about how different this war was from the first one.

During the First World War, the Fish Sales Branch was established under the provincial Department of Game and Fisheries. Their mandate was to secure fish and ensure that they were made available at fixed prices to Ontario consumers.[2] Mary had never been much of a fish eater but had little choice when it was so much cheaper than meat. Canadians had been on their honour to limit themselves to one-and-a-half pounds of butter per person per month. By October 1918, the ration had increased to two pounds per person. Mary remembered eating less "war bread" because it had substitutes for 20 percent of the flour. The hardships were

Courtesy of Gail Horner.

Walter Touchings (Emma's son) and Emma stood on the veranda of the four-bedroom house that Harry built in Elbridge, Alberta, in 1935. His brother Bob was sitting on his horse Pal near their 1928 Chevrolet.

worse then, but they didn't seem to bother her as much. At that time she was only thirty, preoccupied with her family, celebrating her tenth wedding anniversary, and excited about Emma getting married, which reminded her that it was her turn to write. Her sister had been happier since moving to their new home. Mary could only imagine the excitement of owning such a pretty two-storey house with a white-picket fence.

As Mary stepped off the curb, she heard a voice yelling, "Hey lady, watch out!" A car was rounding the corner and nearly hit her. She was thankful that a stranger was looking out for her. The world was becoming such a busy place. There were so few cars on the road twenty-five years ago and everything had been much simpler. Her life now revolved around her son and she anxiously waited for him to come home.

Ross returned in January 1944 after his plane crashed in England. A girl named Rene Enright, whom he'd never met but who had been writing to him for the past four years while overseas, met him at Sunnyside Station. She told him he'd be able to recognize her by her black coat with a silver fox fur collar and silver fox muff.[3]

On October 28, 1944, they were married in Toronto. Mary wore a long, two-tone purple gown and gave them a wedding gift of fifty dollars. As time went by, even though Ross lived in nearby Weston, he had little contact with his mother. Mary missed him terribly and regretted never having grandchildren.

In 1947, Emma and her husband moved to Victoria, British Columbia. Mary wasn't surprised; farming was hard work and they'd been looking forward to their retirement on the island. Harry passed away two years later.

Things were becoming harder for Mary. She was having difficulty finding work as a housekeeper or cleaning lady. "We're looking for someone much younger," was becoming an all too familiar response. In desperation, she found a job cleaning churches and schools at night. It was lonely, backbreaking work that began to take its toll as she grew older.

THIRTY
The Turning Point

"For the first five years of the forties, Canada had been occupied with the business of war, and for the remainder of the decade with the nuts-and-bolts of building factories and mills, homes and highways, and healthy bank balances."[1]

April 1948

Mary's life took an unusual turn in the spring of 1948. She was working as a visiting homemaker for the Red Feather Organization (today the United Way). She was out in the community helping others when she was no longer a young woman herself. At sixty-four she was beginning to feel her age.

She preferred part-time work but that wasn't always possible. A visiting homemaker had to be prepared to stay for as long as required. Mary took the bus to Houghton Avenue in the east end of the city to help a family who'd just had their second child, a little girl born at the Henderson Hospital. She walked up the street to the last house at the top of a slight incline. Mrs. Hewson greeted her at the door holding a tiny infant and with three-year-old Catharine hiding behind her skirt.

Mary, who went by Mrs. Church to strangers, was to help out with the new baby, do some light housekeeping, and prepare meals. She took to Mrs. Hewson right away. She seemed kind, easy to please, and insisted that Mrs. Church take a break mid-morning. They'd sit at the kitchen table while the baby napped and Catharine had a snack, and talk about the weather, the rising cost of food, or a favourite recipe. They seemed to have lots of things in common. Mrs. Church wasn't used to being treated like this. It didn't seem like a job, it felt more like a friendship. They even talked about going to church and she admitted that she should attend more often but found it difficult to go alone.

She was supposed to go every day for two weeks. Her favourite part of the day was caring for the newborn, the little girl who hadn't been given a name yet. Her parents finally decided to call her Mary and Mrs. Church couldn't have been happier. The time past quickly, which meant her visits were coming to an end.

Her last day was one she'd never forget. Mary was napping in the buggy on the front porch, diapers had been taken off the line, the kitchen floor scrubbed, and a meatloaf and sweet potatoes were ready for the oven. Mrs. Church slowly gathered up her sweater and purse. "I think everything is in order. Is there anything else you'd like me to do before I go?" she asked, as she'd done every afternoon before leaving. But today it had a different meaning.

Mrs. Hewson was sitting at the kitchen table with Catharine on her lap. "You've done more than enough. I don't know how to thank you. I'd love to have you stay on but it's not possible," she hesitated. "It's not just having a second pair of hands; I've enjoyed your company and you've taken such an interest in us. I'm going to miss that."

"I'll miss it too," she replied quietly. Mary felt uncomfortable not having had much practice sharing her emotions. "I'll see myself out," she said, turning to leave.

"But you could drop in some time to see how Mary's doing. It seems a shame that she'll never remember you."

"I'd like that."

"Why don't you meet us at Centenary United on Sunday and come home with us after church," she paused, "and stay for dinner?"

And that's how the two-week home care commitment became a rest of a lifetime friendship. Mr. Hewson would wait for her in the front vestibule so they could sit together in church while his wife sang in the choir, Catharine went to Sunday school and Mary stayed in the nursery. Then she'd spend the rest of the day with them and take the bus home after supper before it got dark. It meant that she rarely had to eat Sunday dinner alone, something she'd never enjoyed. She couldn't believe her good fortune to have met this kind family who had adopted her in a way.

While Mary was quite used to living alone and didn't mind her own company, there was something nice about leaving her tiny apartment on

The Hewson Collection.

In July 1948, Mary (Janeway) Church stood on the steps of Centenary Church with the Hewson family on Mary's christening day.

the weekends to spend time with the Hewsons. She liked helping in the kitchen, setting the table, or peeling potatoes and carrots for supper. She never waited to be asked, simply found a job and did it. It seemed as though she liked being busy but that was only part of the reason. It was important for her to feel that she'd earned her keep and would "never be beholding."

She truly belonged to a family now, like a grandma except that everyone called her Mrs. Church, including the parents. She took that as a sign of respect because of her age. After several months Mr. and Mrs. Hewson asked her to call them by their first names Bob and Gladys, the same day they asked her to be Mary's godmother.

As little Mary got older, she liked to snuggle up on the sofa with Mrs. Church to share one of her favourite books, *Dumpy the Turtle*, *Slappy*, or *Scuffy the Tugboat*. She never grew tired of the same stories, and although she couldn't read, knew immediately if something had been missed. Sometimes a grown-up would skip a page but not Mrs. Church; she had all the time in the world. Mary got her undivided attention and what could be better than that to a young child? Gladys could see a special bond developing between Mrs. Church and her younger daughter.

Mary would never forget the day that she got a message that they wouldn't be at church on Sunday. There'd been an accident and young Mary had been taken to the General Hospital. The thought of something happening to the little girl made her panic and brought back painful memories of losing her own daughter. Since she had no phone, she jumped on the bus and headed to the east end of the city, relieved to find out that the youngster was back home with only minor bumps and bruises. An Eaton's delivery truck had backed into her as she peddled her kiddie car across the driveway. An apology from the store manager, a reprimand to the driver, and a doll the same size as Mary was delivered the next morning. She was back to her usual self within a week and the ordeal was soon forgotten.

Occasionally, Mary visited the Hewsons on Saturday. The littlest member of the family would watch at the window mid-morning until she saw Mrs. Church coming and then head out to greet her. She'd grab her free hand, the one that wasn't carrying a purse, and almost pull her up the street. It was wonderful to be needed and made to feel so important. Mary had a soft spot in her heart for the little girl; after all, if it

The Hewson Collection.

During the summer of 1950 young Mary Hewson was taking her dolly for a walk in the stroller.

hadn't have been for her, she'd never have been there in the first place. She always spent the first little while with little Mary before sitting down with Gladys to catch up on things over a cup of tea.

"Lately I've been having a terrible time getting Mary to eat her supper. I don't know what the problem is," the young mother confessed.

"Maybe she just isn't hungry," Mrs. Church replied. "After all it's been warm lately and I find my appetite isn't the same." That evening not only did Mary refuse to eat supper, she wouldn't touch her dessert, which she usually devoured. A few days later the mystery was solved.

"Well, I found out why Mary isn't hungry," Gladys said, as she put the kettle to boil. "She's been going door-to-door asking for treats. Isn't she the limit?" she said, shaking her head.

Mrs. Church smiled, imagining how hard it would be to say no to the little fair-haired girl with big blue eyes. "Are you going to talk to your neighbours?"

"No, Bob made a typewritten sign that I pinned on her jacket, the navy corduroy one she always wears outside to play. It says, "Please do not feed cookies, chips, or candy." Thankfully she can't read yet."

It was little day-to-day things like this that made Mary's life more interesting. It didn't surprise her to hear that the little girl fired the cleaning lady the fall she started kindergarten. Apparently she'd overheard a conversation in which her mother said she wasn't happy with the woman but didn't have the heart to let her go. Gladys was almost relieved that her daughter had dealt with the situation but certainly wouldn't have admitted it.

Mary couldn't get over the young child's spunk and the way her parents dealt with it. She would never have gotten away with those things when she was growing up. Her life as a home child had been so different. Reflecting on her past, she realized how many things had changed since she was that age.

The 1950s were unfolding as a decade of prosperity, a time when people were becoming consumers instead of shoppers. The fifties introduced superhighways, suburbs, shopping plazas, and television, which most considered to be a "passing fancy" and only a slight improvement over the radio.

Who would have predicted that in less than two years over a million televisions would be purchased and people would sit for hours watching anything from health-remedy ads to westerns and cartoons? It was no surprise that television was responsible for closing two hundred movie houses in the first three years.

Mary remembered watching Percy Saltzman, the first Canadian to appear on television, talk about the weather. It was September 8, 1952, and she was working as a housekeeper for a family on Aberdeen Avenue. Working for the well-to-do helped her keep abreast of new technologies like the television. The growing popularity of TV dinners and TV tables meant no one had to miss anything on television during the supper hour; even the test pattern was considered a novelty. Not only were the lifestyles of Canadian families altered, their living rooms were rearranged to accommodate the "big box."

There were those who had a television and those who wished they could afford one. Shortly after they came out, Bob brought a small one home on loan, and it took up a central location on their dining-room table. Mary witnessed the excitement, but without an aerial or antennae they could only get one channel. The girls still sat there mesmerized by *Country Calendar*, a half-hour commentary on farm matters and gardening tips. The television was gone after a couple of weeks. After that the two girls went down the street to Donna Patton's house to see the *Howdy Doody* show. Mary remembered how reluctant Gladys had been, for fear they were taking advantage of their neighbour.

Mary continued to visit the Hewsons, especially looking forward to holiday weekends since it meant staying an extra day. She realized that she'd have been lonely if it hadn't been for them. Taking the streetcar to the market every Saturday and going home to cook for one was something she didn't miss, and she was thankful that she had much more than that to fill her days.

Bob and Gladys were thrilled when another baby came along; this time a little boy named John. A year later they sold their two-bedroom house and bought some land to build a home in the village of Stoney Creek. They hoped to move by the end of the summer, but if it wasn't quite ready they could always stay at their cottage on Lake Erie a little longer.

THIRTY-ONE

A Family at Last

"October 16, 1954: Hurricane Hazel hits central Ontario, flooding homes, roads and crops. The damages for Canada's worst recorded hurricane total $100 million and 80 fatalities are recorded."[1]

1954

Mary was turning seventy that summer and feeling very good. It was the last Sunday in June and she looked forward to her outing with the Hewsons, who were heading to Lake Erie in a few days. She only came to the cottage once a summer because she didn't like the heat and preferred to stay in the city. The outing became an annual event.

She'd always thought summer homes were for rich folks, like those in Goderich where she had worked as a domestic. But the Hewsons didn't act rich at all. It was far different to go to the lake as part of the family rather than work for them. The first time Bob took her out there she felt like royalty, having had few occasions for a ride in an automobile. The Lake Erie shoreline was interesting and the pretty countryside reminded her of the rural setting of Innerkip when she lived on the Jacques farm.

The Hewson Collection.

Mary Church enjoyed a stroll through the Royal Botanical Gardens, but was always a bit shy when asked to have her picture taken.

The white-framed cottage with bright green shutters wasn't exactly fancy but was homey and warm. Bob had built it himself piecemeal over the years. He was proud of its concrete foundation and flush toilet and didn't hesitate to point these features out to strangers. An old pine dinner bell beside the screen door had weathered many storms but Mary could still make out the inscription. A wooden table painted a glossy black swallowed up the tiny kitchen, and a big picture window in the living room overlooked the lake. Mary felt nostalgic when she saw the English-style fireplace with the silhouette of a lady's face imprinted on the wine-coloured mosaic tiles. It reminded her of her uncle's place in Lambeth, England. All that was missing was the coal hod, the black metal pail with a sloped lip for holding the fuel handy on the hearth. Little did she know that she'd be accompanying the family on many walks along the lakeshore over the course of time, looking for driftwood small enough to fit in the hob grate that had originally been designed to burn coal.

She could feel a sense of history in the little cottage the very first time she was there. Perhaps it was because she knew that Gladys had grown up on a farm in Nanticoke, a couple of miles down the road, and taught music in the country schools for years.

Mary was content to sit in the shade high up on the bank a safe distance from the water and watch the kids play on the beach. She'd never learned how to swim. Young Mary tried repeatedly to get her to go down to the beach and had about as much luck with that as she did trying to convince her parents to go swimming. It never occurred to her that they might be afraid of the water. It was a red-letter day when the entire family, with the exception of Mrs. Church, went for a dip, usually on the Labour Day weekend and only if there wasn't an offshore breeze.

This well-worn inscription on the old rural school bell at the Hewson's cottage had been engraved many years ago and reminded Mary of her school days at Blandford School S.S. No. 3, near Innerkip: "The Soul Of Music / Slumbers In The Shell / Ti'll wak'd And Kindled / By The Dinner Bell."

The Pettit Collection.

The summer that little Mary turned six, she finally got Mrs. Church down to the beach to sit at the water's edge. Mary was wearing a navy short-sleeve shirtwaist dress, a pearl necklace, and a floppy-brimmed straw hat. Gladys looked out her kitchen window and was shocked at what she saw.

"Bob, you're not going to believe it," she said, dropping the dishcloth and heading to the door for a closer look. "Mrs. Church has taken off her shoes and stockings and is dipping her feet in the lake. Next thing you know, our Mary will have her wading through the seaweed to catch frogs." Bob wasn't surprised at all. His younger daughter had a way with Mrs. Church that couldn't be explained.

When summer came to an end in 1954, their new house wasn't ready, so Bob boarded in the city, taught school, and worked evenings and weekends to finish their new home. The rest of the family stayed at the lake with a car that would only start in nice weather, a fireplace to take

The Hewson Collection.

Gladys Hewson, holding John in her arms, was taking daughters Catharine and Mary to school. Note the tin lunch boxes that the girls are carrying.

the chill out of the cottage, and no telephone. Times were simpler then. Gladys thought nothing of staying behind with her three children, ages one, six, and nine after all the cottagers left. The girls walked a couple of miles to the two-room rural school in Nanticoke when the car's engine wouldn't turn over.

That fall Mary missed her visits with the Hewsons, especially with young Mary, and anxiously waited for them to return. She knew they had to be back once the lake froze over since there'd be no water and not enough heat to keep them warm. It was mid-October when Hurricane Hazel came up through the States, hit South Carolina particularly hard, and headed for Toronto and Hamilton. The seriousness of this storm was downplayed until the wind and rain were out of control by eleven o'clock on Friday, October 15. Mary sat by her radio, sick with worry, not only for herself but the young family living out at Lake Erie.

The following day Hamilton reported heavy rainfall resulting in landslides on the Mountain brow, downed power lines from fallen trees, flooded underpasses, and cave-ins on James Street, and numerous flooded basements. There was no mention of how widespread the storm had been or how hard Lake Erie had been hit. It wasn't until later that she learned what had happened.

Bob was unable to get to his family and Gladys described how they huddled together under a blanket while the wind howled and tunnelled down the chimney. At one point she looked out on the water to see her neighbour's mahogany boat being ripped out of its hangar and crashing against the shore. She ran down to try to drag it up to where the beach had once been while Catharine, Mary, and John watched from the bank above. In hindsight, she realized how foolish she'd been to risk her own safety.

Two weeks later they closed the cottage and returned to the city to live in a rented house on Tuxedo Avenue until the end of the year. That Christmas Santa brought young Mary a double-gun holster set, an unusual request from a girl. Gladys made both her daughters poodle skirts and bought them pop-it beads to match. Mary was reminded how lucky the girls were to have such caring parents and how fortunate she was to be part of such a loving family.

Their new house was finally ready between Christmas and New Years. Mary had seen it several times under construction but was in awe of the spacious ranch-style home built halfway up the escarpment overlooking the Steel City. At night the lights were a breathtaking sight. The village of Stoney Creek, population of 4,000, became a town the following year, and Bob was elected to sit on the first council. It seemed like a good place to raise a young family. The girls could safely sleigh ride down the hill to the street below since there was virtually no traffic on the road.

Mary had concerns that she might be forgotten once the Hewsons moved and also realized friendships didn't always last forever. The letters she received from her family out west became increasingly more important as time went on. That year, her older sister Carrie died of a heart attack, which meant that she and Emma were all that was left of the Janeway family. However, her fears about not seeing the Hewsons were unfounded. She actually saw more of them after they moved. Bob got into the habit of picking her up on Friday night on his way home from school. She'd be sitting on the steps outside her rooming house, looking patiently down the street for his car.

After church they would drop her off on their way home. It meant eating Sunday night supper alone but it also meant she didn't have to take a bus, which was a strain on her pocketbook. It wasn't easy to say goodbye and head up the steps to her tiny apartment, but she was used to her own company and adamant about not becoming a burden on anyone. However, living alone was quite different than living with a busy family of five, and she looked forward to the weekends with anticipation.

A toddler and a brand new home kept Gladys busy and Catharine was old enough to visit her friends. That meant there were many opportunities for Mary to spend time with her goddaughter. They'd sit with one of her favourite storybooks, go for a walk into town, or head to the nearby Devil's Punch Bowl to see the huge waterfall tumbling over the escarpment. Young Mary would never have been able to venture that far without an adult and her parents were much too busy. It was on these occasions that she began to ask questions. Sometimes they'd come right out of the blue and others times there'd be a reason.

"Do you like your name?" she asked Mary one day as they headed to the IGA for some hamburger buns.

"Church?"

"No, your first name," she replied impatiently.

"Why, it's the same as yours."

"I know. I think it's kind of plain, don't you?" she asked squinting in the sun.

"It's all right," Mary replied. She'd never felt comfortable talking about herself and hoped that this would be the end of it.

"What's your middle name?" the girl persisted.

"I don't have one."

"You don't?"

Mary shook her head.

"Why not?"

"I'm not sure," she replied. Young Mary assumed that everyone had a second name and while she'd never been crazy about her own, at least she had one. Luckily, they reached the store and the topic was forgotten. On another outing, she wanted to know all about her godmother's wedding. Mary tried to say as little as possible, just enough to satisfy the girl's curiosity.

Mary was at the Hewson's the weekend Eaton's delivered a brand new, Viking console, monochrome, Electrohome television made of solid mahogany. It was given a prominent position in the living room. Bob and Gladys wanted their children to enjoy this new form of entertainment but didn't want their lives to revolve around the "big box." They had some television rules that their daughter was anxious to share.

"Mom says piano and homework aren't going to suffer because of the television, so we can't watch any during the week. We get an hour on Friday, another one on Saturday, and that's it!" she said, counting with her fingers and crossing her arms. "And the *Ed Sullivan Show* at eight o'clock on Sunday night if we're ready for bed and have our teeth cleaned," she added, letting out a big sigh.

"Well that seems fair to me," Mary replied.

"I'm going to pick my shows very carefully so I don't waste my time. Oh, and we're not allowed to eat or chew gum in the living room either," she said, rolling her eyes. Her goddaughter tended to be a bit dramatic but invariably amused Mary. She could learn a great deal by spending five minutes with her even though her version of any story, conversation, or problem on that particular day was sometimes different than her mother's.

Christmas became one of Mary's favourite holidays after she met the Hewsons. She'd come home with them after the Christmas Eve service at Centenary United and would stay for three or four days. She loved watching the children open their gifts, which reminded her of how important Santa was to young children. Gladys always gave her practical gifts, a hand-knit scarf, a pair of woollen gloves, postage stamps, and a book of HSR tickets. She never would have insulted Mary by giving her money.

On Christmas Day, Bob would offer her an alcoholic beverage. "Can I pour you a little glass of sherry?"

"Well I guess a little won't hurt," Mary would say, seeming a bit flustered, but decided that since it was a special occasion, she would imbibe. Young Mary watched her father pour this orangey-red liquid in the tiniest glass and her godmother would make it last over an hour. Then he'd asked her if she would like more.

"No, Bob, you're getting me all fired up," Mary would reply, her cheeks having turned scarlet red.

That spring Mary fell ill and wasn't well enough to visit. Bob and Gladys insisted she see her doctor where she was diagnosed with abdominal cancer. Although their daughter was never told the seriousness of her illness, she had surgery and recovered quite quickly, thankful that she wasn't alone and had the Hewson's support throughout.

Mary's visits to Stoney Creek continued to make her feel needed and loved. She could always count on her goddaughter to lift her spirits. It amazed her how often that little girl with the French braids could make her laugh.

"Did you ever really really want something when you were little and you didn't get it?" young Mary asked one day, suddenly stopping in the middle of a hopscotch game with her hands on her hips and feet firmly planted on the numbers seven and eight.

"I'm sure I must have," Mary replied, knowing full well that she was waiting to be asked the same question.

"Me too. I always wanted a wading pool, a three-ringer just like the one Gail Fernihall had."

"But you've got a whole lake at the cottage."

"That's exactly what my mom said," she replied with a big sigh, jumped on number nine with one leg, scooped up the chalk, and continued on with her game. Not only did Mary find her goddaughter interesting, but also her sister. For the longest time she didn't know that Catharine would only eat grapefruit when Mary was there to prepare it.

"I love the way you cut grapefruit, it's so easy to eat," Catharine admitted one morning. "Mom says it takes too much time to cut it on both sides and she never peels celery either," she added with a mouthful of grapefruit. Luckily, Gladys wasn't in earshot.

Shortly after that Catharine came to visit her at her rooming house. Her sister wanted to go too but her parents felt she was a bit young and two girls might be more than Mrs. Church could handle. They went to the market to buy leaf lettuce. Catharine came home with a full report.

"For lunch we had a big blob of English salad dressing rolled up in that special lettuce and stewed rhubarb with lots of sugar that was frosty from being in the fridge. And Mrs. Church had the most beautiful green and rose tablecloth and it wasn't even Sunday."

Later, Gladys relayed Catharine's story to Mary and how much she'd enjoyed her visit. These little reminders told her that she was appreciated and loved. Who would ever have thought it came down to the way she prepared grapefruit, celery, and stewed rhubarb?

After a weekend away, Mary's daily life seemed almost too calm, too tranquil, but as she grew older, she began to appreciate the quiet times as well. When she was alone, she had time to think about the family she'd grown to love. As she washed her supper dishes or got ready for bed she'd reflect on some little thing that had happened while she was there.

Some memories stood out more than others, like the time Gladys told her about young Mary's bursting in while she was having tea with Sadie Brooks next door at the cottage. She was very sorry that she'd "accidentally poked her sister in the behind with a meat fork." Mary could hardly keep from smiling as she tried to imagine the look on Mrs. Brook's face.

Then there was the summer the houseflies were such a problem that the girls were paid a penny for every ten they caught in the cottage. They kept track of the number on their little blackboard. Who would have thought that young Mary would hold the screen door open and invite them in so Catharine could swat them? Mary liked the fact that her goddaughter trusted her enough to confide in her and came to the conclusion that it was children that made life interesting, some more than others.

The following year, 1957, Mary's sister came for a visit. Emma arrived by train from Edmonton, stayed a few days with her, then continued on to Detroit to visit some friends. Mary wished that her apartment had been fancier and a bit bigger. Emma was excited to see the Royal Botanical Gardens, a world-famous landmark in Hamilton. She asked a passer-by to take their photo and it found a special place on her sister's sideboard.

That same spring the Hewsons went to the local SPCA and came home with a chubby little reddish-brown cocker spaniel with long floppy ears. Mary often went with her goddaughter when she took Chum out for some much needed exercise.

"Did you have a dog when you were growing up?" she asked, as they headed down the street.

Mary was always careful what she said since her young namesake was extremely inquisitive. "No, but I had a cat named Mustard."

The little girl brightened up and fired a series of questions at her. The last one was the hardest to answer. "Did your mother let him sleep in your bedroom?" she asked innocently.

Instead of explaining that she wasn't with her family but was a live-in servant, she simply said, "No, Mustard was a barnyard cat and slept in the loft. He was never allowed inside."

"That's awful," she replied indignantly. "Why would your mom be so mean?"

"She had allergies, it wasn't her fault," Mary quickly replied. It was true that Mrs. Jacques had allergies, but she certainly wasn't her mother.

"At least she had a good reason. Mom won't let Chum in our room because she says bedrooms are for people, not animals. I think that's silly. Dogs aren't much different than us; they don't want to sleep in the basement," she said rather indignantly.

Courtesy of Gail Horner.

Mary enjoyed Emma's visit but felt sad when she left, knowing that it was unlikely she would ever see her again. The photo was taken in 1957 at Royal Botanical Gardens in Hamilton.

Mary spent many Saturday afternoons sitting in a lawn chair watching the girls play tag or skip. When young Mary was alone, she'd tie one end of the rope to the garage door handle, ask her godmother to turn the other, and count by twos so she could skip on the driveway. On one of these occasions she asked her if she and Catharine could call her "Nana." Mary never knew what prompted the question but was delighted. Unfortunately, the girls found it hard to change her name after calling her Mrs. Church for so long and it didn't help that their parents called her that as well. The use of Nana was short-lived and the girls went back to what they'd always called her, but Mary knew how they felt and that's all that mattered.

Mary loved to sit on a little stool at one of the long family room windows and watch them play outside while she peeled apples or peaches, darned socks, or shelled peas. No one could ever recall seeing her sit there with idle hands. Bob was convinced that there never would have been as many pies for dessert if it hadn't been for Mrs. Church.

The Hewsons found a local church in their new town, which was more convenient than traipsing into the city every Sunday morning, but Bob continued to pick up Mary on Friday night on his way home from work and she'd stay for the weekend. Sometimes she took the bus home, other times Bob drove her home on Sunday night, especially if it was dark. His young daughter always went with them.

If for some reason he couldn't pick her up after school, they'd go on Saturday morning. Young Mary hoped that one day her godmother wouldn't be out front waiting so she could knock on her door and catch a glimpse of her apartment. But she was always sitting on the steps outside. Mary was a private person and didn't want to share the details of her living arrangements. She never mentioned the other tenants in her rooming house; it was as though they didn't exist.

Mary changed her address every couple of years or so. She'd say that "a better situation had come up" or that she wanted to be closer to the bus route, but every rooming house looked the same from the outside. They were tall, narrow buildings on busy streets in the heart of the city. There was never a discussion about whether she'd come to live with them. There seemed to be an understanding that Mrs. Church would have politely refused if she'd been invited.

As they rounded the corner on this particular day, the little girl could see her perched on the top step wearing a gray hat, her purse looped through one arm, and her little royal-blue suitcase sitting beside her. She wore that hat with the netting and shiny pin on it wherever she went, even on a picnic.

Stoney Creek, a little town tucked underneath the escarpment, had lots of interesting places that were perfect for a picnic. Whenever the children struck out for a picnic, Mary went too, when she was visiting. It was obvious she didn't want to be left behind by her comments: "I wouldn't mind going, the exercise would be good for me," or "I'm sure the fresh air will do me a world of good." It was an unusual sight to see a woman in her seventies, wearing a pillbox hat, head for the escarpment with a picnic basket in hand and several children in tow. She was like a mother duck taking her goslings to the creek for a swim, and she couldn't have been happier.

Picnics were fancier when Mary went along. She made the most delicious egg or ham sandwiches on whole wheat. Young Mary would have preferred white bread but her mother refused to buy it. She'd put pickles in a small Tupperware container, fill a thermos with milk, wash a few apples, and never forget to pack serviettes. The children thought it was wonderful. It was a whole meal away from home. When Mrs. Church wasn't there, they made peanut butter and jelly sandwiches and threw them in a bag.

Mary always wore a dress or a skirt and blouse, never pants. The only time she left her purse behind was on a picnic. She had one pair of black shoes, with two straps across the top, and a slight heel to compensate for being so short. When her goddaughter asked her why she always wore the same pair, she explained that shoes were expensive so she'd chosen a serviceable pair that would do for every occasion. The little girl had no idea what that meant.

Once in the woods, they'd follow the creek bed to one of their usual spots and set up camp. A place would be cleared for a blanket under the shade of a large tree. Mary was content to sit and watch them skip stones in the creek or play tag until they got hungry. She was in charge of the food basket. It was as if they each had their own jobs to do without anyone giving orders, like camp minus the rules.

The spring that young Mary turned nine she perfected the art of balancing on top of those shiny, skinny, railway tracks that ran parallel to the woods. Her godmother never said things like, "that's dangerous, you'll trip and fall" or "I'm afraid you'll sprain your ankle." It seemed like everything the child did was fine with her.

After they'd gone on a number of picnics, Mary suggested taking hot dogs and building a fire. The children thought this was a marvellous idea since they didn't get to eat them very often at home because their dad said they weren't real food. They'd gather kindling for a fire and pile up leaves to smother it out when the time came to leave. Mary liked to be near the creek in case they needed water. It was understood that she'd handle the matches and start the fire. When there was a breeze it was tricky so they'd all hover around to provide enough shelter for the paper to catch on fire and start the kindling. There was nothing more delicious than a hot dog blackened on an open fire and smothered in ketchup.

On one picnic they had no luck with the fire because it had rained the previous day. Since Mrs. Church said the hot dogs were already cooked so it wouldn't hurt to eat them cold, they indulged in a new treat. But young Mary never told her mother for fear she'd never be allowed a picnic with hot dogs again.

There was always a feeling of sadness when it was time to pack up and go home. Once their picnic was over, half the weekend was gone, which meant that Mrs. Church would be leaving the next day. Young Mary actually preferred picnics with just the two of them. She could see her friends any time, but Mrs. Church wasn't always there. It was obvious that a special bond was growing stronger between them. As she grew older, she became more inquisitive and asked her mom to tell her stories about when she first met Mrs. Church.

"She was anxious to please and never refused any job, big or small. I'm sure she had her favourites but never made it obvious with one exception … you," Gladys said. "She'd drop anything if you cried or needed attention. She was good to Catharine too, but you could tell she had a weakness for babies, well one baby for sure!"

"Was it because she didn't have any of her own?" Mary asked innocently.

"That's what I thought until recently when she told me about her son and daughter. Mona had polio and died when she was seventeen. Ross was married and living in Weston but she hardly ever heard from him. I never asked her why. I figured she'd have told me if she wanted me to know." She looked at her daughter. "Mary, promise me you won't ask her," she said firmly. Mary nodded reluctantly.

She kept her word but it didn't stop her from being curious about other things. She learned that Mrs. Church's mother had died when she was five and she had two brothers, an older sister, and a baby sister named Emma. She assumed they must have lived far away since she never talked about them and spent most weekends and holidays with her family.

Over time Mary's stays grew longer. It seemed that she wasn't anxious to leave. Sometimes Bob would pick her up on a Thursday after school or take her home Monday night. She liked being part of the Sunday night Hewson ritual of watching the *Ed Sullivan Show*. She remembered seeing Johnny Wayne and Frank Schuster, two well-known Canadian comedians, make their first appearance one Sunday evening in 1958. They had signed a twenty-six-appearance contract on one of the most popular TV shows in America.

The girls liked it when she stayed a few extra days because their lunch would be ready when they came home from school. Their mom always seemed to be doing a hundred things at once, and if lunch wasn't ready they had to do fifteen minutes of piano practice while she made it. There's nothing worse for a kid than to be starving and have to set the metronome and practise scales. That never happened when Mrs. Church was there. And she wasn't in the habit of listening to "The Happy Gang" on the radio like their mother, which meant they didn't have to whisper. All around it was more fun!

As the children grew older, Bob and Gladys would leave them with Mary for a whole day and once in a while overnight. The girls loved it because she never seemed to be concerned how much time they practised the piano or if they accidentally set the kitchen timer for five or ten minutes less. They were allowed to stay up later than their usual bedtime and she'd make whatever they wanted to eat even if all three of them wanted something different. It was like going to a restaurant. When Mrs. Church was left in charge it felt like no one was the boss.

THIRTY-TWO
A Milestone

"By the late 1950s and early '60s, the deterioration downtown had set in to such an extent that stores were sitting vacant, movie theatres had emptied, and even the market was losing business. The once jammed, noisy, downtown streets that had so much life and vitality were showing clear signs of decay. People were simply not coming downtown in the numbers that they once had, and it was generally agreed that something dramatic had to be done to attract them once again."[1]

1959

Mary was seventy-five when she stopped working. Ever since her surgery she'd been having dizzy spells and problems with her balance. The doctor thought it was best for her to slow down.

With reluctance she gave up her job looking after an elderly lady, only four years older than herself. She'd have to be extra careful living on a fixed income based solely on old age security. Her room on West

Avenue cost $32 a month, which was a great deal but its central location meant that she didn't have to take the bus as often.

She wouldn't miss having to be up and out the door by 8:30 to care for Mrs. Whitaker, but would have a great deal of time to fill now that her days were her own. She'd have been much lonelier without the Hewsons, and, as she put it "was glad they'd taken her under their wing." It was comforting to know that someone was looking out for her.

After quitting her job she found herself more rested and ready to enjoy her weekends. Sometimes Bob and Gladys invited her to go with them to the Hamilton Philharmonic Orchestra or the Players' Guild once Catharine was old enough to babysit. She enjoyed these outings but would have been just as happy to stay home with the children.

In April, young Mary turned eleven and wanted a red skort for her birthday. Gladys worked well into the evenings after her daughter had gone to bed to make the little, permanent pleated skirt without the help of a pattern. Mary sensed the child's disappointment when she opened the gift, and remembered when she was that age how much she'd wanted something store-bought too.

That year ringlets were all the rage for young girls. Gladys tried to please her daughter but her expertise was in French braids, not ringlets. Mary came to her goddaughter's rescue. The two of them went down to the basement and sorted through rag boxes to find a piece of old flannel bed sheet. She ripped it into narrow strips, dampened the girl's thick shoulder-length hair, and section by section rolled it up in the rags, tying each one into a little knot. She was sceptical when she looked in the mirror at her head covered in white cotton bobbles, but the next morning was thrilled with the perfect springy coils that bounced when she walked.

Mary also helped out with "dish duty." Gladys insisted it wasn't her job but the girls were relieved to be off the hook.

"If we had a dishwasher like some of our neighbours, nobody would have to do them," Catharine said. Her sister nodded in agreement. "It would save at least a half an hour every night after supper," she added.

"A dishwasher's nothing more than a dirty-dish cupboard," Mrs. Church replied, grabbing the tea towel. The girls laughed as they hurried out of the kitchen but didn't change their mind about wanting one. She was reminded of this conversation when she cleaned up after supper in her own place. Washing a dinner plate, one fruit nappy, and a cup and saucer was hardly worth mentioning.

Bob and Gladys were adamant that Mary not be alone on her seventy-fifth birthday. She spent it at the lake with everyone except Catharine who was away at Sparrow Lake Camp. She recalled it being a beautiful summer day and Gladys not letting her help prepare the meal. While she did insist on husking the corn while she sat outside in the sun, she did relinquish peeling potatoes and setting the table. Her goddaughter decided that candles in the shape of a seven and a five would have to do since seventy-five of them wouldn't fit on the cake. She reminded her to make a wish before blowing them out. Mary felt like someone had turned back the clock and she was a young schoolgirl once again.

She'd never been comfortable being the centre of attention, but young Mary explained that that was the best part about being "the birthday girl." Gladys gave her a pink and gray paisley scarf and a book of bus tickets, but the present that meant the most was the one from her goddaughter.

The Hewson Collection.

In 1959, Mary Church, Gladys, Mary, Bob, and John, holding his fishing rod, posed for Mary's seventy-fifth birthday at the Hewson family cottage on Lake Erie. Note that Gladys is holding Mary Church's hand.

"I hope you like it, I chose it all by myself," the girl said, handing her an odd-shaped package wrapped in pale blue tissue paper.

"I'll like it because you gave it to me," Mary said, looking at her and slowly unwrapping it, trying hard not to tear the paper so it could be used again.

"Rip it open," she said impatiently. It was a forty-nine-cent bottle of pink Angel Skin hand cream that she'd bought at the drugstore with her own allowance. "This is the best part," she said, moving closer, removing the cap, and putting it under her nose. "What do you smell?"

Mary shook her head, having trouble identifying the sickly sweet odour emanating from the unusual shaped bottle.

"Maraschino cherries," young Mary told her, matter-of-factly.

"That's it," Mrs. Church replied tactfully, "I knew it was familiar." It was far from her favourite fragrance, but would never have admitted that to the little girl she'd grown so fond of.

The year that young Mary turned twelve she was allowed to visit Mrs. Church in her second-floor apartment on King Street. Her godmother was waiting for her on the steps outside. Her apartment consisted of a tiny kitchen, sofa, coffee table, and in the far corner, an iron bed painted brown, a pine dresser with an oval mirror, a squatty glass lamp, and a chair. She was shocked to find that the whole apartment was in one room, but thought it was quite unique that Mrs. Church shared a bathroom down the hall with two other tenants.

She recognized the floral oil tablecloth from her sister's description and a cross-stitch picture of a cottage with "The road to a friend's house is short" embroidered underneath, and was fascinated looking at the knickknacks and trinkets. A ginger-coloured ceramic cat curled into a tight ball appeared to be asleep on a shelf beside a miniature rosebud tea service for two. She mouthed the words as she read several hand-embroidered sayings framed like pictures on the wall: "Love goes where it's sent," "One good turn deserves another," "A stitch in time saves nine."

"I don't know what that means," she said, pointing to the last one.

"If you sew something right away before the hole gets too big, it's easier to fix."

"But if you keep fixing things, you never get anything new."

"New costs money," Mary replied quietly.

A Bible was sitting on her dresser. Mary explained that it'd been a gift from the rector at St. Paul's in Innerkip when she was a young girl about her age and over the years she'd taken to tucking little things between the pages.

"Like what?"

Mary had never shown anyone before. She moved to the sofa and her goddaughter sat down beside her.

"This is a list of the books of the Bible," she paused. "I had to memorize it at the orphanage." Young Mary was tempted to say something but had promised her mother she wouldn't ask Mrs. Church any personal questions. "And here's a bookmark I got from the London Public Library in 1901, long before you were born." As she continued to leaf through, a narrow strip of faded yellow and blue paper woven together fell on the floor. Mary bent down and picked it up.

"That was Ross's first piece of artwork when he was in kindergarten. Ross is my son," she replied sadly, tucking it away. A tattered scrap of paper was sticking out near the back. "It's a poem, 'The Man At The Gate,' one of my favourites," Mary said, closing the book. "Why don't we have some tea?"

After boiling water in her tiny whistling kettle she made a pot of Earl Grey tea and some Ovaltine for her guest, who didn't really like it but was resolved that anything tasted better when it was served in a cup and saucer. She ate five social tea biscuits and her godmother never said a thing.

Young Mary peered out the tall, skinny window that overlooked the alley and realized that had it been open she could have touched the next building. What she didn't notice was Mrs. Church's blue suitcase tucked safely under her bed. At one time it signified being ready for flight, a habit ingrained in her from childhood. Now it was simply a practical place to store it in her small one-bedroom apartment.

They walked downtown, spending most of their time in Woolworth's, a store she had only been in a few times. She felt overwhelmed as they slowly made their way up and down the aisles. She'd brought her

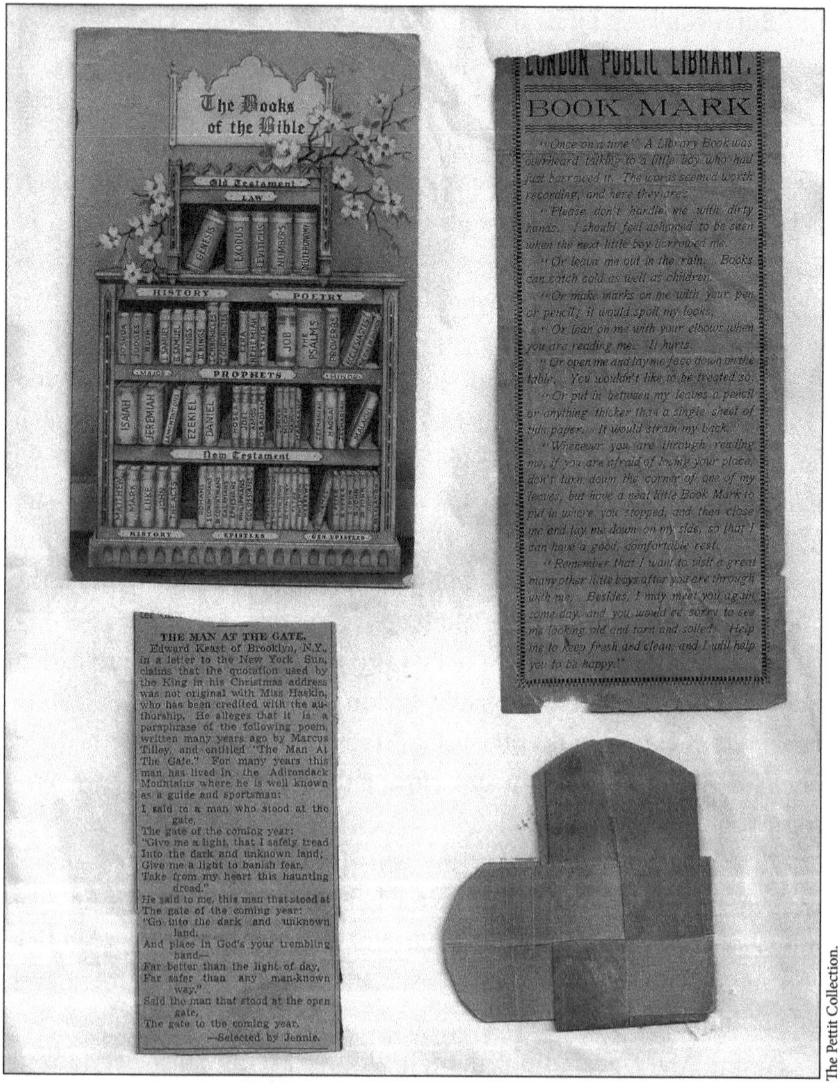

THE MAN AT THE GATE.

Edward Keast of Brooklyn, N.Y., in a letter to the New York Sun, claims that the quotation used by the King in his Christmas address was not original with Miss Haskin, who has been credited with the authorship. He alleges that it is a paraphrase of the following poem, written many years ago by Marcus Tilley, and entitled "The Man At The Gate." For many years this man has lived in the Adirondack Mountains where he is well known as a guide and sportsman:

I said to a man who stood at the gate,
The gate of the coming year:
"Give me a light, that I safely tread
Into the dark and unknown land;
Give me a light to banish fear,
Take from my heart this haunting dread."
He said to me, this man that stood at
The gate of the coming year:
"Go into the dark and unknown land,
And place in God's your trembling hand—
Far better than the light of day,
Far safer than any man-known way."
Said the man that stood at the open gate,
The gate to the coming year.

—Selected by Jennie.

LONDON PUBLIC LIBRARY.

BOOK MARK

"Once on a time" A Library Book was overheard talking to a little boy who had just borrowed it. The words seemed worth recording, and here they are:

"Please don't handle me with dirty hands. I should feel ashamed to be seen when the next little boy borrowed me.

"Or leave me out in the rain. Books can catch cold as well as children.

"Or make marks on me with your pen or pencil; it would spoil my looks.

"Or lean on me with your elbows when you are reading me. It hurts.

"Or open me and lay me face down on the table. You wouldn't like to be treated so.

"Or put in between my leaves a pencil or anything thicker than a single sheet of thin paper. It would strain my back.

"Whenever you are through reading me, if you are afraid of losing your place, don't turn down the corner of one of my leaves, but have a neat little Book Mark to put in where you stopped, and then close me and lay me down on my side, so that I can have a good, comfortable rest.

"Remember that I want to visit a great many other little boys after you are through with me. Besides, I may meet you again some day, and you would be sorry to see me looking old and torn and soiled. Help me to keep fresh and clean, and I will help you to be happy."

The Pettit Collection.

The memorabilia found in Mary's childhood Bible express her sentimental nature, particularly when it came to her son. Note how intricate the bookmark artwork would have been for a five-year-old child.

allowance and finally settled on a small red leatherette change purse and a package of butterscotch drops. Mrs. Church was so patient and didn't seem bothered that it took her almost an hour to make up her mind.

For dinner they had rice, green beans, turnips, and a cottage roll. Dessert was raspberry junket. She was surprised that Mrs. Church said grace since it wasn't Sunday.

"Do you say grace every night?" she asked, having completely forgotten her promise not to ask personal questions.

"It's important to be thankful every day, not just the Lord's Day," Mrs. Church replied. Mary nodded, and ate everything on her plate except the turnip, which she found to be bitter. She poked it around with her fork hoping it would look like some had been eaten.

"It's all right. What suits one doesn't suit another." She liked Mrs. Church's expressions; she didn't always understand them, but they always made her think.

By the second visit, Mary had moved to Ottawa Street in the east end of the city. Her apartment was on the second floor again, but had two, tall, skinny windows, making it brighter than the last one, but she still shared a bathroom down the hall. Mrs. Spink, her landlady, lived in the apartment directly below. This time Mary had her own refrigerator, a second-hand Kelvinator she'd bought for $120, which meant that she could buy a little more produce at the market without it going bad.

THIRTY-THREE

The Final Chapter

"What happened in the historical sixties is that the world changed. A great many issues that had been fermenting near the surface of society for twenty years or more erupted at more or less the same time. There was undreamed of affluence, and that meant survival for almost everyone was assured. There was the gathering pace of the technological revolution which — under the guise of automation — irrevocably changed the nature of work. Women began to demand a new place in society — a place equal to man's."[1]

1961

High-rise apartment buildings began to change Hamilton's skyline, and the one-way street system introduced five years earlier had eliminated some of the congestion downtown. The majority of average Canadian families owned a television set. Paperback books sold for under a dollar, and folksingers like Gordon Lightfoot and Joni Mitchell were making a hit. Men's hairstyles got shorter and women wore their hair shoulder-length.

The Hewson Collection.

Grandma Lindsay, Mary Church, and Bob Hewson with children Mary and John stand in front of the family home in Stoney Creek, 1961. Mary Church is wearing clear-coloured galoshes, a popular yet practical solution to winter footwear.

The Hewson Collection.

Mary Church posed for a picture beside Gladys Hewson's dark-green Morris Minor before heading back to the city, 1961.

Mary never took to the "teased" or backcombed look of the new hairdos, but didn't mind the calf-length sack dresses. She spent the Easter weekend with the Hewsons and Gladys's mother, who came for a visit. She didn't use a cane and had so much energy that thirteen-year-old Mary considered her quite a bit younger than her "real" grandmother.

That summer both sisters were at camp when Mary came to the cottage. It didn't feel like she was imposing as much since the girls didn't have to give up their bedroom. She was slowing down and knew that this would probably be her last trip to the lake. Lately she'd been reflecting on the past, and while she'd had her share of sadness, the last twenty years had been kind to her. She was content with her life and had no regrets.

She'd not only watched a young family grow, she'd been part of it. Over the years Bob had changed schools, become a principal, and worked hard as a town councillor while Gladys stayed home to raise their children, sang in the church choir, and sold Tupperware to buy a piano. She was grateful to have found herself in the midst of a close-knit hard-working family. In many ways she felt that they'd kept her young in spirit, especially her goddaughter.

Mary, now seventy-seven years old, had been worried about living alone for some time. Bob assured her that when she felt the time was right he would help her. That fall he made arrangements for her to move into Idlewyld, a home for the aged on Hamilton Mountain. She no longer had to worry about taking care of herself and making ends meet.

It was late October when she settled into her new surroundings, bought a portable Fleetwood TV for $169, and felt comfortable. She continued her visits to Stoney Creek for a while but began to find it too tiring. She was just as happy to go for a short car ride and be taken back home. Young Mary was growing up and in the last few years had become less dependent on her. It was something she hated to admit but knew it was just as well.

In 1963, when her goddaughter turned fifteen, the Beatles' first big hit, "She Loves You," rocketed the top four from Liverpool to international stardom. Mary couldn't understand what all the fuss was about. The teen was awestruck with the four mop-haired boys from England, bought every one of their records, and couldn't remember being happier.

But that same year Mary Church became very ill, and young Mary couldn't remember a time she'd been sadder. The doctors said the cancer had come back.

In November, Mary went to the Henderson Hospital on the mountain for a series of cobalt bomb treatments that left her tired and frail. It was a sad Christmas for the Hewson family. Her days were numbered. Mary Janeway Church died on February 21.

Just several months shy of her sixteenth birthday, her goddaughter had never lost anyone close to her. She felt a tremendous sense of emptiness and wanted to know more about Mrs. Church after she'd passed away. Her father told her that she'd been separated from her family as a little girl after her mother died and sent to an orphanage in Liverpool. She had come to Canada as a home child. He explained that home children were orphans or had parents unable to look after them and were sent across the ocean in hopes of a better life. Mary shook her head, trying to imagine what it would be like to be separated from her family and sent far away.

"Why didn't she ever talk about it?"

"I'd known her almost ten years before she said anything to me," her father replied.

"Why?"

"Being a home child wasn't something that people talked about. I got the sense she was embarrassed that her father couldn't take care of her. She didn't want you to know for fear it would upset you. Mrs. Church always worried about everybody but herself. That was her way."

Mary nodded. "Please tell me everything. I think I'm old enough to know," she said, slowly sitting down at the table across from her father.

"Her name was Mary Janeway. She was placed with a family on a farm by the name of Jacques," he hesitated as though he were collecting his thoughts. "She was expected to be up by six, bring in the wood, light the fire in the winter, fetch the water, and feed the dogs before the rest of the family got up. If she were lucky, she'd be allowed to go to school, a two-mile walk down the road." Mary shook her head in disbelief.

"She wasn't always treated kindly, was overworked, and sometimes went hungry. She suffered terrible bouts of loneliness and longed to be reunited with her family in England," he paused. "Mrs. Church made it very clear that she wasn't complaining, just describing her childhood and how much she missed her family. She often told me how lucky you, John, and Catharine were to have each other."

Mary realized now why Mrs. Church had been reluctant to talk about her past and would say things like, "I never want to be a burden, I know my place," or "I wouldn't mind coming along if I won't be in the way."

"What happened to her?"

"She was exactly your age when she decided to run away," Bob said quietly, looking at his daughter. "A week before her sixteenth birthday, she hitched a ride into town and took a train heading for London." It made Mary sad to think that anyone could treat a child that way, especially the kind, caring lady that she'd known. It also made her realize how brave Mrs. Church had been to leave. Mary wondered if she would have been as strong as Mary Janeway.

Her father went on to explain how she'd lived through the Spanish influenza that killed so many Hamiltonians, a Depression, and two world wars. Over the years he'd had several conversations with her and she admitted trying not to let her early "home child" years affect the rest of her life. He'd heard it said that home children were of a resilient, forgiving nature and had to be in order to survive. He felt that described Mrs. Church perfectly.

Shortly before her death she told Bob that some of her happiest memories were those spent with the Hewson family. Whether it was sitting down to Christmas dinner, going on a picnic, or gathering kindling for a fire at the cottage, her memories in her later years were happy ones.

She admitted her fondness for young Mary and was proud to have been her godmother. If she hadn't come home from the hospital with her after she was born, she would never have known them. Perhaps it was destiny that Mary Janeway would find the Hewson family and her life would become part of theirs.

Who would have thought that Mary Janeway, the little home child from England, would leave such an impression on another little girl? Not only did they share the same name, they shared beautiful memories. Mary knew Mrs. Church better than her own grandmother. She would never believe that blood was thicker than water; it's just a different colour.

Epilogue

The spring after Mrs. Church died, Mary wrote a poem, "A Quiet Departure," a tribute to her dear friend, which was published in her high school yearbook. Mrs. Church's son Ross died of a massive heart attack eight months after his mother. He was only forty-two years old.

Emma passed away in 1977 in Victoria, British Columbia, at the age of eighty-nine. Both Carrie and Emma had grandchildren and have descendants living in western Canada.

Mrs. Church's daughter Mona died as a young girl and her son Ross never had children. There are no direct descendants of Mary Janeway.

Notes

1. Pierre Berton, *Remember Yesterday: A Century of Photographs* (Toronto: The Canadian Centennial Publishing Co. Ltd., 1965), 62.
2. Richard B. Wright, *The Age of Longing* (Toronto: HarperCollins Publishers, 1995), 129.

Prologue

1. Joy Parr, *Labouring Children* (Montreal: McGill-Queen's University Press, 1980), 126–27.
2. Jean Little, *Orphan at My Door* (Toronto: Scholastic Canada Ltd., 2001), 51, 61, 70, 73.
3. Mary Pettit, *Mary Janeway* (Toronto: Natural Heritage Books, 2000), 100.

One: London

1. Alan Phillips, *Into the 20th Century* (Toronto: Natural Science of Canada Limited, 1977), 14.

Two: Summer in Goderich

1. Tourism Goderich advertisement, back cover *Harrowsmith Magazine*,

per discussion with Bob Marshall, tourism manager, Port of Goderich. *www.goderich.ca.*

2. Interview with Margaret McHolme, January 2002.
3. Pettit, *Mary Janeway*, 77
4. Canada Company commissioner, John Galt, and Dr. William Dunlop, the founders of Goderich in 1827, apparently were great partiers. It is said that while drinking one night they made a joke about switching the plans for Guelph and Goderich but it never happened. Goderich was designed after Roman city plans and the word "square" means "meeting place" and has nothing to do with its configuration. Discussion with Bob Marshall, tourism manager, Port of Goderich.

Three: Back in London

1. Phillips, *Into the 20th Century*, 116.
2. *Ibid.*, 7.
3. Pettit, *Mary Janeway*, 84–85.
4. Margaret Sambrook McHolme, *My Unique Heritage, My Grandmothers' Ways and Sayings* (Goderich, Ontario: self-published,1990), 8.
5. *Ibid.*, 8–9.

Four: Mrs. B. Gets Sick

1. Craig Brown, *The Illustrated History of Canada* (Toronto: Lester & Orpen Dennys Ltd., 1987), 396.

Five: Woodstock

1. Art Williams and Edward Baker, *Woodstock: Bits & Pieces* (Erin, Ontario: Boston Mills Press, 1967), 99.
2. Caroline Routh, *Women's Fashions in Style: 100 Years of Canadian Women's Fashion* (Toronto: Stoddart Publishing Co. Limited, 1993), 6.
3. Williams & Baker, *Woodstock*, 68–69.
4. *Ibid.*, 144.

Six: Hamilton

1. Michael J. Dear, J.J. Drake, and Lloyd George Reeds, *Steel City: Hamilton and Region* (Toronto: University of Toronto Press, 1987), 124, 125,127.
2. *The Crazy Twenties 1920/1930: Canada's Illustrated Heritage* (Toronto: Natural Science of Canada Limited, 1978), 86.
3. Houghton, Margaret, ed., *Vanished Hamilton III* (Burlington, Ontario: North Shore Publishing Inc., 2007), 11.

Seven: The Lunch Pail Town

1. Lois Evans, *Hamilton: The Story of a City* (Toronto: The Ryerson Press, 1970), 181.

Eight: Queen Victoria's Birthday

1. Edward Shorter, *A History of Women's Bodies* (New York: Basic Books, Inc., Publishers, 1982), 156.
2. Pettit, *Mary Janeway*, 5.
3. Phillips, *Into the 20th Century*, 74.
4. Little, *Orphan at My Door*, 46–48.
5. Interview with Dr. Ruth Shykoff (Dr. Sky), September 2001.

Nine: The Church Family

1. Marjorie Freeman Campbell, *A Mountain and a City: The Story of Hamilton* (Toronto: McClelland & Stewart Limited, 1966), 209.
2. Pettit, *Mary Janeway*, 47.
3. Susanna McLeod, "The Russell Motor Car, A Canadian Automobile," *Canadian History. http://susanna-mcleod.suite101.com/russell-motor-car-luxury-built-in-canada-in-1908-a401080*, accessed February 2011.
4. Phillips, *Into the 20th Century*, 66.

Ten: Infantile Paralysis

1. John M. Last, MD, "Polio — Early History, Polio Epidemics, The

Medical Response — Encyclopedia of Children," *www.faqs.org*, accessed February 26, 2011.
2. Naomi Rogers, *Dirt and Disease: Polio Before FDR* (New Brunswick, New Jersey: Rutgers University Press, 1992), 1.
3. Lauro Halstead and Gunnar Grimby, *Post-Polio Syndrome* (Philadelphia, Pennsylvania: Hanley & Belfus, Inc., 1995), 204.
4. Interview with Dr. Ruth Shykoff, June 24, 2001.

Eleven: Unexpected Visitors

1. Campbell, *A Mountain and a City: The Story of Hamilton*, 216.
2. Pettit, *Mary Janeway*, 72.
3. Troon Harrison, *A Bushel of Light* (Toronto: Stoddart Kids, 2000), 88.
4. Little, *Orphan at My Door*, 50.
5. *Waskatenau and Districts Historical Society: By River and Trail* (Waskatenau, Alberta: Waskatenau and Districts Historical Society, 1986), 930.
6. Roger David Brown, *Blood on the Coal* (Hantsport, Nova Scotia: Lancelot Press Limited, 1976), 15.

Twelve: Life Goes On

1. Brown, *The Illustrated History of Canada*, 396.

Thirteen: A Dream Comes True

1. Phillips, *Into the 20th Century*, 76.
2. Historical Committee Public and Safety Information Branch, *Footpaths to Freeways* (Ontario Ministry of Transportation and Communications, 1984), 56, 59.
3. Frank Ernest Hill, *The Automobile: How It Came, Grew, and Has Changed Our Lives* (New York: Dodd, Mead, 1967), 38.
4. Phillips, *Into the 20th Century*, 110.

Fourteen: Hamilton: A City of Firsts

1. Terry Boyle and Ron Brown, *Ontario Album: Images of the Past from*

the Private Files of Terry Boyle & Ron Brown (Toronto: Polar Bear Express, 1998), 14.

Fifteen: Missing Person

1. John Craig, *The Years of Agony, 1910/1920: Canada's Illustrated Heritage* (Toronto: Natural Science of Canada Limited, 1977), 18.
2. Pettit, *Mary Janeway*, 100.
3. Routh, *Women's Fashions in Style*, 27.

Sixteen: Centennial Celebrations

1. "Spectacular Storm Lasted Several Hours," *The Hamilton Spectator*, August 11, 1913, 1.
2. Brian Henley, *Hamilton Back Then* (Burlington, Ontario: North Shore Publishing Inc., 1998), 62.

Seventeen: A Wedding and a War

1. Craig, *The Years of Agony*, 42.
2. *Ibid.*, 50.
3. Pettit, *Mary Janeway*, 49.
4. Doug Symons, "Woodstock of the 1910s: Lights go on as City Enters Great War," in *Woodstock's Centennial 1901–2001: A Look Back at Woodstock and the World* (Woodstock, Ontario: Annex Publishing & Printing Limited, 2001), 12.
5. Taped interview of Emma (Janeway) Touchings by daughter Lois Lamble, Victoria, British Columbia, May 1976.
6. Henley, *Hamilton Back Then*, 73.
7. Craig, *The Years of Agony*, 64.
8. Bill Freeman, *Hamilton: A People's History* (Toronto: James Lorimer & Company Ltd., 2001), 124.
9. Brian Henley, *The Grand Old Buildings of Hamilton* (Burlington, Ontario: North Shore Publishing Inc., 1994), 80.

Eighteen: A Bitter Cold Winter

1. Craig, *The Years of Agony*, 18.
2. Carl F. Klinck, *Robert Service: A Biography* (Toronto: McGraw-Hill Ryerson Limited, 1976), 16.
3. Robert W. Service, *Rhymes of a Red Cross Man* (New York Barse & Hopkins Publishers, 1916), 73.

Nineteen: Armistice

1. Craig, *The Years of Agony*, 107.
2. *Ibid.*, 105.
3. Marjorie Campbell, *A Mountain and a City: The Story of Hamilton*, 208. The reference is to Sir William Hearst, a lifelong temperance advocate, whose Conservative government passed the Ontario Temperance Act barring the legal sale of beer and liquor in licenced hotels.
4. Craig, *The Years of Agony*, 107.
5. *Ibid.*, 107–08.

Twenty: The Roaring Twenties

1. Thomas Melville Bailey, *For the Public Good: A History of the Birth Control Clinic and the Planned Parenthood Society of Hamilton, Ontario Canada* (Hamilton, Ontario: W.I. Griffin Limited, 1974), 3.
2. John Craig, *The Years of Agony*, 32, 36.

Twenty-One: Mr. Jacques's Funeral

1. *The Crazy Twenties 1920/1930: Canada's Illustrated Heritage* (Toronto: Natural Science of Canada Limited, 1978), 34.
2. Interview with Joseph Jacques, grandson of Daniel Jacques, March 2001.
3. *Ibid.*
4. *Ibid.*
5. *Ibid.*
6. Pettit, *Mary Janeway*, 39
7. *Ibid.*, 106

8. *Ibid.*, 108
9. *Ibid.*, 27
10. *Ibid.*, 34–35
11. *Ibid.*, 44
12. Interview with Joseph Jacques, March 2001
13. *Ibid.*

Twenty-Two: A Child Is Born, a Child Is Lost

1. *The Crazy Twenties*, 13.
2. Angus McLaren, *The Bedroom and the State: The Changing Practices and Politics of Contraception and Abortion in Canada, 1880–1980* (Toronto: McClelland & Stewart, 1986), 22–23.

Twenty-Three: Picking up the Pieces

1. *The Crazy Twenties*, 73.
2. Elizabeth L. Post, *Emily Post's Etiquette: The Blue Book of Social Usage* (New York: Funk & Wagnalls Company, Inc., 1965), 671. Original edition, 1922.
3. Freeman, *Hamilton*, 124–25.

Twenty-Four: A Knock on the Door

1. *The Crazy Twenties*, 20.

Twenty-Five: Kingston Penitentiary

1. George Scott, *Inmate: The Casebook Revelations of a Canadian Penitentiary Psychiatrist* (Montreal-Toronto: Optimum Publishing International Inc., 1982), 9.
2. Dave St. Onge, curator of Correctional Services of Canada Museum, Kingston, Ontario, email received on May 17, 2001.
3. Canadian Government Publishing Centre Supply and Services Canada, *Kingston Penitentiary: The First Hundred and Fifty Years 1835–1985* (Ottawa: Kromar Printing Ltd., 1985), 98.
4. *Ibid.*, 99.

5. Paul Pettit read this graffiti scribbled on a wall in the men's washroom at an industrial worksite forty years ago.

Twenty-Six: Ottawa Street

1. Post, *Emily Post's Etiquette*, 677.

Twenty-Seven: Stony Mountain

1. *The Crazy Twenties*, 8.
2. *Ibid.*, 114.8

Twenty-Eight: Freedom at Last

1. *The Crazy Twenties*, 117.
2. Merilyn Simonds, *The Convict Lover: A True Story* (Toronto: Macfarlane Walter & Ross, 1996), 58.

Twenty-Nine: The Great Crash

1. *The Crazy Twenties*, 118–19.
2. S.J. Kerr, *Fish and Fisheries Management in Ontario: A Chronology of Events* (Peterborough, Ontario: Ontario Ministry of Natural Resources, Biodiversity Branch, 2010), 24.
3. Phone conversation with Rene (Enright) Church in 2001.

Thirty: The Turning Point

1. Stephen Franklin, *A Time of Heroes 1940/1950* (Toronto: Natural Science of Canada Limited, 1977), 120.

Thirty-One: A Family at Last

1. Alexander Ross, *The Booming Fifties 1950/1960* (Toronto: Natural Science of Canada Limited, 1977), 72.

Thirty-Two: A Milestone

1. Freeman, *Hamilton*, 156.

Thirty-Three: The Final Chapter

1. Alan Edmonds, *The Years of Protest 1960/1970: Canada's Illustrated Heritage* (Toronto: Natural Science of Canada Limited, 1979), 7.